BROKEN BLOODLINE

HISTORY AND MYSTERY

JOHN J. JAGEMANN

outskirts
press

Outskirts Press, Inc.
http://www.outskirtspress.com

ISBN: 978-1-9772-2569-6

PRINTED IN THE UNITED STATES OF AMERICA

This book is "dedicated" to the memory of my parents Marilyn and Robert, brothers Tommy and Richie, aunts and uncles, and grandparents.

To my other siblings; Bobby, Linda, Jimmy, Kathy, Cynthia, extended family, and friends. A special thank you is extended to my wife Marian and son Johnny for their exceptional patience while I worked to complete **Broken Bloodline.**

Table of Contents

A Shot in the Dark

It was the summer of '69 and we didn't realize we were nearing the end of our fun and carefree times! It was August and the Woodstock festival had just been held on Max Yasgur's farm in the town of Bethel in upstate New York. It featured top headliner musicians of the era as they rocked the bucolic countryside for three full days, supported by some 400,000 herbally and chemically stimulated backup singers!

My name is Pasquale (Patsy) Scallaci, I grew up in Belmont, a tough Italian neighborhood in the Bronx, one of the five boroughs comprising New York City. I lived with my grandparents, Pasquale and Natala and my father, Vincenzo, on Arthur Avenue and 187th Street, the heart of "Little Italy."

About one year earlier my father and my Uncle Johnny Muller, had retired from the New York City Police Department (NYPD) after twenty-two years on the job. Johnny Muller was not my blood uncle by pedigree nor lineage, he was my father's best friend. They met in 1946, as recruits in the police academy. Ever since I could speak, he was known to me as" Uncle Johnny." My old man's post-retirement now finds him working full time with my grandfather at the Scallaci Family Grocery.

I also "helped out" in the store part-time days, before working nights as a licensed security guard. The building I watched over was located in Riverdale, an upscale community situated on the northwest corner of the Bronx, overlooking the scenic and history-laden Hudson River. I had always aspired to be a cop like my father. In February, I completed the NYPD Entrance Exam and awaited results. I knew, though, even then, that if I passed, I had to be 21 before I could be hired, so I was content with being a rent-a-cop for the time being. When I turned twenty-one, all I would have left to do was pass an NYPD physical.

Vietnam Veteran's Memorial

One day I had some time to kill before leaving for my security job. I stretched out on my bed alongside my loyal dog, Bruiser, a large, male, German Shepherd and watched the news on my twelve-inch black and white Zenith television. After I adjusted my rabbit ear T.V. antenna for better reception, it presented combat footage of American soldiers as they fought in Vietnam. In addition, it showed protests and anti-war demonstrations staged across the United States.

Following that, most stations discussed the grisly August 9th in-home murders in Los Angeles, California, of pregnant model/actress Sharon Tate and four others and another similar set of murders which occurred the following night at the LA home of Supermarket Executive Leno La Bianca, and his wife, Rosemary.

It was a time of sex, drugs, and rock-n-roll! They also aired news clips of Hare Krishna, practitioners of a burgeoning religious movement chanting in Central Park. Many young Americans sported long, unkempt, wild hair, and psychedelic headbands. The youth of America expressed feelings of "anti-establishment" by deed and word. Popular fashion reflected the anti-war sentiment with military jackets adorned with peace signs. It had been a sweat-filled summer, city kids kept cool with the unleashed spray of fire hydrants. Families eluded the night's humidity by sleeping on pillowed fire escapes; others languished peacefully on rooftops. Girls wore the ever-alluring and breeze friendly mini -skirt!

During a recent memorable afternoon, my friends and I took our buddy, Irish (who had just returned home on leave from the Marines before shipping out to Vietnam) to the Paradise Movie Theatre in the Bronx to see the current hit, *Easy Rider,* starring Peter Fonda, Dennis Hopper, and newcomer, Jack Nicholson. Our group was extremely patriotic to the red, white, and blue. Most of our fathers and uncles had fought in World War II or during the Korean War. We were proud of the men and women who served their country with valor. We were pissed-off and did not understand why American soldiers, who served their country in Southeast Asia, were greeted with brutal slurs of war protesters and the cold shoulder of many fellow Americans upon their return home.

My closest friends and I were not into the drug culture of the '60s, we were beer-drinking and ass-kicking "**greasers,**" who loved our country. We wore black leather jackets, T-shirts, engineer boots, blue jeans, chained wallets, and Garrison belts with heavy buckles. Most of us still wore slicked back pompadours or duck-tailed hairstyles, buoyed by hair grease such as Brylcreem. We carried switchblades and brass knuckles, or we would break off a car antenna and use it as a weapon or to construct homemade firearms called "zip-guns," all of which served as protection against rival gangs. My gang did not look to start trouble, but we certainly did not run from it either. We were not bullies or hard-core criminals, we just kept the "neighborhood safe." We drove cool hotrods, fast muscle cars, and Harley-Davidson motorcycles. Most of us in the Bronx neighborhood of Belmont were the sons and daughters of Italian immigrants and became a first, second, or third generation of American-born Italians.

In January of '69, Richard Millhouse Nixon succeeded Lyndon Baines Johnson as the 37th President of the United States. "With regard to Vietnam he promised to achieve "Peace with Honor." He sought to negotiate a settlement that would allow the half million U.S. troops "in country" to withdraw, while allowing South Vietnam to survive the scourge of Communism.

In July of '69, one of mankind's crowning achievements occurred when American astronaut, Neil Armstrong, the first human to set foot on the moon, uttered the immortal words "…that's one small step for man, one giant leap for mankind."

Five months earlier, my old man ran into his police sergeant from his early days when he was assigned to the 41st precinct in the South Bronx. They got to talking:

"Vinny, I retired two years ago," he told my dad, "after a thirty two-year career and have started a security company that's grown. By the way, how's your son doing?"

"Good, he just took the New York City Police Department's entrance exam and is waiting to hear the results, but he's only eighteen."

"Would he consider a job as a security officer?"

"I don't know, but I'll ask him."

The guy handed him his business card.

"Thanks, I will definitely ask."

When my old man got home, he reported:

"Patsy, I ran into my old police sergeant today. He has branched out with his own security agency. Are you interested in becoming a security guard?"

"Let me think on it."

The following day, I gave him my answer of yes.

He phoned his friend: "My son wants to know when he can start."

After his company ran an FBI background check on me and saw that I had no serious convictions or felonies, thanks to the old man, — I was hired.

I completed security guard training and received my license to carry a firearm. I had to take a Firearm and Safety training course - no big deal, I grew up with guns. My father and Uncle Johnny taught me how to shoot a rifle at the age of ten and a handgun at the age of twelve. When I completed the safety course, my old man bought me a brand new "in the box" Smith and Wesson Model10 .38 caliber special revolver, and with practice I became a fairly good shot.

I was assigned to the graveyard shift: midnight – 8 a.m. I did not mind working nights. I reasoned that under the cover of darkness is when most crimes are committed, and I wanted to be there to stop them.

I stood 6 feet 3 inches tall and weighed 200 pounds. Because of my size, I guess I looked somewhat intimidating and formidable. Around my neighborhood, I was known as someone you "didn't want to mess with." I had a reputation as a tough and fierce street fighter who would unleash the well-known Scallaci temper when provoked. The Scallacis had a history of being peasant farmers and Mafioso in Palermo, Sicily.

I drove a cherry, custom built 1955 Chevy Bel Air, which ran like a "raped ape," a popular term for the time. On this day, it had been extremely hot and muggy, the skies appeared menacing. As I pulled into the parking lot of the upper-class community, I ran into Bubba O'Brien, the security guard I was relieving. He had just finished making his rounds of the property and reported all was quiet. He told me to enjoy my weekend and got into his car and drove away.

We had a small guard shack equipped with air conditioning for the summer, heat for the winter, a bathroom, desk, telephone, transistor radio and a small refrigerator. I had to patrol and monitor the entire complex on foot every hour, making sure that everything was safe and secure and that there were no signs of any criminal activity going on.

There were two entrances to the parking lots: the main entrance, where the guard shack was located, and another entrance located in the rear of the complex. The parking lots were full of expensive cars. The area was a bit rural, but well lit. The rear parking lot had a gate, which was locked at dusk. The four pm to midnight guard was responsible for closing and locking the gate chain. The property was now only accessible via the main gate. During my first summer working there, the biggest crime to take place was, occasionally, I caught kids on hot and muggy nights jumping the fence to take a dip in the huge in-ground pool. I would tell them, "You have five minutes to cool off," then they would have to leave. Other than that, it remained without incident.

Since Bubba had already patrolled the area, I did not have to make my rounds for another hour, so I sat down at my desk and began reading my book the *Godfather* by Mario Puzo. Even though I wanted to be a New York City policeman like my old man, I had uncles and cousins who were raised around and belonging to the lifestyle glorified in that book. These "men of honor," commanded respect and were feared in the neighborhoods of New York City.

I patrolled the area hourly, and my logbook entries often consisted of little more than, "All quiet throughout the complex property," so back to reading my book I went, only taking breaks to rest my eyes for a bit.

I was born with two different colored eyes, a condition known as heterochromia. My left eye is **brown** and the right one - so I have been told, is a piercing **blue**. My eye doctor opined, "Having two different colored eyes probably doesn't have anything to do with the occasional tearing, burning, or redness. It's probably caused by an undetermined allergy." He could not explain why my right eye and not the left one was primarily affected. This condition itself, he stressed, "was usually a result of an unexplained genetic mutation."

On this particular day, soon after I had finished making my 3:00 a.m. patrol, the sky opened up with immense lightning and thunder, followed by torrential rains. This kept up into my next patrol. Then to top it off we experienced a "blackout." It was not just our complex that lost electricity, though—the surrounding streetlights were also darkened. Because the neighborhood of Riverdale sits on a higher elevation, I saw that the borough of Manhattan and other areas of the Bronx were also without lights. The only light emanated from a full moon and continuous lightning strikes. Other than that, it was pitch black. In a city known for being well lit when it got dark out even back then, darkness of this extent was haunting.

I carried on with the aid of a small pen light until I located the large flashlight, we kept in the desk drawer. Unfortunately, when I turned it on, the light was quite dim. I searched the rest of the desk drawers for batteries, only to find out we were all out of spares. So, with my pen light, I located my raincoat, put it on over my security guard uniform and went on my way, using my mini-light and the light of the full moon to navigate my way around the complex to complete my rounds. All was quiet, except for the sounds of crickets and bullfrogs echoing from the pond area, and the crack of thunder.

As I approached the rear entrance parking lot, I noticed what appeared to be a light in the distance. I figured one of the homeowners must have been awakened by the sound of thunder and realizing he had no lights, ventured outside with a flashlight to investigate the situation. As I approached the clubhouse, I heard a raspy voice say, "Hurry up, Chains."

As I got closer, I saw the shadowy figures of two people. Moving even closer, I observed a man holding a flashlight for another man trying to pry open a car door. It looked like he was using a Slim Jim, a thin piece of metal used to manipulate the locking mechanism so the door would open. The clubhouse had huge cement columns that supported a portico—the perfect place to hide. I was not sure what to do. My adrenaline skyrocketed. As I peered around the column, the person who held the flashlight who was obviously the lookout, while the other person was trying to break into the car caught a glimpse of me and yelled to his partner, "we have company!"

With my hand on my .38 Special, I exited from behind the column and confronted the two maggots. The lookout pointed his flashlight in my direction. Fortunately, the light of the full moon supplied sufficient light, or so I thought. It permitted me to see him grab with his free hand what appeared to be a shiny pistol from his pants waist brandishing it toward me in either an attempt to scare me or shoot me. It happened so fast, I pulled my handgun out of its holster as fast as I could, and, anticipating that he was going to fire his gun, I aimed mine.

From about twenty-five feet away, with a firm grip on my weapon, I squeezed the trigger three times until I heard a thump on the ground. I then sought the protection of the cement column, thinking the second person might return fire. Hearing no return gunshots, I scanned the lot with my small flashlight and slowly walked over to where the body laid.

I remembered my old man telling me, "Never touch anything at a crime scene because you can contaminate the evidence."

I inspected the area with my penlight, but did not see any sign of a weapon, the flashlight, Slim Jim, or the second suspect. I then heard a vehicle peeling out.

My first thought was that I had found no weapon near the lifeless body. My mind raced as reality started setting in. Did I mistake another object for a weapon and shoot, possibly killing an unarmed man? After all, there was poor visibility.

After I fired my weapon and heard the person fall, I retreated behind the column for about fifteen to twenty seconds. I wondered if the time I had spent hiding behind the protection of the column had given the second suspect enough time to grab his partner's gun and flashlight and run off to a waiting vehicle.

After all, I did hear a vehicle spinning its wheels and leaving in a hurry. It was a short distance from the town road to the entrance of the rear parking lot where the sports car that they were trying to steal was parked. I thought it best to get to the guard shack and call 911 to report the incident. I got there and, again, using my trusty pen light, found the phone. Thank God it had a dial tone! I dialed, tried my best to remain calm, and explained the situation and my location to the 911 operator.

Upon completion of the call, I returned to the crime scene and waited for the NYPD to arrive. While I waited, I lit a cigarette and took a few heavy drags to calm my nerves. I realized that after I finished the 911 call, I should have called my old man. I assumed, because of the thunder, no one had heard or recognized the gun shots. It was still pitch-black out, except for the lightning in the distance, and I probably had a dead man lying on the ground. The atmosphere had turned extremely eerie.

I gazed up at the full moon and the ominous sky. Did this really just happen, or was it just a bad dream?

Within minutes, three NYPD patrol cars with rooftop lights flashing and sirens blasting pulled into the parking lot of the complex and hurried to the crime scene. A heavyset sergeant who must have been the patrol supervisor got out of his squad car and started barking orders to the other officers. The paramedics who arrived in the ambulance checked the suspect for vital signs as he lay in a pool of rainwater and blood.

The paramedics reported to the sergeant that the person was deceased.

The sergeant then used his patrol car radio to contact the Precinct Station House, telling the desk sergeant, "We have a confirmed DOA, [Dead on Arrival]. Send a detective squad, medical examiner, and a "spot truck" [which had battery-operated spotlights to illuminate a crime scene].

The sergeant directed his men to preserve the area for the detective's arrival. Just before the detective squad and the spot truck arrived, the sergeant approached me, asked some basic questions and for my driver's license. When the detectives showed up, they further questioned me about what had transpired. They conducted a thorough survey of the crime scene, directing the crime scene investigators (CSI) to take pictures and to make drawings. The detectives then put me in the back of a squad car and took me to the 50th Police Precinct Station House for my formal statement. During the ride, power to the area was restored. When we arrived at the station house, I requested to call my father to explain to him what had happened and was told, "No problem."

My father raced to the precinct. When he arrived, several of the police officers recognized him. Detectives asked me, "Why didn't you tell us who your father was?"

I shrugged. I was not looking for any special treatment. Vinny, as he was called, was a retired, but highly decorated and well-respected, former Homicide Detective Sergeant for the Borough of the Bronx.

As my father sat by my side, I explained to the detectives, in great detail what had transpired. I also told them I was a licensed security guard at the Riverdale Community and licensed to carry the firearm the officers at the scene had confiscated. I had shown them my carry permit for my weapon and told them, "I think the dead suspect called his partner, Chains."

The detective's expression was grim. "The dead person's name is Billy Cunningham, son of State Senator and former Bronx District Attorney, William H. Cunningham."

He began.:

Billy Cunningham's driver's license listed the address of his father's residence in the luxurious complex that you work at. The 1969 Ferrari Daytona that they tried to break into was also registered to his father.

My father replied, "I worked with the Senator when he was the Bronx DA., I did not like him. We had 'words' several times. Besides being arrogant, he was more concerned with his political career than he was about putting the bad guys behind bars. The current Bronx District Attorney was an assistant DA under William H. Cunningham. Mr. Cunningham was instrumental in getting him elected as the new Bronx District Attorney."

Fortunately, the detectives investigating the case were satisfied that this was a clear case of self-defense in the shooting of the suspect.

The lead detective went on to say:

"The evidence found at the crime scene corroborated what you told us. Even though we did not recover a weapon at the scene, we have identified scratch marks on the car's driver side door and damage to the window's weatherstripping by the door lock, which would be consistent with someone using a Slim Jim to break into the vehicle. We found the chain and lock that held the rear gates closed and it was cut, probably by bolt cutters, and there were also visible tire tracks left on the pavement outside the gates on the town road."

I chimed in:

"The tire tracks were probably left by the vehicle I heard spinning its wheels as it hurriedly exited the premises."

The detective nodded in agreement:

"This wasn't the first-time young Billy had a run-in with the law," he concurred "But though the kid's been arrested a few times before for car theft, and for carrying an unlicensed firearm, he's never been convicted of a crime. Unfortunately, because of the Bronx DA's association with the dead suspect's father, we have been told to keep this case open and investigate it further. You could be summoned to appear in front of a Grand Jury."

It was about 2:30 p.m. on a stormy Saturday afternoon when I was finally released from the 50th Police Precinct located in the northwest corner of the Bronx. My father drove me back to my job to pick up my '55 Chevy and followed me home. When we got there, we both went into the Scallaci Family Grocery to talk with my Grandfather Pasquale, to let him know I was alright.

While I was there, I grabbed a cold six-pack of Pabst Blue Ribbon beer and a pack of Lucky Strike cigarettes.

"Thanks, Dad, for being there, I love you."

He squeezed my shoulder. "You had quite a night - you okay, Patsy?"

"Yeah, I'm just really tired." I glanced at my father and grandfather. "I'll see you both later."

I walked next door to our apartment building. When I opened the door, I was greeted by my dog, Bruiser. Even though I was exhausted, I was still pumped up by the morning's events. I cracked open a cold brew, lit up a cancer stick, sat and relaxed on the covered porch, listened to the thunder, and watched the lightning strikes amidst the continued deluge.

The somehow-familiar violent storm triggered a memory of a story that my grandfather had told me on this very same porch when I was a boy. It was during another August thunderstorm, the worst I had ever experienced. That night, the thunder, lightning, wind gusts and monsoon-type rain was alarmingly similar. I was scared shitless, and that is when he told me the Scallaci Story of immigration from the island of Sicily, across the Atlantic Ocean to America. He explained the obstacles, struggles, and hardships that the Scallacis and other immigrants endured.

I embraced slumber, escorted into yesteryear by an ancestral remembrance.

2

Continental Exodus

Told against and woven into the backdrop of U.S. history, our story animates the trials and tribulations Italian immigrants experienced in pursuit of the elusive American dream. Although our journey began at the onset of the 1890s, it encompassed: mounting uncertainties of the early 1900s, decadence expressed during the1920s, destitution endured throughout the 1930s, brutalities inflicted within the 1940s, flourishing achieved during the 1950s and the turbulent times of the 1960s.

Secondarily, it poses a tale from a resurrection from the abyss of an uncertainty shrouded in mystery to the jubilance of recognizing a self-worth built upon the backbone of ancestry strengthened by the foundation of family loyalty and the bond that blood is thicker than water. It is the trail of the "**Broken Bloodline**".

The Scallaci history of immigration began in 1893, my grandfather's in 1905. When he was six years old, his family fled their homeland of Palermo, Sicily in hopes of completing the voyage across the great Atlantic Ocean, toward the shoreline and promise of the United States. He was accompanied by his father, Amerigo, his mother, Giovanna, and his older brother, Vincenzo. They steered their way to Ellis Island; and were both terrified and hopeful of what they would encounter upon arrival.

The family's history began in the capital city of Palermo, Sicily, the largest island in the Mediterranean Sea. Sicily had experienced centuries of invasion and occupation by foreign powers. In 1861, northern Italy on the Mainland, southern Italy and the Island of Sicily merged under one consolidated flag. This Italian unification caused already unstable economic conditions to considerably worsen.

The newly formed Italian government was dominated by the northerners. Southerners were hurt by high taxes and protective tariffs levied upon northern industrial goods. Additionally, soil erosion, a scarcity of cultivatable land, deforestation and a lack of coal and iron ore required by industry further impacted the eroding national economy. The future did not look promising for the Scallaci. They were peasant farmers who cultivated durum wheat, used in the process of making pasta.

During the 1890s, Sicilians experienced severe deteriorating economic conditions. The Italian peasant was not the only one who suffered from the general poverty of the south, skilled workers could no longer find employment either. Thousands of men left their families to seek employment in America. As a result, my grandfather's Great Uncle Natale and his son, Tommaso, left their place of birth in pursuit of the American dream. They packed their few belongings, expressed their sad goodbyes to family and friends and headed to the port town. Traveling from rural areas to the port town was difficult as there were no cars or local train service. Many immigrants traveled with someone from their village. Support from people they knew was critical during the voyage and upon arrival.

Uncle Natale and Cousin Tommaso traveled with two other families from their village. When they reached the port, they purchased two third class tickets with their meager life savings. The price of a single ticket cost thirty dollars. They would begin their new life in America with just eight dollars!

The ferry terminal was crowded with hundreds of men, women and children waiting to board. After the 1893 immigration law went into effect, each passenger had to answer up to thirty-one questions before boarding the ship. Their first medical inspection was subsequently carried out. Shipping companies did not accept the ill or infirmed as passengers. In any case, they would have been rejected upon arrival to the United States. Disinfection of both immigrants and baggage was standard practice. Vaccinations were routinely performed at the port.

No problems ensued!

Uncle Natale and his paisanos (countrymen) boarded the steamship. When it was full of immigrant passengers, the steamship departed across the Atlantic Ocean heading for New York Harbor.

Dense fog, hurricanes and icebergs were among the many natural dangers encountered during travel across the Atlantic Ocean. They were greeted by the Statue of Liberty upon arrival, but before they could embark on their new lives in the United States, they had to undergo medical examination and inspection. This meant a stressful procession through the buildings of Ellis Island. Inspectors boarded the ship to perform a hasty inspection of first- and second-class passengers. The government thought that passengers who could afford first or second-class tickets were less likely to become a health burden to the public. Passengers were sent to Ellis Island for possible quarantine only if they failed the cursory health exam. Meanwhile, lower class passengers (third class) were transported from the pier or ship to Ellis Island on barges or ferries, often in crowded and unsanitary conditions.

Passengers routinely lingered for hours on these barges before entering Ellis Island. They lacked basic amenities such as food, water, toilets, or protection from the elements. As immigrants filed through Ellis Island's large registry room, doctors would briefly scan each immigrant for obvious physical or mental health issues. Doctors or nurses used chalk to write letters on an immigrant's clothes to indicate possible health problems. An "H" indicated a possible heart condition while "LCD "signified loathsome contagious disease.

Eventually, these rapid-fire physical health inspections came to be known as "**six-second**" physicals. The most common medical rejection related to the contagious eye disease, trachoma. Inspectors were routinely overwhelmed and rushed. Due to the rush, echoing noise of the vast registry hall and the inspector's unfamiliarity with many

European languages and dialects spoken, many immigrants found themselves leaving with new shorter "American" versions of their last names. Italians without proper paperwork had tags hung from their shoulders with the letters "WOP" written upon it. "WOP" denoted without papers. The term "WOP" hence became widely used as an ethnic slur describing Italian immigrants as a class of undesirables.

The U.S. Immigration Service collected arrival manifests from incoming ships. The manifests contained passenger names and answers to several questions about potential destinations and employment prospects.

Much has been written about suffering and discrimination Italian immigrants faced in the United States, but this must be measured against what they left behind at home in Italy. The immigrant at this time left one thing behind, poverty. At home, there was unemployment, under-employment, high mortality, little or no medical care, minimal schooling, poor housing, exploitation, and semi-starvation. A dismal circumstance to say the least.

For the average Italian, migration to America offered an opportunity for liberation and hope for a better life. After all, wasn't the United States supposed to be the land of opportunity, where the streets were paved with gold? All went well for Uncle Natale, Tommaso and the "paisanos" from their village! They were finally finished with the grueling intake and inspection processes!

One year earlier, Giuseppe Scallaci, his wife, Maria, and their son, Giacomo immigrated from Palermo. They were the first of the Scallaci Family to come to America! Cousin Giuseppe met them at Ellis Island and brought them to their new home on the Lower East Side of Manhattan, New York City. Most immigrants faced daunting language and cultural barriers. The Italians faced hostility from other more established Americans, thus they settled in friendlier communities known as "Little Italys." living among other immigrants from their native regions.

Sicilian immigrants lived in tenements, houses divided into and rented out as separate residences or a block of apartments, especially ones that were typically run-down and overcrowded. Sharing a three-room apartment were Natale, Tommaso, Giuseppe, and his family, along with the two families that took the journey with Uncle Natale for a total of thirteen. Uncle Natale and his son, Tommaso, found work as street vendors, peddlers selling fruits and vegetables from pushcarts on the Lower East Side of Manhattan.

The earliest arrived Italian immigrants were northern Italians who became prominent as fruit merchants in New York and wine producers in California. The northern Italians had long considered southern Italians inferior to them and harbored a traditional animosity. Sicilian-American immigrants often faced unjust stereotyping and discrimination, even from other Italians. Tensions between Italian regions had not been entirely resolved with unification. Northern Italians had many "sayings" that unjustifiably painted Sicilians as untrustworthy and dishonest.

Lower East Side Peddler's Market

The late 1800s saw a massive wave of immigrants from southern Italy. It took some time for the Scallaci to adjust to their new country and life in New York City. As the years passed, with hard labor, Uncle Natale persevered, working to expand his business operations.

Natale knew he would need help. He contacted his nephew, Amerigo, in Palermo to ask if he and his family wanted to come to America for the opportunity of a better life. Amerigo had been close to his uncle; his own father had died when he was just a boy. Uncle Natale managed to save money in the eleven years he had been living in America and would send some to Amerigo for him and his family to pay for their passage if they decided to come. After much thought, Amerigo decided to bring his family to America. He contacted his uncle and agreed to come with his family. Natale sent him the money to purchase four third class steamship tickets for Amerigo, his wife, Giovanna, and their two sons, Vincenzo, eight years old, and his younger brother, Pasquale, six years old.

3

From Sea to Shining Sea

My grandfather, Pasquale, and his family packed their paltry possessions, expressed their goodbyes to family and friends and headed to the
port town. They were reluctant to leave their birthplace, but knew they
faced a truly bleak future. They began the trip with one other family
from their village. When they arrived at the port-town, they were told
they would have to wait around twelve days for their ship to arrive.

Amerigo's wife, Giovanna had an aunt and uncle who lived nearby
the port town. Naturally, that was where they stayed until their steamship arrived. When their ship arrived, they purchased third-class tickets.
Finally, with questions answered, medical exams completed, vaccinations still stinging and disinfectants still reeking, the immigrants were
led to their onboard accommodations.

Third class "steerage" passengers were led past the tiny deck space,
squeezed past the ship's machinery, and directed down steep stairways
into the enclosed lower decks. They were now in "steerage," which was
to be their "Hades" for the rest of the ocean journey. The hellish voyage
across the Atlantic Ocean to New York Harbor took about ten days.
They arrived at the harbor in 1905, and just like the Scallaci who immigrated before them, Amerigo and his family boarded a ferry from
the steamship to Ellis Island, for processing and medical examinations.

If all went well, they would be completed in one day--it did. They were greeted by Uncle Natale, they hugged and kissed. This was the first time that Natale had laid eyes on his great nephews. A jubilant re-union ensued! Having just ten dollars in a deep pants pocket, Amerigo and his family followed Natale to the neighborhood of Elizabeth Street, where they would share a tenement apartment.

Nine Scallaci would now live in a "newer" four-room tenement with better living conditions than Uncle Natale, Tommaso, Giuseppe, and his family's earlier tenements had provided. The Italians created ethnic enclaves; the first such communities were settled on Mulberry Street. Though New Yorkers labeled the newcomers Italians, immigrants identified primarily with their home region or village and segregated their neighborhoods accordingly.

Mulberry Street was distinctly Neapolitan, Mott Street held the Calabrese, Elizabeth Street strictly Sicilian. Individual blocks were inhabited by natives of a specific Sicilian town. New York City welcomed millions of Italian immigrants throughout the late 19th and 20th centuries, becoming home to the nation's largest Italian population. Amerigo worked on the cluttered streets of the Lower East Side, selling fruits and vegetables from a pushcart like his Uncle Natale and Cousin Tommaso. At eight years of age, Vincenzo sold newspapers and shined shoes. His younger brother, Pasquale, at six years old, performed chores in the tenement.

His mother, Giovanna, and Maria Scallaci were skilled seamstresses and undertook "piece work" from home. Sometimes they went days without seeing sunlight. Everyone contributed income to the family. For the most part, Italian immigrants were ignorant of the laws and customs of America, except for what they observed. Contact with Americans was limited to those who probably exploited immigrant labor - paying wages as low as possible, or with landlords who greatly overcharged for rent. Pasquale Scallaci, my name-sake grandfather told me about his voyage through hell and about the hardships of living in and growing up in overcrowded tenements.

Third class passage, steerage, was the cheapest and the most common way poor immigrants traveled. They were called "steerage" passengers because their quarters were located below the ship's deck, situated next to the ship's steering mechanism and engines. It was virtually the same as the baggage compartment, without portholes or other ventilation. They were low ceilinged, narrowly corridored crowded spaces, with triple layered bunks fitted with coarse mattresses, if any at all.

Men and women were separated - sometimes only barely, by a sheet hung over a rope. The nearly intolerable experience was worsened by stifling smells of oil lamps and ceaseless engines. Passengers endured the odors of vomit, urine, and fear. Their few personal belongings were often stolen. Diarrhea was prominent among the passengers. Starvation, dampness, and filth became the breeding ground for cholera and death. Corpses were weighed down and tossed into the sea like yesterday's trash. Food was poorly prepared, infrequently served and typically consisted of herring. Barrels and barrels of herring!

Seasickness was prevalent day and night. Crying could be heard echoing along the massive interior. For many, steerage passage across the Atlantic Ocean was remembered as a kind of Purgatory. Not all immigrants planned on staying in America permanently, some would return to their birthplace, traveling back and forth several times. They would usually arrive in the spring and returned to their countries before Christmas, bearing money they were able to save. They had a phrase for these migrants; they were referred to as "birds of passage."

Then one day, the magic words, "la merica, la merica, "statua liberta" were shouted and widely heard. Passengers rushed up to the top deck so they could get a good look at "la statua liberta" as the ship slowly moved past the Statue of Liberty and Ellis Island, but the ship did not stop, continuing through the bay into the Hudson River to a pier.

Resentful steerage passengers watched as first and second-class passengers "were allowed to bypass Ellis Island," disembarking directly from the ship onto a pier on the west side of Manhattan. Third class immigrant passengers wondered, "Will we ever set foot in "la merica?"

With first-and second-class passengers finally unloaded, the ship would turn around and head back down the Hudson River to deep waters, just beyond Ellis Island. When their turn finally arrived, the waiting passengers were ferried to the island, where they would be examined and processed.

The name "Ellis Island" often struck fear in the hearts of Italians, for they had heard stories of families being sent back or separated for various reasons, thus the nickname "The Isle of Tears" was coined. Many immigrants arrived penniless, having exhausted their savings on the cost of the journey. Those few with a meager savings, soon fell prey to the waterfront "sharper" (swindler).

In the early 20th Century, many Americans believed Sicilians were an inferior race destined to remain in ignorance and poverty. In Sicily, the Scallaci were peasant farmers; education beyond the third grade was out of the question for them. If the voyage on the steamship did not kill them of disease, there was a high probability life in the tenements would.

When the Scallaci first arrived in America in the early 1890s, the tenements they lived in were the "old" type, located on the Lower East side of Manhattan, NYC. The landlords let the buildings rot and decay. They were the slums of the "Five Points District," a breeding ground for crime and pestilence - amid filth and disease, they lacked proper drainage and "sufficient ventilation."

Immigrants lived in damp, smelly cellars, or attics with up to six or ten men, women, and children packed into a crowded single room, where filth left undisturbed for so many years and pestilence wiped out hundreds of lives annually. This was the worst-case scenario of tenement life. Trash collection had not yet been systematized. Slop and garbage from the houses were thrown into the streets, left to fester in the scorching sun.

Upon entering the overcrowded tenements, visitors were greeted with a nauseating stench emanating from unwashed bodies, rags, stale cooking odors, old bottles, and accumulated garbage heaps. Decaying grease, adhering to waste pipes from kitchen sinks added to the putrid odor and foul emanations. These tenement buildings were dangerous fire traps as well as a breeding ground for hordes of murderous rodents that would kill babies in their cribs.

The indigent tenants did not have the luxury of running water, especially if they lived on the top floor. Water had to be carted upstairs from street-level fire hydrants or hand pumps located in rear yards and they were frequently frozen in the winter.

Later buildings generally had a sink and water closet in the hallway of each floor. There were frequent issues with vermin, rats, mice, and roaches. For many years, pigs roamed the streets with reckless abandon. Adding to the horrendous and unsanitary conditions, were shared "outhouses" the landlord provided, but neglected to maintain. These outhouses "were located in the rear yard of the premise." The stench from the "outhouses" creeping into the building was enough to choke a horse. Because of massive overcrowding, infectious disease overwhelmed communities.

Cholera, yellow fever, typhoid, and similar epidemics swept through the slums on a regular basis. Tuberculosis was a huge killer; infants were infected at high levels. Nearly twenty-five percent of babies born during the 19th Century in cities died before reaching the age of one. Trash was routinely dumped upon the streets or into waterways. Old sewage pipes dumped the waste directly into rivers or bays. These rivers were sadly often used as a primary water source!

Along the streets, one would find dead dogs, cats, and rats in various stages of decomposition. Children slept many to a single bed, which clearly reduced heating issues during winter. Throughout summer months, when the heat was intense, people often slept on the fire escapes or roofs to avoid overwhelming temperatures.

Even near the end of the 19th Century, city streets were riddled with horse manure. Worse still, horse carcasses abounded. In 1880, the city removed 15,000 such dead horses. It is estimated that each horse produced fifteen to thirty pounds of manure per day. The horse population in NYC during the 1880s, was about 175,000. That meant that there were 3 to 4 million pounds of "horse shit" piling onto city streets daily.

By the 1890s, electric streetcars had replaced horse drawn vehicles. They ran above or below ground to avoid the increasingly crowded streets. During the early 1900s, the horse had become unprofitable and a serious environmental hazard. The automobile, the modern-day environmentalist's nemesis, was at the time considered to be a savior.

Everyone who lived in the apartment had to do their share, even children worked long hours. Sometimes, these children were forced by their parents to earn their own livelihood. How many greedy men amassed great wealth from the blood, sweat and tears of these poor immigrants?

As the 20th century began, the plight of the urban poor was heard by more and more social reformers, like Jacob Riis and others--meaningful change subsequently arrived. While most tenements were crowded; "the majority of tenement apartments were as clean as soap and "elbow grease" could render. After living in tenements built in the early to late1800s, Uncle Natale, Cousin Tommaso, Uncle Giuseppe, and wife Maria, son Giacomo, nephew Amerigo, wife Giovanna, and their two sons, Vincenzo, and Pasquale moved into a newer four-room tenement built in 1903. It had more amenities than Natale's and Giuseppe's families were previously availed. This would be the Scallaci home for the next five years, and their first taste of 'prosperity.' As time went by, they all settled into a daily routine of hard work, long hours, and little sleep.

4

Consumption Presumption

Uncle Natale's son, Tommaso experienced early evidence of tuberculosis. He started to have a persistent problem, coughed up thick white phlegm and sometimes blood. He also presented other symptoms such as fatigue and night sweats.

During the 19th and early 20th centuries, Tuberculosis was the leading cause of death in the United States and one of the most feared diseases in the world. There was no reliable treatment for TB. Some physicians prescribed bleedings and purgings, but most often, doctors simply advised their patients to rest, eat well and exercise outdoors.

Between 1873 and 1945, Saranac Lake located in the Adirondack Mountains of Upstate New York became a world-renowned center for the treatment of tuberculosis. Medical staff developed treatments that involved exposing patients to as much fresh air as possible under conditions of complete bed rest. These venues were commonly referred to as "cure cottages." These prescribed methods were simply not practical for Tommaso.

The spread of TB played a role in the movement to prohibit public spitting, except into "spittoons," a receptacle especially designed for users of chewing and dipping tobacco. It was also known as a cuspidor. They were stationed **in** pubs, brothels, saloons, hotels, stores, banks, railway carriages and other places where adults (especially adult men) gathered.

With the start of the 20th century, medical doctors urged tuberculosis sufferers to use personal pocket spittoons instead of public ones; these were jars with tight lids which people could carry with them to spit into.

TB was primarily a disease of the city, where crowded and often filthy conditions provided an ideal breeding environment for incubation of the highly contagious disease.

Urban poor represented the vast majority of TB victims. Tuberculosis was also known as "consumption". In the early 1900s, it was not uncommon for such a death to strike at any age. In the coming weeks, Tommaso wasted away and died in 1909, at the age of twenty-three.

Natale, who had buried his wife, Domenica, one year before they arrived in America would now have to enshrine his only child. He had seen death on a daily basis and understood that death was clearly part of the human experience. He would make arrangements for the ceremony marking his son's death. There would be a two-day home-wake for his son, Tommaso, in the parlor of the Scallaci tenement apartment, a service at the Roman Catholic Church, and an interment at the church cemetery.

Tommaso's remains were embalmed and prepared for the traditional open casket viewing. Open casket funerals were common, as it was customary to kiss the deceased's cheek or forehead. That kiss was symbolic of one's respect for the decedent. The superstitious Sicilians believed that a person's soul did not want to leave Earth. As a result, survivors performed a variety of rituals to help them transcend to the hereafter. Many Italians did not speak of the dead once the period of mourning ended, as they did not wish to summon them back to earth. They buried the deceased with their favorite material possessions like cigarettes, matches, photographs, jewelry, and books in hopes this would encourage them not to return to Earth. Sicilians held much respect for death. Some families even left all the windows open so that the soul could depart unencumbered.

Flowers adorned Tommaso's coffin; everyone dressed in black. After the final rites of the wake completed, all attendees paraded by foot in a funeral procession to the church and grave site. The coffin was loaded onto a horse-drawn hearse pulled by two black stallions. The funeral mass was performed at the neighborhood Roman Catholic Church. At the cemetery, mourners paid their final respects and final words were spoken by Uncle Natale. As the coffin was lowered and touched ground, family and friends threw a handful of earth onto the coffin. All family members and closest friends returned to the Scallaci tenement. Upon hearing of Tommaso's death, friends and neighbors brought food, wine, casseroles, fruit, and desserts.

This all had to be eaten before spoiling, so the Scallaci women prepared and served the food to their guests. The next day, the Scallaci men were back on the streets of the Lower East Side selling their wares. One day, not long after the burial, on the crowded streets of Lower Manhattan, Uncle Natale ran into his father's childhood friend from their village in Palermo. They hugged and kissed each other on the cheek. They were surprised and overjoyed at seeing one another.

Uncle Natale did not know it at the time, but this encounter would forever change the Scallaci family future. They had a conversation in their native dialect. The older gentleman was accompanied by two men.

"Natale, would you and the rest of the Scallaci like to move into a four-story apartment building with twelve four-room apartments and four storefront shops beneath them, which I now own?"

"You could occupy two storefronts, where you could sell your fruits and vegetables, along with an assortment of other Italian food products - creating a neighborhood grocery."

"That would be a dream come true."

"The Scallaci Family could live in one of the apartments rent free and just pay rent on one of the store fronts."

"What can I do for you in return?"

"In return, the Scallaci would be responsible for maintaining the property and you would be the live-in landlord of the building collecting all rents. The only drawback would be that you and the rest of the Scallaci will have to relocate because the building is located in the Bronx.

"That's great news!"

The man was Don Luigi Sabatino, "Boss" of a powerful Mafia Clan back in Palermo, Sicily.

The Mafia began as a way of life, a way to protect one's family from the injustices of the Sicilian government. So, one might wonder what environment fostered such violence, slander, and camaraderie among men? Sicily's violent and oppressive history of government and its numerous corrupt and inconsistent rulers nurtured an atmosphere of governmental distrust, self-reliance, and cooperation among the people. This reliance and respect "were induced by fear, instilled by violent threats, and fortified by a hierarchy of families and friends."

Sicilians banded together in groups to protect themselves and carry out their own form of justice. In Sicily, the term "Mafioso," Mafia member, initially bore no criminal connotations. It referred to a person suspicious of central authority. By the 19th Century, some of these groups emerged as private armies, who extorted protection money from landowners. They eventually became the violent criminal entity known as the Sicilian Mafia. The Mafia emerged in an area that is still its heartland. It was initiated where Sicily's wealth was concentrated; in the dark green coastal region among modern capitalist export businesses, based in the idyllic orange and lemon groves just outside Palermo.

Even though Natale's father had been a long-time trusted friend of Don Luigi and had many offers to work for him and earn significant money, he chose the life of a peasant farmer like his father and grandfathers before him, right up until his death. Uncle Natale followed in his footsteps. Although Natale's father would not accept any financial help or favors from his old friend, his oldest son, Pasquale, did not want to be a farmer and instead, he became a soldier (enforcer) for the Sabatino crime family and served as Don Luigi's personal bodyguard. He was also killed protecting the "Don" from an assassin's bullet. He was the father of Amerigo and older brother of Natale.

Don Luigi arrived in America to oversee construction of a wholesale import distribution market in hopes of selling his export of citrus fruit and Italian food products from Sicily. Don Luigi acquired significant farmland in and around Palermo. In addition, he operated protection rackets and other criminal enterprises along with legitimate businesses in Sicily. Don Luigi wanted legitimate businesses and his goal was to establish a foothold in America. He intended to implement his plan accompanied by two bodyguards and his widowed brother-in-law. He had been married to the Don's younger sister, who died two years earlier. His name was Vito Anastasi, a trusted lieutenant in the Sabatino Mafia Family.

Vito arrived with his two sons, Angelo, the eldest at 24 years old and his younger brother, Santo, 23 years old. Don Luigi would leave Vito in charge of the Sabatino operations in America. Vito, along with his father, uncles, and brothers were master craftsmen who had built some of the most beautiful villas, cathedrals, civic buildings, and "palazzos" for the Sabatino construction companies in Sicily.

Don Luigi had just purchased one hundred acres of wooded land. The property abutted the railyards and docks. Vito, his two sons, along with several Sicilian immigrants from his village in Sicily, who had also emigrated to America would be responsible for building and creating two separate businesses on a portion of the property. One business would be the "Sabatino Wholesale Market;" the second business would be the "Sabatino Construction Company of the Bronx."

Vito had to clear some land for the buildings and to provide easy access for transportation of horse-pulling wagons to the railyards and docks to unload or load their merchandise. The four-story apartment building is where the Anastasis' and the Sicilian immigrants that worked for the new Sabatino businesses would reside. If the Scallaci accepted Don Luigi's offer, they would live there as well. The building was brand new and sat on twenty-five acres of property.

The Bronx had become a part of NYC in 1898. The quiet suburban streets and farms of the Bronx yielded to rapidly expanding factories and urban neighborhoods. The construction of the Bronx Zoo, the New York Botanical Gardens, and other large commercial projects brought many labor-force immigrants to the area.

It was now April of 1910, and Don Luigi remained to oversee the

construction of his new companies. Now that they were fully operational, it was time to return home to Sicily to his family and businesses.
Before his voyage back home, he met with Natale to discuss his decision of relocating to the Bronx. Natale, patriarch of the Scallaci family
in America after much deliberation, accepted Don Luigi's generous offer to move to the Bronx. Don Luigi was delighted with his decision!

The Sabatino and Scallaci families had been extremely close to
each other for many years. Natale was now responsible for collecting
all the rent money and handing it over to Vito. Don Luigi's business
in America was now complete! Natale and the Don hugged and kissed
each other on the cheek and spoke their goodbyes. He left with his two
bodyguards enroute to the Lower West side of Manhattan to meet his
steamship for his voyage across the Atlantic Ocean to his beloved Sicily.
They traveled in "first class."

The next day, the Scallaci Family packed up their possessions, conveyed their goodbyes to friends and neighbors, and left the Lower East
Side of Manhattan for the Bronx. Vito Anastasi had sent his two sons
to the Scallaci tenement in Manhattan, each pulling two horse-drawn
wagons. They picked up the Scallaci Family, along with their belongings, and escorted them to their new home.

Upon their arrival in the Bronx, they set up their four-room apartment. The apartment was located directly above Natale's soon-to-be grocery store. Vito and his crew of craftsmen merged two of the storefronts
at the end of the building and combined them into one big store. They
built counters, cabinets, and racks of shelving. They next installed two
large ice boxes to keep the produce fresh. A gift from Don Luigi!

When Vito finished the renovation, the Scallaci ensured the new
store was spotless! They stocked it with Italian food products such as;
assorted pastas, jarred sauces, fruits, vegetables, dried and cured meats,
assorted cheeses, baccala, sardines, coffee, espresso, figs, pine nuts,
almonds, garlic, onions, mushrooms, peppers, lentils, capers, fennel,
spices, homemade wine and the list goes on. Everything was purchased
at the Sabatino Wholesale Market in preparation for the grand opening.

Natale had a huge sign constructed for the exterior of the storefront written in big black letters, "Scallaci Family Grocery" in Italian, with the colors of the Italian flag (green, white, red) in three equal parts as background to the sign. As the sign was hoisted up, you could see the tears of joy and accomplishment on Natale's face. The new store was located on Arthur Avenue at East 187th Street, the heart of the Italian community.

Arthur Avenue was named in honor of the 21st president of the United States, Chester A. Arthur. The apartment/storefront building was located in the Belmont neighborhood of the Bronx. The location was convenient for the Scallaci, they just had to walk down a flight of stairs to get to work! They had never experienced any type of convenience before in their lives! No more pushing carts on the overcrowded and cluttered streets of the lower East Side of Manhattan.

The new store afforded an ample kitchen in the back where the women would make jarred sauces. The store also had its own bathroom and a large basement where Giuseppe and his son, Giacomo, produced wine and homemade pastas from durum wheat.

The store opened and experienced great success, as did the Sabatino Wholesale Import Market. Elder family members did not speak much English, consequently, as Vincenzo and Pasquale learned to speak English in school, they would teach them.

The adult Scallaci were peasant farmers sent to work at young ages. Most had only completed a third-grade education but swore to ensure that the next generation of Scallaci would get a high school education. Many of the Sicilian immigrants that ventured to America in the mid-19th through the mid-20th centuries were illiterate. Even though Natale's son, Tommaso, was not alive to see it, Natale knew he would also be proud of how far the Scallaci had progressed since coming to America.

In one of the darkest moments in America's industrial history, the factory for the Triangle Shirtwaist Company in New York City burnt down in 1911, killing 145 workers. It was a sweatshop in every sense of the word. The factory was a cramped space, lined with workstations, and packed with immigrant workers comprised mostly of teenaged Italian women who did not speak English.

5

The Ice Man Cometh

Living together in such segregated communities created little more than a microcosm of the society they had left in Europe. Some enterprising criminals exploited this and extorted the more prosperous Italians in their neighborhoods. A criminal undertaking that would eventually snowball into an epidemic known as the "Black Hand."

People paid the Black Hand extortionists based upon a fearful belief that American Law Enforcement had no understanding of, nor power to help them. The myth of the Black Hand spread through the "Little Italys" of America. A strong despair was instilled in the communities when even the mention of "la mano nera (black hand)" caused people to cross themselves with the hope of divine protection.

Intended prey would receive a letter demanding a specified amount of money be delivered to a specific place at an exact time. It was decorated with threatening symbols, such as a smoking gun, hangman's noose, skull, a knife dripping with blood or pierced human heart. In many instances, signed with a handheld up in the universal gesture of warning, imprinted or drawn in thick black ink.

Italian folklore spoke of gangsters being able to cast the evil eye and possessing other magical powers. Such fables mixed with the reality of bombings and murders highlighted in the local press only helped to compound the effectiveness of the Black Hand legend. In its most basic form, the evil eye was thought of as a look given to inflict harm, suffering, or some form of bad luck on those it is cast upon. To this day, some Sicilians still believe in the "evil eye." They also try to remember to put their first stocking on their left leg in order to ensure a day of good luck.

Uncle Natale received a letter he could not read, but by looking at the threatening symbols, he had an idea of what it was. He handed the letter to his nephew, Amerigo, who could read Italian. He read the letter to Natale:

"If you have not "sufficient courage," you may go to people who enjoy an honorable reputation and be careful as to whom you go. Thus, you may stop us from persecuting you as you have been adjudged to give money or life. Woe upon you if you do not resolve to buy your future happiness you can gain from us by giving the money demanded."

The letter demanded a specific amount of money and directed that it was to be delivered to a specified location. Natale, normally a calm man, but when angered exposed a volcanic temper. After Amerigo finished reading the letter to him, Natale's face turned beet red and veins protruded from his forehead. The other family members realized Natale was extremely angered. He was getting older but was still as strong and powerful as a bull from farming the fields at a young age. He was a robust man with a big black bushy mustache. He was clearly upset and wanted to discuss this matter with Amerigo in private. After they talked, they decided to show the letter to Don Luigi Sabatino's lieutenant, Vito Anastasi, who by now had built up his own gang for the Sabatino family in America.

After showing Vito the letter, he looked him straight in the eye:

"What do you make of this, Vito?"

"Not to worry Natale, we will take care of this. By no means should you pay the extortion money! Leave the letter with me and tell no one else about this."

"Grazie (Thank you), Vito."

As Natale and Amerigo prepared to leave, Vito told him:

"I've received word from Sicily that your brother Salvatore and two of his sons are coming for a visit to the Bronx."

"When do they sail?"

"I'm not sure, but I will find out for you."

Natale was one of three brothers: Pasquale, the oldest, Salvatore, the middle, and Natale, the youngest. His brother, Salvatore, also chose not to become a peasant farmer and followed his older brother, Pasquale, into a life in the Sicilian Mafia, "and also worked" for Don Luigi Sabatino. First as a loyal soldier, and now as a high-ranking lieutenant.

Salvatore had four sons: the oldest, Pasquale named after his older brother, Salvatore Jr., Paolo, and Francesco, the youngest. Uncle Salvatore's oldest son, Pasquale, married his childhood sweetheart, Gianna. She gave birth to twin boys who were the same age as Amerigo's youngest son, Pasquale. Two weeks passed and Natale had not heard anything or received any more extortion letters from the Black Hand. Vito confirmed he would take care of it – and it appeared he did! Natale eventually received word that his brother, Salvatore, along with his two sons would be arriving at the pier on the lower Westside of Manhattan sometime tomorrow.

Salvatore had sufficient money for his two sons and himself to travel second class. They would bypass Ellis Island and disembark from the steamship directly to the streets of Manhattan. Natale and the rest of the Scallaci Family were thrilled to see their family members from Palermo. Uncle Natale, accompanied by his nephew, Amerigo, would meet them at the pier and bring them to the Bronx the next day.

Natale and Amerigo arose early the next morning. They hitched up their wagon with a pair of horses and journeyed to the pier. They waited ten hours for the ship to arrive. When it did, it took another two hours or so before second class passengers could disembark. As Natale and Amerigo waited near the ship's off-ramp, they searched for Salvatore. At the same time, they caught Salvatore searching for them. They experienced much joy and elation at the reunion! When they exited the ramp, Natale and Amerigo were right there to greet them. They hugged and kissed each other.

"Last time I seen you two, you were just bambinos (children). Look at you, you are both all grown up!"

Amerigo was elated to see his Uncle Salvatore and his two cousins. Natale was finally reunited with his sibling! When Natale and his son, Tommaso, left Palermo in 1894, he did not know if he would ever see his brother or his nephews and the rest of the Scallaci family living in Sicily again. It was 1913. Today was an incredibly emotional day for the Scallaci, especially for Salvatore and Natale.

They grabbed their bags, climbed up on the wagon and headed home. When they finally arrived at the Scallaci Family Grocery, it was late, but all the Scallaci were there waiting for their family reunion with the new arrivals from Sicily. There was plenty of Sicilian food and wine. They reminisced about the old days. They ate and drank until their bellies were full.

Salvatore and his two sons stayed with Natale and the rest of the Scallaci in their four-room apartment. The following day, Uncle Salvatore, his two sons, Sal Jr. and Paolo took a horse drawn wagon to Sabatino's Wholesale Import Market where they met with Vito Anastasi and his two sons, Angelo, and Santo, to discuss business. Uncle Salvatore would explain Don Luigi's plan for the future of the Sabatino family in America.

First off, he told the Anastasis:

"It was Don Luigi's decision that I become "underboss" of all operations in America. I will now be running Sabatino Wholesale Market and my son, Paolo, will be joining me. Vito, you will be in charge of all construction. The Don wants you to expand Sabatino Construction Company to one location in each of the five boroughs that make up NYC, along with the suburbs of Long Island and Westchester County. Your first priority is to establish a new company in Manhattan."

He also wanted Vito and his sons to get involved in the building trades and to infiltrate the labor unions. Salvatore told Vito's son, Angelo:

"You will now be in charge of the Sabatino Construction Company of the Bronx. Your younger brother, Santo, will now be working for you. Your uncle, the Don promoted you to lieutenant of our Bronx crew."

Don Luigi's son, Luca, was now underboss of all Sicilian operations. Luca and Salvatore had been best friends since childhood and now both answered only to the Don. Vito Anastasi and his son, Angelo, now reported to Uncle Salvatore. Salvatore and his older brother, Pasquale had fearsome reputations as enforcers for the Sabatino family in Sicily back in the day. They were lethal in the use of stilettos (daggers), guns, and their fists. Now it was Vito and his son, Santos', turn to explain in detail and to show Salvatore and his sons the daily operation of the Sabatino Wholesale Import Market of the Bronx. Salvatore "was in charge of" the huge Sabatino's Wholesale Export Market in Sicily, so he would not have any problem running the smaller Bronx Market. Salvatore even had some great ideas to expand Sabatino's American businesses. He told them:

"Don Luigi conveyed to his son, Luca, and godson, Salvatore, all his business knowledge and both men excelled at it."

After Salvatore and Vito talked in private for some time, they hugged and kissed each other on the cheek. Vito and his sons exchanged their goodbyes and headed out. Vito left for Manhattan to purchase a four-story apartment building for him and his talented crew of tradesmen to live in. He intended to purchase property along the Hudson River for the new location of the Sabatino Construction Company of Manhattan, where they would be constructing tall buildings (skyscrapers).

Uncle Salvatore, Sal Jr., and Paolo inspected the entire wholesale markets operation. The Scallaci said their hellos to the immigrant workers they knew from their village and region. They even brought them news from their families back home. After they were done with that, the two sons followed their father to his new office upstairs in the Wholesale Market to talk business.

Salvatore explained his agenda:

"I along with Paolo will run Sabatino Wholesale Import Market and expand its business not only to the Bronx, but to the entire East Coast."

Before Salvatore and his sons left Sicily, the scale of pasta production had increased via many factories in the immediate suburbs of Palermo which Don Luigi owned. The transformation of Sicilian wheat into pasta for export to the United States, Britain, France, Argentina, Brazil, and other European and South American countries was a huge money maker for Sabatino Wholesale Export Market in Sicily. In addition to exporting boxes of assorted Sabatino brand pastas, the factories also produced dried cakes of tomato puree reduced to a thick dark paste, tin cans of skinned pulverized tomatoes lightly cooked in sauces and canned olive oil.

Salvatore had big plans for Sabatino's Wholesale Import Market and for other Sabatino operations in America. Uncle Salvatore being the oldest Scallaci, would now be the patriarch of the family in America. A huge motivator was his remembrance of his childhood, working in the fields of Palermo in the scorching sun alongside his two brothers, father, grandfather, uncles, and cousins cultivating the soil to grow durum wheat. He wanted to be successful for the entire Scallaci Family, and for all of them to prosper. He harbored big plans for the future of the Scallaci Family.

Uncle Salvatore wanted to create a new Scallaci business. This new business would be run by Salvatore Junior. Uncle Salvatore believed that it would be a big money maker. He wanted to get into the "frozen ice" industry. The ice trade began with the harvesting of ice from ponds and rivers during the winter, to be stored for the summer months ahead in ice houses. The ice needed to be at least eighteen inches thick to be harvested, as it needed to support the weight of the workers and horses and be suitable for cutting into large blocks.

Ice cutting involved several stages and was usually carried out at night, when the ice was at its thickest. Natural ice typically had to be moved several times between being harvested and used by the end customer. A wide range of delivery methods were used including wagons pulled by horses, railroads, ships, and barges. These ponds and rivers were typically located near industrial factories which spewed out pollution. With metropolitan growth, many sources of natural ice became contaminated from industrial pollution or sewer run-off. In the early 20th Century, new technology was used to create refrigeration cooling systems and manufactured plant ice. This would be the way Uncle Salvatore would proceed! He would have Angelo Anastasi build an ice manufacturing plant, next to the Sabatino Wholesale Market, where it would be close to rail lines and docks. They would develop routes to distribute the plant ice to their final domestic and commercial customers.

Ice began to be used in refrigerated cars by the railroad industry, allowing the meatpacking industry around Chicago and Cincinnati to slaughter cattle locally, sending dressed meat East for use in the internal or overseas markets. Chilled cars and ships created a national market for vegetables and fruit that could previously only have been consumed locally. The ice trade revolutionized the U.S. meat, vegetable, and fruit industries. This revolution further enabled significant growth in the fishing industry and encouraged the introduction of a range of new drinks and foods. The final part of the supply chain for domestic and commercial customers involved the delivery of ice using ice wagons.

In the United States, ice was manufactured or cut into twenty-five, fifty and one hundred-pound blocks, then distributed by horse-drawn ice wagons. "Similar to the milkman or coal delivery man," the iceman was a local fixture. Displaying an "Ice Today" card visible in the window, an iceman driving the cart would then deliver ice to the household using ice tongs to hold blocks, then place it over his back or shoulder and perhaps walk up two, three or even four tenement flights. Deliveries occurred either daily or twice daily.

"In order for a domestic or commercial customer to use ice," it was necessary to be able to store it for a period away from an icehouse. As a result, iceboxes were a critical final stage in the storage process. Without them, households could not have used or consumed ice. In addition to the temperature ice was held at, there was also a need to efficiently drain off melted water as this water would further melt the remaining ice much faster than warm air would.

Non-electrical iceboxes were used in the early 1900s. Blocks of ice obtained from an icehouse or manufacturing plant and stored inside the unit were necessary to keep the contents cold. These containers were usually constructed of wood with hollowed walls lined with tin or zinc and packed with various insulating materials such as cork, sawdust, straw, or seaweed. A large block of ice was held in a tray or compartment near the top of the box. Cold air circulated down and around storage compartments in the lower section. An expensive model featured a spigot for draining melted ice water from a holding tank. Economy models utilized a drip pan, which was placed under the unit and had to be emptied frequently.

A constant supply of ice was required to maintain refrigeration. This practice would become common until the invention of the electric refrigerator. New York City, home to numerous hotels, businesses and restaurants consumed more ice than any other city in the United States. Uncle Salvatore had just one little problem, he had some of his own money to invest in his new venture, but he knew he would need more! Salvatore would need a partner with plenty of money along with the resources to make the operation prosper. He would contact Don Luigi Sabatino about his idea. He had plenty of money and owned property that led to the rail lines and docks, which would be the perfect location for the new business. For years, the Sabatino's businesses in Sicily had been represented by a prominent lawyer, Gaetano Romano, who ensured all legitimate business matters were conducted legally and advised the Don in his illegal activities.

Gaetano had sent his oldest son, Alfonso, to America in 1895. He excelled intellectually, attending the finest schools and universities. He spoke and wrote in perfect English. He enrolled at New York University School of Law, worked diligently, and received his law degree. He had been working at a law firm for several years now and was just barely making it. His father, Gaetano, who was good friends with Salvatore, sent Salvatore a message asking him if he could give his son, Alphonso, a job. Salvatore, who was an astute businessman, but had no education beyond the third grade needed someone who could advise him in legal and non-legal matters. Alphonso, who could read and write in both Sicilian and English, was hired by Salvatore. There was a storage room situated behind Salvatore's office that would now serve as Alphonso's office.

Alphonso would now strictly work for the Sabatino family in America and the Scallaci businesses in the Bronx. When Alphonso arrived at the Sabatino's Wholesale Market in the Bronx, Uncle Salvatore, Sal Jr., Angelo Anastasi, and he discussed the idea of the ice business Salvatore wanted to create with Don Luigi as his partner.

Salvatore wanted to craft an arrangement that would be fair to both the Sabatinos and the Scallaci. The four men spent several days discussing Salvatore's plan and doing their research on the operation. To propose his idea in a plan to the Don, he had Alphonso Romano detail such in a letter written in Sicilian. Don Luigi, who could not read or write, would have Gaetano Romano read and discuss this new business arrangement with him and his son, Luca, in his Palermo office.

Salvatore would now have to wait for his boss's decision. Meanwhile, "all of the Sabatino's legal and illegal operations were thriving in Sicily and America. While Salvatore was waiting for Don Luigi's yes or no decision, he thought of ideas regarding how to export back to Europe products that were in demand. Sabatino's Wholesale Market in Palermo now owned and operated three cargo ships that exported their products not only to America, but also to other European and South American countries. These ships typically delivered their cargo to their destinations and returned empty. Salvatore mused—instead of leaving empty-handed, he wanted to fill the ships' hold back up with cargo of American manufactured products and American-grown produce.

As a result, Sabatino's Wholesale Import Market in the Bronx became an import/export business. The main hub for Sabatino's Wholesale Market in Palermo was now an export/import market. If Salvatore's proposition for the ice company was approved by the boss, the Sabatino Wholesale Market and the Scallaci Family Grocery would have an endless supply of ice, which they and the rest of New York City needed. Accordingly, Natale and Salvatore had been quite busy in the weeks following Salvatore and his son's arrival to America and had not spent much time together.

Tomorrow was Sunday! The religious festival or festa that honored the patron saint, Rosalia, was to be held. The festa marked not only a day of celebration but also reinforced emotional ties immigrants held to their native villages.

6

Misfortunes of War

Natale planned to hold a celebration for his brother, Salvatore, and his two sons, welcoming them to America, on the day of the festival. Sunday arrived and they started early on this joyous day. All the Scallaci, Anastasis, friends and neighbors gathered. There would be traditional Sicilian singing, dancing, puppet shows and other forms of Sicilian entertainment. The women dressed in traditional costumes.

The festival involved an elaborate procession through the streets in honor of a Patron Saint, in which a large statue was transported by a team of men, with musicians marching behind. This was followed by food, fireworks, and general merriment. The "Festa" became an important occasion that instilled immigrants with a sense of unity and common identity.

This was the first time Salvatore and Natale really got to talk to each other, as they both worked long hours.

"Natale, I am sorry for the loss of your son, Tommaso. My original plan for coming to America was to visit you and the rest of the Scallaci Family. Then after spending a month in America, I would "return back to Sicily," leaving my two sons to start up a new Scallaci family business based in the Bronx. My plans changed after a meeting with my boss, Don Luigi Sabatino."

Don Luigi had different plans for me in America. Salvatore did not know if he would ever return to Sicily. He would send for his wife, Anna, oldest son, Pasquale, and his family along with his youngest son, Francesco, to come to America."

"I like living here in la merica. It really is the 'land of opportunity'."

There was an available apartment in the Sabatino building, across the hall from Natale's apartment, so Salvatore, Sal Jr. and Paolo moved in. Soon, the family would be reunited! Salvatore discussed his idea for an ice venture he wanted to start up. It would be a Scallaci and Sabatino family partnership.

"Natale, this new business would be legitimate; I would not involve you or the Scallaci family under your care in any illegal activity."

As they were having their conversation, Sal and Natale noticed two New York City Police Officers talking and showing something to their guests.

"Let me see what they want."

He approached them. They looked Italian. One of them spoke Sicilian and identified himself and his partner as detectives and members of the New York City police "Italian Squad" Homicide Division.

"We are investigating the murder of an unidentified man."

He held a photo of a man who appeared dead.

"Would you take a look at the photo?"

Even if Natale could identify him, he would not say anything. "Omerta," the code of silence is how all Scallaci were raised and what they lived by. He gave the photo a good look. It showed a man with a letter lying on his chest, held down by a stiletto through his heart, with his throat slashed from ear to ear. He did not know the man's name but had seen that face before around the neighborhood. He did, however, recognize the letter as being the "Black Hand" extortion letter he had received and gave to Vito Anastasi, who told him, "Don't worry, I will take care of this." He handed the photo back to the detective.

"I have never laid eyes upon this man before."

Natale did not feel any emotion, as he thought the man had got what was coming to him.

He returned to where Salvatore was.

"What did they want?"

"They were asking around if anyone knew the dead man in the photo."

"I told them I didn't, I guess no one else did either, because they both left without knowing the man's identity."

Salvatore continued his conversation with his younger brother, conveying more about his idea to manufacture plant ice and distribute it all throughout New York City.

"I think you have a good idea. When will you get started?"

"I'm waiting to hear back from Don Luigi. I am now in charge of Sabatino's Wholesale Import/Export Market in the Bronx. I have hired a lawyer, Gaetano Romano's son, Alphonso, who now strictly works for the Sabatino family and the Scallaci businesses.

With that, the fireworks show commenced, indicating that the sacred rituals of the Festa honoring the patron Saint of "Saint Rosalia" were coming to an end.

It was back to work for the immigrants. In the coming weeks, Uncle Salvatore sent money back to Palermo for steamboat passage for the rest of his family to immigrate to America. He also received a message from his boss giving him the go ahead to create his manufactured plant ice. With this news Salvatore wasted no time implementing his plan. He had Angelo Anastasi and his construction crew clear some wooded property next to Sabatino's Wholesale Market. He then ordered them to construct a factory to house his refrigeration cooling systems that would produce his "manufactured plant ice."

They would also construct additional buildings to house his many horses and wagons. Sal Jr., Angelo, and Alphonso would work with engineers who possessed the latest technology along with the best refrigeration equipment available to create a state-of-the-art ice manufacturing plant! Angelo had built a sawmill next door to the Sabatino Construction Company of the Bronx, so all the trees they cut down to clear the area for the new ice company could be milled for lumber and used in the construction of these new buildings. These projects would keep them all busy for some time.

It was now 1914, and there was mounting tension among European countries. Differences in foreign policies and the assassination of Austrian Archduke Ferdinand became the "casus belli" for the beginning of World War I, the great war" or "the war to end all wars." The two main sides were the Allies, which included France, Great Britain, Russia, and their opponents, the central powers of the German and Austro-Hungarian Empires. In total, thirty countries were involved in the conflict. Soldiers fought largely in trenches. The trench network of WWI stretched approximately 25,000 miles from the English Channel to Switzerland. The area was commonly known as the "Western Front."

President Woodrow Wilson at the onset of WW I, declared the United States as remaining neutral. The U.S. endowed major contributions in terms of supplies, raw material, and money - serving as an important supplier to Britain and other Allied powers. While war in the trenches is described in horrific, apocalyptic terms--the mud, the stench of rotting bodies, the enormous rats--the reality was that the trench system also protected the soldiers to a large extent from the worst effects of modern firepower used for the first time during that conflict.

Thousands suffered from stress known as "shell shock." Approximately thirty different poisonous gases were used during the war. Mustard gas was the deadliest. It was fired into trenches in shells. It was colorless and took twelve hours to take effect. Effects included blistering skin, vomiting, sore eyes, and internal and external bleeding. Death could take up to five weeks. The WW I machine gun was primarily used as a defensive weapon, inflicting appalling casualties. Thousands of men charging toward the enemy line were mowed down by the rapid fire of these devastating weapons.

As WWI raged on, Uncle Salvatore oversaw the construction of his new ice manufacturing operation. He was in the process of planning distribution network routes for residential and commercial delivery of his blocks of ice. Also, his wife Anna, son, Pasquale, along with his family and youngest son, Francesco arrived from their voyage across the Atlantic Ocean. They also traveled in second class.

Pasquale, the oldest son, who helped his father manage Sabatino's Market in Sicily would now be in charge of the market in the Bronx. His brother, Paolo, would serve as his right-hand man. Francesco would work for his older brother Salvatore Jr. at the new Sabatino and Scallaci Ice Company.

Salvatore's wife, Anna and her daughter-in-law, Gianna, would help Amerigo's wife, Giovanna and Giuseppe's wife, Maria in the Scallaci Family Grocery kitchen preparing Italian sauces and soups that they jarred and sold in the store. Relationships with customers were quite personal in the early 20th Century and at the Scallaci Family Grocery you could send a kid down to the store and say, "put it on our tab," and pay for it later. Natale and Amerigo knew their customers; that is because when they visited the store, they held conversations, resulting in Natale and Amerigo getting to know all the families in the neighborhood quite well!

Uncle Natale, now 45 years old, developed a bad cough, experienced night sweats and fatigue, and presented the same symptoms that his son, Tommaso, showed before he died of tuberculosis. Natale, who did not want to miss a day's work, finally listened to his nephew, Amerigo's, advice and visited a doctor, accompanied by his brother, Salvatore. After the doctor examined him, his diagnosis was dire--Natale indeed had T.B. The news devastated the Scallaci Family. Natale was loved and well respected by all. He refused to go to a sanatorium and be isolated from society. He chose to spend his final days with his "la famiglia" (family). In the weeks to follow, Uncle Natale, a robust and extremely powerful man, experienced severe weight loss. The disease seemed to consume him.

Tuberculosis, one of the leading causes of death in the United States had taken Natale's life in the year 1915, six years after it took his son, Tommaso. This was the saddest day for the Scallaci since immigrating to America. They had just started to get a small taste of the American dream, thanks to Uncle Natale. Natale worked up to the day he died without complaint. Salvatore, patriarch of the family, took care of all the arrangements for the wake and burial of his younger brother. The one thing which all Italians share, however, from whatever region they immigrated from was the habit of spending much of their resources on ritual behavior.

The cemetery plot itself performed an important social function for the immigrant. The type of plot, plantings and stone selected stood as a permanent visual record for all to see, testifying to the status of the deceased and his survivors. Salvatore, busy at this time creating his ice business, left his sons, his lawyer, and Angelo along with his crew of tradesmen to complete his ice operation. Salvatore devoted all of his attention to taking care of Natale's funeral and burial arrangements. He arranged for the wake to be held at the Tarantino Funeral Home located in the neighborhood.

He purchased a large family plot in a peaceful Roman Catholic Cemetery in the Bronx where future generations of the Scallaci family, upon their deaths would be buried. He had stone columns built, adorned by ornamental iron railing and gates adorned with the letter, 'S' which stood for the first letter of the Scallaci surname. The area was landscaped with beautiful plantings. The church yard cemetery where Natale's son, Tommaso, had been buried in Manhattan was by now filled to capacity. Salvatore had his nephew's body exhumed from the church cemetery and relocated to the Scallaci family plot in a new casket. The ceremony occurred in a basement church called our "Lady of Mount Carmel," located on 187th Street and Belmont Avenue. An Italian-speaking priest who spoke their regional dialect would perform Natale's final mass.

Salvatore selected an ornate casket and bought Natale a new suit for the traditional open casket viewing. The room at the funeral parlor where the embalmed body lay peacefully was magnificently arranged. His casket was adorned with many beautiful flowers. It was packed with people who spent quality amounts of time around the casket praying and mourning. They showed much regard and respect for Natale during this time. People gave respect to death rather than fearing it. Natale was genuinely loved and mourned by the Scallaci family and the entire neighborhood.

After the two-day wake ended, the casket was loaded into a hearse by family, taken to the church for the mass and finally, to the cemetery. The casket was placed near the grave site. Uncle Salvatore spoke for Natale. The Roman Catholic priest spoke the final benediction. The casket that held Natale's body was lowered and all the mourners threw a handful of dirt on the casket as a show of their respect to a great man. Natale was now resting in peace alongside his son, Tommaso. Life after the funeral, was a time of deep mourning, to let Time heal, and to show regard for the deceased.

Although Natale's wife had died one year before Natale and Tommaso emigrated to America, Italian women rarely left their homes except to attend church or church-linked events such as baptisms, weddings, and funerals. Language isolated women even more than it did the men since few of the women had attended school in Italy. Few spoke standard Italian and could communicate only in their regional dialects, which was understood only by those who had immigrated from the same area. It was this problem of language teamed with suspicion of people from other villages that caused Italian immigrants to split into regional factions.

Salvatore arranged an elaborate funeral with all the traditional Sicilian rituals for Natale whom he would miss very much. The next day, Uncle Salvatore stopped by the Scallaci Family Grocery to talk to his nephew:

"Amerigo, before Natale died he told me his last wishes. He directed 'Amerigo, my beloved nephew' to be the new owner of the Scallaci Family Grocery and that all his savings and possessions were also bequeathed to him, whom he always considered as his son."

It was Natale's dream that one day the Scallaci Family would prosper as a successful business family, transforming from Sicilian peasant farmers into well-to-do Americans! Amerigo would continue Uncle Natale's dream toward prosperity in America. It was now Amerigo's turn to follow in his footsteps. As one Scallaci dies, a new Scallaci is born. Uncle Giuseppe's son, Giacomo married a Sicilian girl, Lucia, who gave birth to a son. Vincenzo, Amerigo's oldest son, was now 18 years old and eager to enlist in the American Army.

With Italy entering WWI on the Allied side in 1915 and America still neutral in the war but helping support Great Britain and its allies, Vincenzo felt it was his patriotic duty to serve in his country's military! Vincenzo enlisted in the United States Army and was subsequently sent to a stateside training camp. Upon completion of his training, he was then sent to the Mexican border in Texas to join his new outfit, First Division as an infantry soldier, with the punitive expedition U.S. Army. It was a military operation conducted by the United States Army against the paramilitary forces of Mexican revolutionary, Francisco "Pancho" Villa.

Uncle Salvatore had completed all the finishing touches on the Sabatino and Scallaci Ice Company and was pleased with the way it turned out. Salvatore was meticulous and had a lot of pride. He favored quality over quantity, which was one of the Scallaci family traits. The ice manufacturing plant was now one hundred percent operational, running smoothly and efficiently. Business was flourishing!

America entered World War I following the interception of a note from the German Foreign Minister to a Mexican diplomat promising that if Mexico would join forces in attacking the United States, Germany would ensure Mexico got back territories it had lost during the American Mexican war. This was referred to as the "Zimmerman Note." In addition, the sinking of an American ship, the "Housatonic" and four more U.S. merchant ships by German U-Boats enraged the American populace. President Woodrow Wilson appeared before Congress and called for a Declaration of War against Germany.

The United States entered WWI in 1917. The Italian American community wholeheartedly supported the war effort. Its young men, both Italian and American-born, enlisted in large numbers in the American Army. The United States joined its allies Great Britain, France, and Russia to fight in WWI under the command of Major General John J. "Blackjack" Pershing. More than two million soldiers would fight on battlefields in France.

On May 2nd, 1917, a month after the American declaration of war, Major General John J. Pershing received word that he was to travel to

France with four infantry regiments and three artillery regiments to form a division. It would be the First division, which had recently seen field service under Pershing's command on the Mexican border. The First Division, with which Vincenzo Scallaci proudly served, earned a reputation for excellence and "esprit dé corps." World War I was the first time in American history that the U.S. sent soldiers abroad to defend foreign soil.

The First Division, also called the "Big Red One" was the most experienced of the five American divisions. The final Allied offensive of WWI, the Meuse-Argonne Offensive, also known as the "Battle of the Argonne Forest," the largest in United States military history, involved 1.2 million American soldiers, stretched along the entire Western Front. By the beginning of 1918, the tide of WWI had turned, the German armies began to retreat. Demoralized German workers suffering from food and fuel shortages threatened revolution at home.

German leaders, fearing a communist takeover, eventually asked the Allies for peace. The Armistice went into effect on November 11,1918. With the war over, the Scallaci family patiently waited for months to hear from Vincenzo. Finally, they received a telegram, but it was not from Vincenzo; it was an official Army form. Pasquale, the only Scallaci who could read and write in English, read the telegram aloud. It read, "We deeply regret to inform you that your son, Corporal Vincenzo Scallaci, was killed in action on 2 November1918 during the battle of the Argonne Forest in France." The news shocked everyone! Amerigo, though saddened, understood like his Uncle Natale, who taught him at a young age that death is just another path - one that we all must take!

Giovanna took the death of her oldest son extremely hard. It would take quite some time for her wounds to heal—maybe never. Vincenzo was buried in France at the Meuse-Argonne American Cemetery alongside his fellow "doughboys" (soldiers). The Scallaci also received a letter from his commanding officer saying, "that before he was killed in action he was responsible for eliminating two German machine gun nests (positions)." For his brave and heroic act, he was posthumously awarded his Second Silver Citation Star for combat gallantry and a Purple Heart Medal.

Pasquale, who always looked up to Vincenzo, was proud of his older brother for having served his new country and for his bravery on the battlefield. He vowed to his mother and father, "Someday, I will travel to France and place flowers at Vincenzo's grave."

Pasquale, 19 years of age, had been working at the family grocery full-time for a couple of years now. He worked sixteen-hour days, Monday through Saturday, and a half day on Sunday. The rest of Sunday, the family attended church, then would visit the Scallaci Family plot to spend time with Uncle Natale and Cousin Tommaso.

Uncle Salvatore had a huge headstone built for his brother, Natale, and a smaller one for Tommaso. When they left the cemetery, the entire family would sit down to a big multi-course meal accompanied by wine and completed with dessert, strong coffee, and a cordial.

In 1918, the first cases of one of the worst influenza epidemics in history were reported at Fort Riley, Kansas. Influenza would eventually kill more than a half million Americans and more than twenty million worldwide. The influenza pandemic of 1918 was commonly referred to as Spanish flu" or "la grippe." It was a global disaster. In Paris, diplomats representing the combatant nations of WWI signed the treaty of Versailles, which promised to sustain peace through the creation of the League of Nations, but also planted the seed for future conflict by imposing mercilessly stiff war reparations upon Germany.

7

The 1920s, The Lions Roar

By the turn of the century, temperance societies became a fixture in communities across the United States. Women played a strong role in the temperance movement as they viewed alcohol as a disruptive force to family life and marriage. During the 19th Century, alcoholism, drug abuse, gambling addiction and a variety of other social ills and abuses led to activism in an attempt to cure the perceived maladies of society.

In 1906, a wave of attacks against the sale of liquor led by the Anti-Saloon League and driven by reaction to urban growth, as well as the rise of evangelical Protestantism and its view of saloon culture as corrupt and ungodly.

In 1917, after the U.S. entered WWI, President Wilson instituted a temporary war-time prohibition in order to save grain for producing food. That same year, Congress submitted the 18th Amendment, which banned the manufacture, transportation, and sale of intoxicating liquor for state ratification. The amendment was ratified on January 29, 1919.

The 18th Amendment went into effect a year later on January 16th, 1920. The Federal Volstead Act shuttered every tavern, bar, and saloon in the United States. This drove the liquor trade underground. People simply patronized nominally illegal "speakeasies" where access to spirits was controlled by bootleggers, racketeers, and other organized crime figures. It was not illegal to drink during prohibition. The Volstead Act which established prohibition actually had a significant loophole. Alcohol consumption in and of itself was never deemed illegal.

Because alcohol was now thought to be inaccessible to most Americans, supporters of the act believed consumption would taper off and eventually cease. Prohibition was supposed to lower crime and corruption, reduce social problems, lower taxes needed to support prisons and poor houses, and improve health and hygiene in America.

Instead, alcohol became more dangerous to consume. Organized crime blossomed, courts and prisons became overloaded, endemic corruption of police, and public servants occurred. Organized crime received a major financial boost from prohibition. Gangsters historically limited their activities to prostitution, gambling, and theft until 1921, when organized bootlegging emerged in response to prohibition. A profitable black market for alcohol flourished. Alcohol distribution once the province of legitimate business was taken over by criminal gangs, which fought each other for market control. Violent confrontations including murder sprang forth. Gangsters such as Chicago's Alfonse Capone and New York City's Lucky Luciano became wealthy and gained local and national prominence. It is widely believed that the term "bootlegging" originated during the American Civil War as soldiers snuck liquor into Army camps by concealing pint bottles within their boots or beneath their trouser legs. There remained a substantial demand for alcohol as a staple commodity. Uncle Salvatore now had a new and profitable enterprise for the Sabatino family. With the Sabatino's factories in Sicily producing Sabatino brand pastas packaged in boxes, Uncle Natale's cousin, Giuseppe, and son, Giacomo, who prepared all the homemade pastas to sell in the grocery now simply produced pasta on a much smaller scale. They decided it was time to open their own Scallaci business. The Bonacasa cabinet shop previously located at the opposite end of the Sabatino building had moved and relocated to Long Island. The storefront was now available. Uncle Giuseppe and his son opened up the "Scallaci Butcher Shop." Giacomo and Lucia now had two sons and a daughter to add to the ever-expanding Scallaci family. Amerigo, with help from Uncle Salvatore, struck a deal with Don Luigi to purchase the apartment/store front building and property they occupied on Arthur Avenue and 187th Street for more than a fair price. The Scallaci were now property owners!

The 1920s was a period of dramatic social and political change. For the first time, more Americans lived in cities than on farms. The nation's total wealth more than doubled. People from coast to coast bought the same goods, thanks to nationwide advertising and the spread of chain stores. In addition, residents now listened to the same music, did the same dances such as the Charleston, Foxtrot, Texas Tommy, and even uttered the same slang.

Many Americans were uncomfortable with this new urban exodus and sometimes racy mass culture. In fact, for many, even most people in the United States, the 1920s brought more conflict than celebration. However, for some young people in the nation's big cities, the 1920s roared!!

The decade following WWI, would be memorialized as the "Roaring Twenties." Nothing quite like it had ever happened before in America. By the mid-1920s, jazz was being played in dancehalls, roadhouses, and speakeasies all over the country. The blues which had once been the province of itinerant black musicians, the poorest of the Southern poor, had grown into an industry; and dancing consumed a nation that seemed convinced prosperity would never end.

Advances in technology led to the age of electricity and America, especially in the industrialized cities, were suddenly powered up. Access to electricity in the 1920s provided Americans with the power required to run new labor-saving devices. The 1920s were also a time of prosperity for many Americans. There was access to easy credit, making it possible for people to take advantage of the decade's innovations.

Even though Henry Ford's Motor Company introduced the Ford "Model T" in 1908 at nearly one third of the price of any other car on the market, most Americans could still not afford it. In 1908, it cost $850. Assembly line production innovation allowed the price of the touring car to be lowered to less than $300 by 1925.

In the early 1920s, the Sabatino and Scallaci Ice Company started delivering coal to residential dwellings and commercial businesses for heating. All Sabatino and Scallaci men traded in their horses and wagons for cars and trucks.

Salvatore became extremely successful and earned a ton of money for his boss, Don Luigi, and the Scallaci as a bootlegger in the smuggling and sales of illegal alcohol. He consequently began his rise in organized crime and, along with fellow gangster, Lucky Luciano, would become one of the biggest bootleggers in NYC. He employed several different ways to smuggle illegal alcohol into the city. The most frequently used method that he employed was the Sabatino's cargo ships to transport the "hooch" into offshore waters. Then, faster smaller boats would take the illegal liquor to landing spots along Long Islands coast, for further distribution.

Once it reached shore, the liquor would be unloaded onto trucks disguised as fruit or vegetable haulers or other transport vehicles with false bottoms which concealed the contraband. In the days of "rum running," it was common for captains of these ships to add water to the alcohol to stretch their profits or to relabel it as "superior, more expensive goods."

Cheap sparkling wines became French champagne. Unbranded liquor miraculously became top-of-the-line name brands. The Sabatino family bootlegging operation had a reputation for never watering their booze and for only selling actual top brands in their speakeasies and to others.

Some bootleggers sold poor quality home distilled hard liquor called "bathtub gin" in the cities and "moonshine" in rural areas. One of the common side effects of prohibition was alcohol poisoning. Since bootleg alcohol was not produced in distilleries under government supervision and was not, except in rare instances, distilled under the direction of chemists, its quality was extremely suspect. The chances of obtaining "real stuff" were never better than eight in one hundred! In most cases, it had been spiked with chemicals and poisons to give it a "kick." As a result, deaths from alcohol poisoning increased dramatically. Over time, more people drank illegally so a lot of money ended up in gangsters' pockets. The Sabatino crime family smuggled whiskey from Canada, Scotch whiskey from Scotland, gin from England, rum from the Caribbean and wines and champagne from France. In addition to all that, they purchased their beer from Dutch Schultz the "Beer Baron of the Bronx."

Not only did they have to elude the police, the Sabatino family also had to fend off other bootleggers looking to steal their precious cargo for their own benefit. Bootlegging grew into a vast illegal empire in part because of widespread bribery. Many public officials and enforcement agents received monthly "retainers" to look the other way. The Sabatino family also operated over one hundred "speakeasies," thriving establishments that illegally sold alcoholic beverages. Uncle Salvatore's son, Paolo, was heavily involved with running these night clubs for the family. Patrons had to whisper or speak easy through a small opening in a door, either providing the name of the person who had sent them or a secret code or password to gain access through a door that appeared to lead to an ordinary apartment, deli, tailor or soda shop.

Once inside though, there was plenty of drinking and entertainment including torch and cabaret singers, vaudeville acts. and a whole lot of "jazz." At one time, there were thought to be over 100,000 speakeasies in New York City alone. Prior to the Amendment, women drank moderately and even then, perhaps just a bit of wine or sherry. Just six months after prohibition became law in 1920, women achieved the right to vote! Coming into their own, they quickly loosened up, tossed their corsets, and enjoyed their new-found freedoms.

The "jazz age" quickly signified a loosening up of morals, the exact opposite of what prohibition advocates had intended. A new breed of women emerged called "flappers" who liked to smoke and drink, listen to jazz, and talk about sex. With short skirts, bobbed hair, powdered faces, bright red lips and bare arms and legs, they embraced an abandon never before displayed by American women. They flooded the Speakeasies! None of this was considered lady-like at the time; it was new and shocking! Flappers enjoyed the changing times with more freedom to express themselves. There is no doubt the flappers had a lot of style. The names of some of the more popular speakeasies flappers favored were The Cotton Club, The Stork Club, 21 Club, Connie's Inn, and Chumley's of New York City. The interiors of some of the finest speakeasies were quite lavish, with fine restaurants and underground passageways. Many, however, were drab makeshift saloons in basements or tenements located in shabby parts of town. Pasquale Scallaci, son of Amerigo and Giovanna was now engaged to a neighborhood girl, Natala Ruggiero, the 17-year-old daughter of Giuseppe Ruggiero, owner of the Italian Barber Shop in the now Scallaci building. They were to be married in one week at the Roman Catholic Church of "Our Lady of Mount Carmel" in the year 1923. The wedding celebration that would follow the church ceremony would take place outdoors, directly behind the Scallaci building in the newly constructed backyard.

Glamourous Flapper Girl

Uncle Salvatore had Angelo Anastasi and his crew of master craftsmen build a bar, a stage for the brass band and a dance floor for the celebration's entertainment. They crafted stone walls and added a fountain, statues, lighting, a magnificent garden, and beautiful landscaping. Angelo had created a lavish estate type backyard! This would be a wedding gift from Don Luigi and the Sabatino family to Pasquale and Natala Scallaci. Everything was ready for the big day! With Uncle Salvatore's connections, Salvatore hired Beniamino Gigli, the famous Italian opera singer and tenor to perform for the wedding celebration.

The Scallaci family expanded at a rapid rate and their quality of life was improving. Pasquale was ready to settle down and raise a family of his own to carry on the Scallaci family lineage. Salvatore took care of all the alcoholic beverages, soft drinks, chairs, tables, food, and drink servers, ice, and the entertainment.

The Italian people cherished many customs, traditions, superstitions, and rituals. The night before the wedding, Natala wore a green outfit as this was considered to bring good luck and the promise of fertility. Sunday was considered the only day for a wedding if the married couple were to enjoy a life of happiness. Any other day was considered to be unlucky. The groom would carry a piece of iron (toc ferro) in his pocket to ward off evil spirits or malocchio, the evil eye. The bride will make a small tear in her veil to welcome good luck.

Pasquale also must not see Natala before the wedding ceremony. Tomorrow was indeed a big day for the Scallaci and Ruggieros! Everyone showed their excitement and joy for the Sunday morning ceremony. The weather as well as the bride were beautiful! Natala's mother passed down her wedding dress to her daughter who looked stunning!

The wedding party consisted of her married cousin, Angela, maid of honor, and her daughter, Chiara, flower girl. For the groom, his cousin, Giacomo, best man (witness), and his young son, Mateo, ring bearer.

Traditionally, the Italian bride would prepare a "trousseau" or hope chest of household items and clothing for herself and sometimes even clothes for her future husband. Her family would provide her a "dowry" of monetary and possibly domestic goods. They would add items collected throughout her childhood and have it ready at the time of the wedding, as the newlyweds would move in together right after the honeymoon. During the ceremony, a ribbon was placed across the door to the church. This represented the couple's harmony and showed anyone passing by that a joyous event is taking place inside.

Pasquale, keeping with Italian tradition, provided the bride's bouquet as the last gift from the groom as boyfriend. The bride would later throw the bouquet - the girl who caught it was believed to be the next to marry.

The church was crowded! The Ruggieros and their guests were seated on the left side of the church, the Scallaci and their guests on the right side. Pasquale stood at the altar with his best man, Giacomo. He waited until Natala stepped in accompanied by her father, Giuseppe who walked her down the aisle and then gave her away.

He shook Pasquale's hand, lifted Natala's veil, kissed his beautiful daughter, then strolled back to the first row and stood next to his lovely wife, Antonina. A neighborhood Catholic priest performed the wedding vows speaking in their Sicilian dialect. It truly was a beautiful ceremony! When Pasquale and Natala exited the church, all the guests shouted "Auguri" (best wishes), clapped, and threw paper confetti, rice, and grain symbolizing money, prosperity, and fertility. The newlyweds, wedding party, family, and guests paraded a few blocks to the wedding celebration reception located behind the Scallaci Family Grocery. When they arrived at the celebration, they heard the splendid sounds of the brass band. Tables and chairs surrounded the dance floor, providing seating for 200 guests.

The large bar was manned by three bartenders to serve drinks. The bar was set up with all different types of liquors, wine, champagne, beer, and soft drinks for the children. Most of the guests were Sicilian immigrants from the Scallaci and Ruggiero's villages in Sicily. The brass band, along with the young Italian opera singer, Beniamino Gigli, (who became one of the greatest Italian operatic tenors of the period) performed "all of the Italian classics." The wedding guests danced to the "Tarantella," perhaps the most iconic of Italian dances. It was part of a folk ritual intended to cure the poison caused by tarantula bites. The bride carried a satin bag at the reception for guests to place envelopes of money in. A tradition called the "bustle."

After the numerous courses of delicious Italian cuisine were served, guests stuffed their bellies with food and drink. Following dinner, they relaxed for a short time then danced some more. Then everyone's eyes lit up when the dessert courses arrived, which included an array of decadent delights--such as pastries, cannoli, cassata cakes, fruit, coffee, and espresso.

They had a beautiful white tiered wedding cake symbolizing purity, topped with figurines of a smiling bride and groom all laid out on a Viennese dessert table. The bride and groom broke a vase! The number of shattered pieces predicted the number of years of "married bliss." All the guests had a wonderful time. It was a lavish wedding and the weather could not have been any nicer for the outdoor celebration. The splendid yard provided an air of elegance! The food, drink, service, and entertainment were all four-star. As a finale, an extravagant fireworks display lit up the evening sky.

At the end of this beautiful wedding day, just before all the guests left, Natala and Pasquale gave small gifts to their guests as a "thank you." The Italians called them "bonbonniere," consisting of confetti (sugared almonds), and painted ribbons. Bonbonniere is the symbol of family life. The number of confetti is significant and should be an odd number preferably five or seven, each being a good luck number. Pasquale and Natala intended to live with his mother, Giovanna and father, Amerigo, in their four-room apartment above the Scallaci Family Grocery.

Uncle Giuseppe, wife, Maria and son, Giacomo along with his wife, Lucia, and their three children now had their own apartment on the third floor, across the hall from the Ruggieros. The Scallaci building housed all the Scallaci, Anastasis, Ruggieros and friends from their village in Palermo.

Pasquale and Natala spent the night at the Plaza Hotel in Manhattan for their honeymoon. Subsequently, they moved in with Pasquale's parents. Pasquale returned to work at the family grocery after the Honeymoon!

Natala's mother a seamstress, and Natala, designed dresses to sell in the Garment District. Pasquale and Natala wasted no time starting a family. She gave birth to a healthy baby boy in 1924. They named him Vincenzo after Pasquale's older brother who was killed in WWI. One year later, she gave birth to another baby boy, Rocco, who along with their Italian American born cousins, became the first generation of Scallaci born in America.

However, across the Atlantic in Italy, all was not well. Italian dictator, Benito Mussolini, capitalizing on public discontent rose to power in the wake of WWI. As a leading proponent of fascism, Mussolini organized a paramilitary unit known as the "Black Shirts," who terrorized political opponents and helped increase fascist influence. By 1922, as Italy slipped into political chaos, Mussolini dismantled all Democratic institutions and by 1925 had pronounced himself dictator, taking the title "Il Duce" (leader).

Herbert Hoover became the 31st President of the United States running on a slogan of "a chicken in every pot and a car in every garage." In 1929, the Saint Valentine's Day Massacre, the single bloodiest incident in a decade-long turf war between rival Chicago mobsters fighting to control the lucrative bootlegging trade occurred. Members of Al Capone's gang murdered six followers of rival, Bugs Moran.

Post-war prosperity ended with the 1929 stock market crash. Plummeted stock prices led to losses between 1929 and 1931 of an estimated 50 billion dollars, ushering in the worst depression in the nation's history. What roared at the beginning of the 1920s disappeared in an instant with the stock market crash, taking the accumulated prosperity of the decade with it!

8

The 1930s, Depression Aggression

On October 29th, 1929 "Black Tuesday" pummeled Wall Street as investors frantically traded some 16 million shares on the New York Stock Exchange. Billions of dollars were lost, wiping out thousands of investors. In the aftermath of Black Tuesday, America and the rest of the industrialized world spiraled downward into the Great Depression, which lasted from 1929 to 1939.

After the initial crash, a wave of suicides occurred in New York's Financial District. The Great Depression set in and lasted some ten years. Unemployment reached 25 percent of the total workforce. People who lost their homes, often lived in what were called "Hoovervilles" or shanty towns, named after President Herbert Hoover. As the Depression worsened in the 1930s, severe hardship afflicted millions of Americans, with many looking to the federal government for assistance.

When the government failed to provide relief, President Hoover was blamed for the entire intolerable economic and social conditions. Shanty towns cropped up across the nation, primarily on the outskirts of major cities. The highly unpopular Hoover believed that government should not directly intervene in the economy and that it did not have the responsibility to create jobs or provide economic relief for its citizens.

"Hooverville shanties" were constructed of cardboard, tar paper, glass, or wood from crates, tin and whatever other materials people salvaged. Some were not buildings at all, but rather deep holes dug in the ground covered by makeshift roofs laid over them to keep out inclement weather. Some of the homeless found shelter inside empty conduits and water mains.

No two Hoovervilles were quite alike! The camps varied in population and size. Some were as small as a few hundred people, while others in bigger metropolitan areas boasted thousands of inhabitants.

People who lived in Hoovervilles did not have access to medical facilities. Living conditions in these shanty towns bred sickness and disease. Inadequate sanitation, lack of clean drinking water and poor nutrition led to a variety of diseases and illnesses such as tuberculosis, diphtheria., diarrhea, rickets, influenza, pneumonia, eczema, and psoriasis.

By 1935, soup kitchens sprang up in every major town and city in America as there were few government-based welfare programs to help the unemployed, starving, and destitute populace.

President Hoover believed that private charities and local communities, not the Federal Government could best provide for those in need. Due to Hoover's beliefs and his slow response to the Great Depression, the soup kitchens had to provide the main form of sustenance for the poor, needy, unemployed, and homeless. The staple diet offered, depending on the Center's location, consisted of soups, stews, and bread. An unemployed factory worker and father during the Depression may have stayed away from home at mealtime so as not to eat the food his children needed. Instead, he may have gone to wait patiently in a bread line, with hundreds of other men for a meal consisting of soup, bread, and coffee.

During the worst years of the Depression, Uncle Salvatore and my great grandfather, Amerigo, became benefactors of a soup kitchen. All the Scallaci women with the aid of neighbors prepared soups, stews, bread, and coffee in the family grocery's kitchen. They served it to the unemployed, homeless men, women and children who waited in long lines on Arthur Avenue.

In the mountain communities of Appalachia, whole families were reduced to dandelions and blackberries for their basic diet. Some children were so hungry they chewed on their own hands.

The Great Depression changed family life in several ways. Many couples delayed marriage. Divorce and birth rates plummeted. Some men even abandoned their families. To add to the devastating Stock Market crash, the Dust Bowl, the name given to the Great Plains region devastated by drought during the1930s Depression-ridden America burgeoned. This 150,000 square mile area encompassing the Oklahoma and Texas Panhandles and neighboring sections of Kansas, Colorado, and New Mexico, had little rainfall, "light soil" and high winds—a potentially destructive trifecta.

With the onset of drought in the 1930s, over-farmed and over-grazed land began to blow away. Winds whipped across the Plains, raising billowing clouds of dust. The sky darkened for days, leaving even well-sealed homes with a thick layer of dust on the furniture. In some places, the dust drifted like snow, covering farm buildings and houses. Nineteen states in the heartland of America became a vast dust bowl. With no chance of making a living, farm families abandoned their homes and land and fled Westward, hoping to become migrant workers. In his 1939 book, "The Grapes of Wrath," John Steinbeck aptly described the flight of families from the dust bowl.

By 1932, Hoover was so unpopular that he harbored no realistic hope of being re-elected. Governor Franklin Delano Roosevelt, of New York won that year's Presidential Election by a landslide. FDR projected a calm energy and optimism, famously declaring, "that the only thing we have to fear is fear itself." Roosevelt took immediate action to address the country's economic woes. Firstly, he announced a four-day bank holiday, during which all banks closed so that Congress could pass reform legislation and reopen banks determined to be sound.

Secondly, he addressed the public directly over the radio in a series of talks. These so-called "fireside chats" contributed toward restoring public confidence. Lastly, during his first 100 days in office, his administration passed legislation that aimed to stabilize industrial and agricultural production, create jobs, and stimulate recovery. After thirteen long years, the government finally realized that Prohibition was not working. It had in fact, created more problems than it solved! Finally, the government abolished the Prohibition laws.

In early 1933, Congress adopted a resolution proposing a 21st Amendment to the Constitution that would repeal the 18th Amendment. In New York City, Lucky Luciano and Meyer Lansky murdered old-line Mafia heads and formed the new "American Mafia." Lucky Luciano then formed a group, "The Commission," consisting of five mob bosses, who all shared equal power in hopes that this arrangement would eliminate future conflict, settling disputes in a voting style system. The "Five Families" referred to the five major New York City organized crime families constituting the Italian American Mafia as first recognized in the United States in 1931.

Although the Sabatino crime family was not one of the five families, they conducted business with all of them. They limited their area of operations to the Bronx and Westchester County. They sought to establish additional legitimate businesses and to maintain a low profile on their illegal operations in the US. The Great Depression did not adversely affect the business of organized crime to the degree it affected many other elements of the legitimate economy.

After Prohibition ended in 1933, major criminal organizations diversified and became increasingly powerful in the process. Gambling, loan sharking and the growth industry of narcotics distribution became important sources of criminal revenue. An increasingly significant area of enterprise during this period involved racketeering. The International Longshoreman's Association and The International Brotherhood of Teamsters were among the best-known examples of labor organizations affected by racketeering. When the 1933 repeal of Prohibition rendered buying liquor legal once again, the Sabatino crime family of the Bronx resorted to those traditional sources of illegal gain as well as engaging in racketeering. The Sabatino crime family in America earned millions of dollars during the thirteen years of

Prohibition. During the Depression years the Sabatino crime family was still making money as were the Scallaci businesses.

The Scallaci family did not invest in the stock market and certainly did not keep their money in any bank, so their finances were secured during the Great Depression. Uncle Salvatore had a small bank vault (strong room) built with steel reinforced concrete in the basement below the Scallaci Family Grocery to protect their savings and valuables from fire or theft.

During Prohibition, Uncle Salvatore lost his third oldest son, Paolo, and several Sabatino soldiers to deadly turf wars with rival gangsters. Paolo was buried in the Scallaci Family Plot. During the early1930s, Salvatore's youngest son, Francesco, had married. His wife, Concetta, gave birth to a son whom they named Paolo, after his brother.

As the Depression swept through the United States, it also laid waste to the continent of Europe. We Americans were concerned about our way of life, but little did we know that the greatest threat to the American way of life lay within that continent we so casually regarded. As America embraced democracy and capitalism, some European nations turned to fascism and aggression.

In May of 1938, Uncle Salvatore received word from Sicily notifying him of the death of Don Luigi Sabatino. After leaving Sicily during the 1920s, to escape a fascist crack-down on the Sicilian Mafia, the family returned in 1937. While keeping a low profile and living in hiding, Don Luigi was able to die peacefully and be buried in his homeland.

Salvatore completed arrangements to pay his final respects to his mentor, boss, and Godfather. His plan was to voyage back to Sicily aboard a Sabatino cargo ship delivering imported Italian food products from Sabatino Wholesale Market of Sicily to Sabatino Wholesale Market of the Bronx. He would make the return voyage back to Sicily to pay his respects to Don Luigi, who always treated him like his son. Giuseppe Scallaci, Salvatore's cousin would accompany him. Giuseppe still had two younger brothers and a sister living in Palermo. He had not seen them in over forty years!

Their ship would arrive in New York City in one week. After unloading its cargo, it would be reloaded with merchandise to export. It would then head back to Sicily with Salvatore and Giuseppe onboard.

Uncle Salvatore had smuggled a lot of "hooch" (illegal alcohol) during Prohibition and would now have to smuggle Giuseppe and himself in and out of Sicily. Wary of Mussolini's fascist regime, they stayed anonymously in Sicily for two weeks. Salvatore and Uncle Giuseppe would return to the Bronx via Palermo.

While in Sicily, Giuseppe was reunited with his siblings and had the opportunity to meet all of his nieces and nephews that he had never met. Because Sicily was a bad place to be, under Mussolini's totalitarian dictatorship, the Sabatino Family fled to South America in 1924. They returned in 1937, in complete secrecy, living in a remote area of Sicily.

Don Luigi was buried in a temporary gravesite without a headstone. When the time came that it was safe, Don Luigi's body would be moved to a more elaborate gravesite in Palermo.

His son, Luca, was anointed the new boss of the Sabatino Family operations in Sicily, America, and elsewhere. Uncle Salvatore and Giuseppe paid their respects to the Sabatino Family and to all Scallaci Family members and friends who still lived in Palermo. Salvatore and Don Luca were like brothers and spent time together catching up on old times and discussing the future of the Sabatino Family legal and illegal operations in Sicily and America.

Luca Sabatino told Salvatore that Don Luigi wanted him to inherit the Sabatino half of the Sabatino and Scallaci "Ice and Coal Company," all of its buildings and the property on which the business stood. This was a last departing gift from the Don to his godson, whom he loved like his own son. Uncle Salvatore and the Scallaci Family had always shown much respect, loyalty, and devotion to the Sabatinos. Salvatore also gave Don Luca the balance of the money Amerigo owed his father for the purchase of the Scallaci building in the Bronx. That would be Uncle Salvatore's gift to his nephew, Amerigo, and his family. They now owned the building and property free and clear!

The instability and insecurity of the 1920s and 1930s gave rise to political extremism in many European countries. People looked to authoritarian leaders as a political alternative. Fascist leader, Benito Mussolini, ascended to power in Italy in 1922, subsequently, all aspects of Italian life came under State control. In Germany Adolph Hitler became Chancellor in 1933 and established a Totalitarian one-party state under the Nazis. Political opposition was violently repressed. Hitler exploited the popular belief that Germany had been humiliated after the First World War. He promised economic recovery, national revival, and that Germany would return to international prominence. Germany withdrew from the League of Nations in October 1933. Hitler announced German rearmament and reintroduced conscription (military draft), which was prohibited under the Treaty of Versailles. The ultranationalist governments of both Italy and Germany pursued aggressive foreign policies of territorial expansion that threatened to destroy world order established by post-war peace settlements.

In March of 1939, German forces occupied what remained of Czechoslovakian territory. This convinced Britain and France that there were no limits to Hitler's territorial ambitions. They were now determined to prevent German domination of Europe, by force if necessary. In April, Hitler ordered preparations for the invasion of Poland. He strengthened ties with Japan, the main threat to Britain's Empire in the Far East. In May, he signed a military alliance with Italy. On September 1st, 1939, Germany launched a lightning war (Blitzkrieg), and invaded Poland. Two days later, France and Britain declared war on Germany, thus beginning World War II.

The outbreak of war did not come as a surprise. Tensions in Europe had been building for several years. There was a growing sentiment that German aggression needed to be confronted with force.

Pasquale's two sons, Vincenzo, and Rocco were now at the age where they would get into fights at school and in the neighborhood. Vincenzo got into fights protecting the boys who did not want to fight or who were too afraid to stand up to bullies. Rocco, on the other hand, just liked to fight and would find his way into trouble only to get bailed out by his overprotective big brother, Vincenzo.

When they were children, they played "cops and robbers." Vincenzo the cop (good guy) and Rocco a robber (bad guy), which turned out to be that way in years to come. Pasquale thought if they both liked to fight so much, he would introduce the two to a friend, a retired prize fighter and now a trainer at Gleeson's South Bronx Gym. Pasquale made a deal with this man. If he would teach his two sons how to box, he would pay him in groceries. The deal was accepted! He agreed to teach them after school. When they were done with their training, they would go home and continue their studies.

Natala and Pasquale wanted their two sons to graduate from high school-that was their number one priority. The boys would work in the Scallaci Family Grocery all day Saturday and a half day on Sunday. Vincenzo took his boxing training seriously and showed tremendous promise. Rocco also showed that he had talent to fight, but when he sparred against an opponent and got hit, he would go berserk on the guy. Rocco, although younger than Vincenzo, was a much bigger kid, so he just stuck to lifting weights.

In 1940, Vincenzo would win the New York Daily News Golden Gloves Championship at Madison Square Garden. He wanted to transition from an amateur boxer to professional boxer upon graduating from high school. With his father's help, they convinced his mother, Natala, to let him turn professional after graduation. For now, he would train hard and in one year would be ready when his chance came.

9

The 1940s, War and Peace

On September 1, 1939, Adolph Hitler's Germany invaded Poland, officially starting World War II. Two days later, Britain and France now obligated by treaty to aid Poland declared war on Germany. Just after war broke out in Europe, President Roosevelt hurriedly called his Cabinet and military advisers together. It was agreed that the United States would stay neutral in these affairs. One of the primary reasons given was that unless America was directly threatened, they had no reason to be involved. This reason was valid, as it was American policy to stay neutral in affairs not having to do with them, unless American soil was threatened directly.

It was now 1941, young Vincenzo came of age, graduated high school, and turned professional boxer. Vincenzo would have his first professional fight this night at the Bronx Coliseum. He fought in the middleweight class. His opponent, a tough Irishman, Paddy O'Sullivan from "Hell's Kitchen" in Manhattan hailed with a professional record of 6 - 0, with five of those wins by way of knockout.

There were to be three six-round bouts (fights) on the undercard and a ten round main event. With Uncle Salvatore's connections, all of the Scallaci men, young and old, got ringside seats. Uncle Salvatore also bought tickets for friends and neighborhood "Paisanos." Vincenzo would have plenty of support in attendance. He was scheduled for the third bout. The Scallaci Family were all seated and ready for the first fight to start. The first two fighters were lightweights and they would go the distance to the sixth round, with the fight ending in a draw. In the second fight, the bout again lasted all six rounds, with a win by unanimous decision.

Finally, the fight they had all been waiting for! As Vincenzo stepped into the ring, his name was announced - the crowd cheer was raucous. The referee gave his instructions to both fighters in the middle of the ring. The two boxes touched gloves and returned to their corners awaiting the bell.

Vincenzo was an orthodox boxer (right-handed), the Irishman was a Southpaw (left-handed). The bell rang, both boxers came out fighting, exchanging jabs (quick straight punches).

The Irishman was more of a brawler, with tremendous punching power while Vincenzo was more of a finesse fighter. During the first round, both fighters battled furiously. When the round was over, they navigated to their corners, sat on their stools, drank water, and rested for a minute, while taking instruction from their trainers. Vincenzo was attended to by his trainer, younger brother, Rocco as inspirational motivator and a seasoned cut man.

The bell rang, round two began! More jabs were unleashed, then uppercuts, hooks and crosses exchanged. Towards the end of the round, the Irishman threw a hard-left-cross, connecting to Vincenzo's face - leaving him dazed as the bell rang, ending the onslaught. Vincenzo had a minute to shake it off, take a swig of water, and ingest relevant advice from his trainer. The bell rang for round three, with more of the same; the Irishman landed more of his punches. Vincenzo seemed to be in trouble most of the round. At the end of the third round, Vincenzo returned to his corner, sat on his stool, and sipped some water as the cut man worked on his bleeding right eye.

His trainer and Rocco provided encouragement. The bell rang, and he stood for the fourth round. His opponent sensed that he had hurt Vincenzo and became more aggressive, getting the best of him. He connected with all of his punches and was going in for the knockout.

He opened the cut above Vincenzo's right eye with another solid blow. Vincenzo was in serious trouble. His vision foundered - the right eye was completely closed. At this time Uncle Salvatore stood up and pounded his right fist into his left hand, shouting in Sicilian:

"Occhio del tigre," eye of the Tiger in English.

Vincenzo heard his uncle's war-cry and with a tremendous surge of adrenaline directed a powerful barrage of punches landing to the Irishman's face. He continued, landing a solid right cross, which knocked his opponent to the canvas. His opponent was given the dreaded ten-second count. Unable to get up, the Irishman was finished. Vincenzo was awarded a knockout win in his first professional fight. He jumped into the arms of his brother, Rocco, in triumph. The referee raised Vincenzo's arm in victory. All the Scallaci stood up and clapped with great pride. Vincenzo returned to the locker room and had his eye tended to. He washed up, got dressed, and joined his family to watch the main event.

All the Scallaci, close friends, and neighbors congratulated Vincenzo! Uncle Salvatore hugged and kissed his great nephew and told him, "This is a proud day for all Scallaci. You never gave up or surrendered. You reminded me of your great grandfather, Pasquale. You both had the refuse-to-lose attitude and determination to win at any cost."

The next day, Vincenzo was hard at work training for his next fight scheduled to be held in Chicago in three weeks' time.

Uncle Salvatore now owned all of the Sabatino & Scallaci Ice and Coal Company and added oil delivery for heating to the list of services his company provided. With the invention and growth of electricity, the household refrigerator gradually replaced the ice box. The manufacture of plant ice declined. As an astute visionary, he created another new business called "Scallaci Brothers Heating: Installation, Repair and Servicing Company." It was to be located next door to Scallaci Ice, Coal, and Oil company.

Vincenzo left for Chicago for his second professional fight, and he earned a win by split decision. He then traveled to Detroit for his third fight, in which he garnered a win by unanimous decision. His next fight occurred one month later. It was a ten-rounder against the most experienced fighter he had yet faced. The bout was held at Madison Square Garden in New York City, on Saturday December 6th, 1941.

The undercard featured several top contenders. The main event was a championship bout between two heavyweights. The day came, again all the Scallaci male family members, friends, and neighbors would be there to root for the "Kid" from the Bronx!

By the time Vincenzo's bout was scheduled to begin, the Garden exuded odors of sweat and leather. Thick clouds of cigarette and cigar smoke billowed. The house rocked!

Vincenzo's opponent, a hard-hitting African American boasting a record of 28 – 1 appeared. Twenty-five of those wins came by way of knockout. This boxer was a serious contender for the championship. The fight was surely a slugfest. Both fighters took a beating, exchanging solid blows! The 10th and final round began. Vincenzo's opponent had the edge, dominating six of the nine rounds. If Vincenzo was going to win, he needed a knockout. The bell rang, both boxers came out swinging, exchanging blows to the head and body. Vincenzo got knocked to the canvas. His opponent went to a neutral corner.

The referee gave Vincenzo the dreaded "ten-second" count. Vincenzo's corner and all the Scallaci were yelling for him to get up. After the referee counted out nine seconds, he struggled to his feet, shook it off, and resumed fighting. Energized, he then sneaked a hard right-cross to his opponent's chin, dazing him. Next, he hit him with a combination of solid punches, sending him crashing to the canvas. He was unable to get up. Vincenzo had won his fourth and toughest fight to date.

The crowd certainly got their money's worth watching this fight!

The next day, Pasquale and Vincenzo, while taking inventory in the Scallaci Family Grocery, listened to the Giants and Dodgers football game on WOR radio; a sudden interruption on this otherwise tranquil Sunday afternoon, December 7th, 1941 overtook the AM airwaves.

An Associated Press Bulletin at 2:22 EST (Eastern Standard Time) first reported the Japanese attack on Pearl Harbor to mainland news organizations and radio networks. After confirming the initial bulletin with the government, the major radio networks interrupted regular programming beginning at 2:30 PM, bringing news of the attack in progress. Just before 8:00 AM on December 7, 1941, after months of planning and practice, hundreds of Japanese fighter planes attacked the American Naval Base, Pearl Harbor, near Honolulu. The Japanese plan was simple, destroy the U.S. Pacific Fleet. That way the Americans, they hoped, would not be able to fight back as Japan's armed forces spread across the South Pacific.

The day after the attack, President Roosevelt addressed a Joint Session of the United States Congress. Roosevelt called December 7th, "a date which will live in infamy." The attack on Pearl Harbor immediately galvanized a divided nation into action. Public opinion had been moving toward support for entering the war during 1941, but considerable opposition remained until the attack. Overnight, Americans united against Japan in response as calls to "Remember Pearl Harbor" echoed nationally!

The closest ally Franklin Delano Roosevelt had in developing an Allied Alliance, British Prime Minister Sir Winston Churchill, stated that his first thought regarding American assistance to the United Kingdom was that "we have won the war!" Soon after the U.S. had been attacked, President Roosevelt asked Congress to declare war on Japan. Congress swiftly ratified the Declaration of War. Three days later, Japanese allies, Germany and Italy also declared war on the United States. The U.S. Congress reciprocated. More than two years into the conflict, America had finally joined World War II.

The nation rapidly geared itself for mobilization of its people and its entire industrial capacity. "All of the nation's activities" including farming, manufacturing, mining, trade, labor, investment, communications, education, and cultural undertakings were in some form or another brought under new and enlarged controls. The Western Allies decided that their primary military effort was to be concentrated in Europe, where the core of enemy power lay, while the Pacific Theater was to be secondary.

With a huge feeling of patriotism, and a huge shock to his family, Vincenzo decided to hang up his boxing gloves for a rifle and serve his country. He told his family that he wanted to enlist in the United States Army. His grandmother, Giovanna, who had lost her oldest son, Vincenzo, in World War I was totally against his decision to enlist, but young Vincenzo had already set his mind. He knew what he had to do. He wanted to enlist in the Army like his Uncle Vincenzo did and serve his country with honor!

He put a promising boxing career on hold. He felt that serving his country was more important. He completed his Army training in the states and was assigned to the 82nd Airborne Division in 1942, as one of its pioneering paratroopers. In the spring of 1943, the 82nd "All Americans" became the first Airborne Division deployed overseas.

Tunisia served as the departure point for the division's first combat drop, the invasion of Sicily. It was a successful operation, the 82nd Airborne and the Allied invasion drove the German and Italian troops from Sicily. Vincenzo was proud of his Sicilian heritage like all the Scallaci, but his country was America, and he would fight to the death to defend her freedoms.

After combat in Sicily, Vincenzo and the 82nd fought their way through Southern Italy on the mainland. Their next big operation arose during D-Day, the airborne invasion of Normandy, France. The 82nd saw more action in Belgium during the Battle of the Bulge. On April 12, 1945, President Roosevelt, the longest serving President in American history died, three months into his fourth term in office, leaving Vice President Harry S. Truman in charge of a country still fighting the Second World War and in possession of a weapon of un-precedented and terrifying power, the "atomic bomb."

The final battles of the European theater of WWII as well as the German surrender to the Western Allies and the Soviet Union took place in late April and early May,1945. Following the surrender of Germany, the 82nd Airborne was ordered to Berlin for occupation duty. At approximately 8:15 AM on August 6, 1945, a US B-29 bomb-er, the Enola Gay dropped an atomic bomb on the Japanese city of

Hiroshima, instantly killing some 80,000 people. Three days later, a second bomb was dropped on Nagasaki causing the deaths of 40,000 more.

On August 15th, six days after the bombing of Nagasaki and the Soviet Union's declaration of war, Japan announced its surrender to the Allies. The surrender occurred just over three months after the surrender of the Axis Forces in Europe. The 82nd Airborne would return to the United States on January 3rd, 1946.

Vincenzo earned the rank of staff sergeant and was awarded for valor and gallantry in combat the Distinguished Service Cross, two Silver Star Medals, two Bronze Star Medals, numerous foreign medals, and two Purple Heart Medals for being wounded in action.

World War II jettisoned the U.S. out of the Great Depression. After the war, life in the United States began to return to normal. Soldiers returned home in search of peacetime employment. Industry stopped producing war equipment and began to produce goods that made peacetime life more pleasant.

The American economy was stronger than ever! Some major changes began to take place within the American population. Many Americans were not satisfied with their old way of life. They wanted something better! Many people earned enough money to look for a better life.

Millions of Americans moved out of our cities and small towns to buy newly built homes in the suburbs. When Vincenzo arrived home, he was greeted by the entire Scallaci Family who were all proud and happy to see him. As he fought in Europe, he received a letter from his younger brother, Rocco, informing him that Uncle Giuseppe and Uncle Salvatore had both died.

The Scallaci Family was extremely close, both his uncles were sorely missed, but never forgotten, just like all the other Scallaci before them. Uncle Salvatore was one of the last of the "mustache petes," to die. These were immigrant members of the Old Guard Sicilian Mafia who wore large bushy mustaches and usually committed their first killings in Italy.

At first, Vito Anastasi became the new underboss of the Sabatino crime family in America, taking over for Uncle Salvatore. His younger brother, Pietro, was named a Capo and was now in charge of Sabatino Construction of Manhattan. Vito's reign as underboss of the Sabatino crime family was however short-lived as he died a year later. That honor was next bestowed to Vito's son, Angelo Anastasi. His brother, Santo, was also promoted to capo of his own crew and was now in charge of Sabatino Construction of the Bronx and Westchester County. Uncle Salvatore's oldest son, Pasquale, was still in charge of Sabatino Wholesale Import/Export Market in the Bronx and ran its day to day operations along with his four sons.

Uncle Salvatore's second oldest son, Salvatore Jr. was in charge of Scallaci Ice, Coal and Oil Company and the Scallaci Brother's Heating Company. Uncle Giuseppe's son, Giacomo, was now the sole owner of the butcher shop and had his three sons working for him. He was rapidly expanding his business!

Amerigo, who owned the Scallaci Family Grocery was now the patriarch of the Scallaci family in America. His son, Pasquale worked there and now his grandson, Vincenzo, would join them. Rocco Scallaci worked for "Sabatino Construction of the Bronx" so it was kept all in the family.

The fascists were defeated in WWII and the Sicilian Mafia rose once again. Luca Sabatino now the Don of the Sabatino family in Sicily and America, emerged out of hiding and reestablished his illegal and legal operations.

Now that Vincenzo was back in the Bronx, he would work in his grandfather's store until he decided what his plan for the future" was. He had seen so much fighting and death in the war that he no longer wanted to resume his career as a professional fighter, thus making his grandmother and his mother incredibly happy. Meanwhile, on Saturday, Vincenzo's grandfather and father planned a Welcome Home Party for him at the American Legion Hall in the Bronx.

Vincenzo took a couple of days off before starting work in the grocery. He borrowed his father's car and drove to the family plot to pay his respects to Uncle Salvatore, Uncle Giuseppe, and the rest of the Scallaci buried there. He passed the morning there in contemplation. He spent the rest of the day and the next day visiting with family and neighborhood friends.

The New York City that emerged from World War II was a dramatically different place than it had been four years earlier. The changes were owed in large part to the war itself, which had lifted the city out of the Depression and ushered in an era of unparalleled prosperity. In four years, an explosion in commercial activity brought on by the war had reignited the city's economic engine, carrying it to a level of economic power and dominance like never before.

The weekend arrived; the homecoming party for Vincenzo ensued. Vincenzo was excited, as were the rest of the family. Some 100 guests attended. A band played music of the era for entertainment and a dance floor filled with celebrants. There were tables and chairs set up for the guests and buffets of homemade Italian foods prepared by the Scallaci women. A bar served beverages, wine and beer for the adults and soda for the kids. The Hall was decorated in a patriotic theme.

Vincenzo had grown in size since his enlistment in the Army - his old suit did not fit him anymore, so he wore his Army dress uniform. He looked dashing with his jet-black hair and olive colored skin along with his muscular physique. His uniform fit well and with all those medals and his shiny paratrooper jump boots, he looked wholly distinguished. Vincenzo and his father, Pasquale, greeted all family members and their guests at the Hall's Entrance. Suddenly, his eyes lit up! To his surprise one of the guests was his high school sweetheart. He ended their relationship before joining the Army, not knowing if he would return home alive from the war overseas. Her name was Angelina Falcone! She attended with her parents, Nunzio and Carmela Falcone, dear friends of Pasquale and Natala.

Vincenzo assumed she had found someone else after being apart for almost four years. He could not believe how grown up and bella (beautiful) she looked. He still had feelings for her. He couldn't have been happier surrounded by family, which had grown in size" while he was away. With his neighborhood friends and the only girl, he ever cared for in attendance to enjoy this happy occasion, he became overwhelmed by emotion! He escorted her and her parents to their table, then returned to his father's side and greeted the rest of the guests.

When all the guests had arrived, he stopped and chatted with everyone at each table, saving the best one for last. When he finally traversed over to Angelina's table, he sat down and chatted with her and her parents for a while. As the band played a romantic love song, Vincenzo asked Angelina:

"Would you like to dance?"

"Yes."

He helped her out of her chair and escorted her to the dance floor. They danced closely and talked about old times.

"I've waited for your return and remained single."

He was happy and shocked to see her and could not believe how stunning she looked. Holding her in his arms while dancing with her was a dream come true. Angelina's hair exuded fragrance of spring flowers. Vincenzo sensed electricity between them and hoped she felt it too. When the song was over, he asked her:

"May I call on you?"

"You'd better."

He hugged, kissed, and escorted her back to her table.

Angelina's mother and father had always liked Vincenzo and hoped that their daughter and he would one day marry. It had been a great evening; the music, food, drink and most of all, Vincenzo shared it with family, friends, and Angelina. The next day, all he kept thinking about was Angelina. He could not get her off his mind!

When the weekend ended, it was back to work at the grocery. An old customer and family friend ventured into the store. The man was a New York City Police Lieutenant. He had not seen Vincenzo since he left home for the Army. They started talking:

"What are your plans for the future?"

"I'm not completely sure."

"Vincenzo, the department is hiring new police officers. If you are interested, I'll give you the address to police headquarters so that you can fill out an application."

Vincenzo did not yet know what career he wanted to pursue but took down the address anyway. Later that night, he borrowed his father's car and took Angelina to the movies at Lowe's Paradise Theater in the Bronx to see the movie, "The Best Years of our Lives" starring Myrna Loy, Frederick March and Best Supporting Actor Awardee and Veteran double-amputee, Harold Russell.

After the movie, they stopped to get a bite to eat and catch up on lost time. They seemed so comfortable with one another. He would see her the next night, the night after and every night that he could. Prior to joining the Army and going to Europe, Vincenzo had courted Angelina for three years. They were now happily ensconced in a serious relationship. With much thought about his future career, he decided to go to the New York City Police Headquarters to fill out the employment application.

While he served in the Army, he enjoyed the camaraderie of his fellow soldiers and thought he would experience that with fellow police officers. One month later, while working in the family grocery, he received a letter in the mail. He noticed the return address on the envelope read, "New York City Police Department." He thought that this must be about the application he had filled out. He opened the letter and read it. The letter stated that Vincenzo had to report to police headquarters within one week of receipt to take physical and mental examinations. It also stated that if he passed both examinations, he would be accepted as a candidate trainee to the New York City Police Academy.

He took the exam. They told him that he would find out his results no later than the second week of June. If all progressed well and he passed, he would start training at the Academy on June 20th. Vincenzo continued to work at the grocery and would until his test results were posted.

He purchased his first automobile, a 1944 Ford Deluxe Coup in great condition with low mileage. By now, Angelina and he were completely in love and spent all their free time together. Vincenzo knew what his heart beckoned. He invited Angelina's father, Nunzio Falcone out to dinner at his favorite neighborhood Italian restaurant, "Mama Leone's."

Vincenzo picked him up at his home and drove them to the restaurant. When they arrived, they sat down at a table and engaged in conversation:

"Mr. Falcone, may I have your permission to marry your daughter?"

Nunzio never hesitated!

"Yes, I would be more than proud to have you for a son-in law."

After they finished dinner, they returned to the Falcone home, where upon Nunzio and Carmela exited for their nightly walk. Nunzio conveyed the good news.

Vincenzo and Angelina were now alone at the house. Vincenzo got down on one knee, held a ring box and reminisced about the first time he laid eyes upon Angelina, awestruck by her beauty, patience, and kindness to others.

"Angelina, life is so much better with you in it. I am hoping you will spend the rest of your life with me! Will you marry me?"

Angelina was surprised. She knew she would get engaged to Vincenzo someday but did not expect it would be today.

"Yes."

They hugged and kissed. The date fittingly was Saint Valentine's Day, February 14th, 1946. Vincenzo slipped a beautiful diamond engagement ring on her finger, kissed her again and handed her a dozen red roses. They then shared a bottle of champagne to celebrate this happy occasion!!

Angelina's parents returned from their walk, kissed the betrothed couple, and conveyed heartfelt congratulations. Angelina showed off the engagement ring and all four of them raised their glasses, toasting the engagement. When they were finished celebrating, Vincenzo said his goodnights to all and headed home to tell his family the good news. When he strutted through the door to the apartment his parents were having a conversation with his grandparents. He exclaimed:

"Mi scusi, Mi scusi," ("excuse me, excuse me"). And announced: "Angelina and I became engaged to be married tonight!"

They all rose with surprise and excitement and congratulated him with hugs and kisses. They loved Angelina from the beginning and were overjoyed that he had chosen her.

"We haven't set a date yet but are anxious to get married, hoping for a May wedding."

With much thought and discussion, they decided to get married on May 26, 1946. Angelina's father, a prominent tailor, crafted some of the finest suits in New York City. His wife, Carmela, was a talented dressmaker. They owned Falcone's Tailor Shop in Manhattan. They sold their high-end clothing to wealthy businessmen, prominent wise guys, celebrities and professional athletes, and their families.

Angelina's parents would pay the total cost of the wedding and wanted to have it at an Italian wedding hall in the Bronx, equipped with a majestic ballroom, great Italian food, and a grand orchestra. With the approval of Angelina and Vincenzo, Natala, and Pasquale, Carmela, and Nunzio finalized all the arrangements. The Sunday in May that Angelina and Vincenzo picked to get married on was available at the church and the wedding hall.

Accordingly, the invitations were sent out! There would be 300 guests invited. It was now nearing the end of February. The big day would be in three months. Both of them were counting the days and kept busy by working. Meanwhile, all the Sabatino- and Scallaci-owned businesses were doing well. Amerigo had a brand-new apartment building built by Sabatino Construction on vacant property he owned, next to the first Scallaci building. This building was five stories high, with sixteen five-room apartments and six storefronts.

Amerigo and Giovanna along with their son, Pasquale, and his wife, Natala, and son, Rocco, moved into one of the five-room apartments on the second floor. Vincenzo would stay in their old apartment and when married, Angelina would join him. The Scallaci family was multiplying like rabbits, and the first Scallaci building was getting crowded, so some of the other Scallaci followed them as well.

Angelo Anastasi, now the underboss of the Sabatino family in America, believed, due to the end of WWII, that there would be a massive migration of New Yorkers moving out of the city to the suburbs. With Don Luca's permission, he started buying hundreds of acres of undeveloped rural land in anticipation of a huge housing boom on Long Island. He also sent his brother, Santo, and his second oldest son, Gino, to Nassau County on Long Island to start up a new Sabatino construction company to build affordable housing.

His oldest son would now "be in charge" of Sabatino Construction in the Bronx and Westchester County. Gino attended college at Columbia University, studied to be an engineer, and received his degree. The new Sabatino Construction Company of Long Island, along with the Sapienza Architectural firm, were building planned communities and developing towns and villages into some of the first modern suburbs in the United States.

Don Luca Sabatino, who was Uncle Salvatore's son, Pasquale's godfather offered to sell Pasquale the Sabatino Wholesale Import/Export Market in the Bronx. Pasquale, who had been in charge of the Sabatino Wholesale Market for many years, jumped at the opportunity. Don Luca gave Pasquale the deal of a lifetime, the business, the buildings, and the property.

The lawyer for the Sabatino and Scallaci families, Alfonso Romano, took care of all the legal paperwork and the deal was finalized.

Now Pasquale had something to leave his sons, who all worked there and knew the business inside and out. The new sign would go up, "Scallaci Wholesale Import/Export Market." Pasquale now knew how Uncle Natale felt when the sign for the Scallaci Family Grocery was first hoisted in 1910. With Santo Anastasi's relocation to Long Island, Pasquale was promoted to capo of the Bronx crew. Life was good for the Scallaci family! They sure had come a long way since emigrating to America in the 1890s.

The big day was tomorrow, May 26th, the long-awaited day of Angelina and Vincenzo's wedding. With a night of tossing and turning in anticipation of the next day's nuptials, they both awakened bright and early in the morning.

Angelina's mother had sewn her the most beautiful white wedding dress and Nunzio had tailored Vincenzo an elegant suit. Their wedding party consisted of seven bridesmaids and seven groomsmen, a flower girl, and a ring bearer. It was a beautiful sunny warm day. The ceremony would take place at the Roman Catholic Church, where Vincenzo's parents were married. The priest performed the wedding vows and they were pronounced man and wife. The Falcones spared no expense on their only daughter's wedding!

Most of the guests were Sicilian immigrants who immigrated from Sicily to America during the late 1800s and early 1900s. Most of them had never experienced such quality of extravagant luxury before at such a beautiful banquet hall. It was a truly magnificent wedding and the reception was enjoyed by all. They did not go on a honeymoon; instead, they bought all new furniture for their apartment. Angelina moved right in after the wedding and settled into their new home. They were so extremely excited about starting their future together! Finally, in the second week of June, Vincenzo found out he had passed the New York City Police Exam!

The next day was June 20th. Vincenzo would start his police training at the New York City Police Academy, located at Seven Hubert Street in Lower Manhattan. He was up early. He was eager and excited to get started! His training would be twelve weeks long, with instruction in self-defense, weapons and safety, police procedures, etc.

Recruits would start their rigorous physical training immediately. The mission of the New York City Police Academy was to transform new recruits into well trained police officers. This was the first group of recruits following WWII - there were 2000 of them. The reason for so many was that limited hiring took place during the Great Depression and war years. The New York Police Department (NYPD) is one of the oldest police departments established in the United States, tracing its roots back to the first Dutch Eight-Man-Watch in1625, when New York City was New Amsterdam. Around the turn of the century, the New York City Police Department began to professionalize under the leadership of Police Commission President, Theodore Roosevelt.

The new Scallaci Wholesale Market was now supplying Scallaci brand tomato puree and pulverized tomatoes, along with Italian sauces, olive oil, and an assortment of Scallaci boxed pastas, and other Scallaci Brand Italian food products to expanding chain-store supermarkets on the East Coast.

The Scallaci Family Grocery along with the Scallaci butchers were thriving as well. The Sabatino family still owned the wholesale market in Sicily along with several construction companies in Sicily and America. They were raking in millions. Everything was booming!

Within the last year, Anna Scallaci and Maria Scallaci had passed and were buried alongside their husbands. All the Scallaci were busy building and expanding their businesses.

Vincenzo was to graduate the following day from the Police Academy. Three months of instruction passed by quickly. Vincenzo excelled in all aspects of the rigorous training and graduated with honors. The day arrived! It was a nice ceremony with most of the Scallaci, Ruggiero, and Falcone family members in attendance. Vincenzo had received his shield and weapon the day before and was assigned as a rookie police officer at the 41st Precinct Station House, located at 1086 Simpson Street in the South Bronx. While he was at the police academy, he met and became friendly with a fellow recruit, Johnny Muller, who had also been assigned to the 41st precinct. Johnny was a giant of a man, he stood 6 feet 8 inches tall and weighed 295 pounds of solid muscle. He was from Yonkers, NY Located just north of the Bronx in Westchester County, where he lived with his family. Both Vincenzo and Johnny's first assignment was foot patrol, walking a beat on the streets of the South Bronx. They would remain in that role for the next several years.

Harry S. Truman was the 33rd President of the United States stepping up from vice president upon the death of Franklin Delano Roosevelt. In a dramatic speech to a joint session of Congress, President Truman implored the U.S. to aid Greece and Turkey to forestall communist domination of the two nations. Historians have often cited Truman's address, which came to be known as the Truman Doctrine as the official declaration of the Cold War. It was the start of a containment policy to stop Soviet expansion. It was also a major step toward igniting the Cold War.

Vincenzo, now called Vinny by his fellow police officers, and Angelina thought it would be the right time to start a family of their own. But although Vinny and Angelina had been trying to have a child, Angelina could not get pregnant. They had been trying to conceive for some time now with no luck. They decided to see a fertility doctor. They fulfilled the appointment; both were tested for their infertility issues. When the test results were found normal, the doctor's diagnosis was "unexplained infertility," in which standard infertility testing has not found a cause for the failure to get pregnant. Another way to explain it is the doctors cannot figure it out. They were both disappointed in the doctor's findings but decided to give it a little more time. If that did not work, they would consider adoption. Angelina so wanted to have a child and Vinny wanted more than anything to give her one.

10

The 1950s, Adopted Bloodline

During the early months of 1950, Angelina still could not get pregnant and knew she had to go a different route. Vinny and Angelina decided to check into adoption. They did their research and found out the information they needed to know on how to adopt.

After talking to a few adoption agencies, they were told that there were long waiting lists and they could not say for sure how long it would take. Angelina did not want to wait one or two years or perhaps even longer. With this news, she grew even more disheartened and Vinny did not know what to do. He thought about asking his Uncle Pasquale who had all kinds of connections, but then decided against it. He wanted everything to be on the "up and up," especially when dealing with adopting a child.

A few weeks passed, Vinny finished up his shift as did his now best friend, big Johnny Muller. It was Friday, and they decided to visit the neighborhood bar for a few cold ones. Vinny and Johnny got to talking. Vinny, as tight lipped as Johnny about family business, told him about his problem of trying to have a child and about the complicated adoption process.

By now, Vinny trusted Johnny with his life and vice versa.

He told Johnny, "For the first time in my life, I feel helpless."

"I might have a solution to your problem, Vinny."

"Please, tell me more."

It turned out Johnny's younger sister, Helen, was pregnant. She was a high school senior. Her English teacher seduced the attractive and naive Helen into having an affair with him. According to his sister, he was young, handsome, persuasive, and a real smooth talker. Because he was already married, he would not take responsibility or even acknowledge the child was his. Having this child out of wedlock would bring shame to the Muller family who were devout Catholics. Johnny's father, a retired doctor told Helen:

"You could give birth to the child, but the day it was born, you would have to give it up for adoption."

Johnny described Helen to Vinny:

"She is sixteen years old, doesn't drink alcohol or smoke, is athletic and healthy, and did well in school."

"She sounds like a special young lady, Johnny."

"I do not know much about the teacher except that his name is Antonio Russo. I hurried to the high school to confront him the other day, but a school administrator noted he had not showed up for his classes and they had not heard from him either.

"Vinny, I will discuss this matter after dinner tonight with my father, older brother, Carl, and Helen. I'll let you know my father's decision first thing in the morning at work."

"Johnny, how many months has Helen been pregnant?"

"My sister is under the medical care of Carl, a medical doctor. He believes she is between one and a half to two months."

Johnny assured Vinny of total secrecy regarding this matter.

"Only myself, my father, Carl, and of course, Helen, will know the details."

Vinny had never met Helen or Johnny's father, but had met Johnny's older brother, Doctor Carl once. Carl's look and demeanor were the complete opposite of Johnny. You would never in a thousand years guess that they were brothers. Carl was short, scrawny, unathletic, wore glasses, sported balding brown hair, was soft-spoken, and well-educated. Johnny on the other hand, was massive and built like a brick "shithouse." He was loud, possessed a hair trigger temper, and could become extremely violent when provoked. Johnny was of Scandinavian heritage, born in the country of Sweden, blessed with ancestral thick blonde hair, and piercing blue eyes. He reminded Vinny of a story he read way back in history class about Norse Mythology describing a Viking warrior, the God of Thunder--"Thor" wielding a huge hammer from his giant frame. That was Johnny!

Vinny could not wait until the next morning to find out about the decision of Johnny's father. He was not about to tell Angelina about this great news yet. If the decision was a negative, he did not want her to get even more upset than she already was. However, if Mr. Muller's decision fell the other way with a "Yes," he would explain to her in detail about this wonderful news tomorrow night.

The next morning, Vinny arrived at the 41st Precinct Station House early, in anticipation of Johnny's arrival with his father's decision. He was pacing back and forth when Johnny entered. He knew Vinny was dying to know so he just yelled out:

"Yes!"

Vinny was extremely excited and happy! He hugged the big guy, "Thank you so much." He just hoped his wife would be as happy as he was with this arrangement.

Vinny started his shift; the day seemed like the longest day of his life. It dragged on endlessly. All he kept thinking about was getting home to tell Angelina this wonderful news. Finally, his shift was over. He was heading home; his car never moved so fast! When he got home, he strode across the street to Lou's Liquor Store and bought a bottle of red wine. He returned to his apartment, opened the door, hugged and kissed his wife.

He then entered the kitchen, filling two glasses of wine.

"Please sit down, sweetheart. I have wonderful news to tell you!"

He handed her one of the glasses and began to explain the whole situation to her. Vinny was a bit tense as he did not know how Angelina would react to this news. She was ecstatic. She started asking Vinny a bunch of questions.

"Is she in her early stages of pregnancy?"

"Is she healthy?"

"Has she seen a doctor?"

"Helen is due to give birth in around seven to eight months and would spend her pregnancy and childbirth at her aunt's house in Westchester County along with her uncle; they had no children of their own."

"Is her aunt looking after her?"

"When her aunt was younger, she worked as a midwife, a specialist in pregnancy and giving birth. She fulfilled the role of looking after pregnant women and their babies during pregnancy and birth. They lived about a half hour drive north from the Muller house. Helen's mother had died one year earlier during a freak accident, falling from the top of the stairway, breaking her neck."

Angelina and Vinny had their own details to work out. After discussing the matter with her mother, it was decided that she would stay at her aunt's house in the suburbs. Aunt Rosa and Uncle Vic Fatale lived in a quiet waterfront community, Oceanside, on Long Island. It was around an hour's drive from their Bronx home. Angelina would reside there for one month after the birth of their adopted child.

Everyone agreed that her aunt, a nurse would provide excellent care for all and that the peace and quiet of the suburbs would be a restful place to give birth. Angelina and Vinny felt conflicted, they certainly did not want to lie or deceive their relatives or friends about the fake pregnancy or the adoption. It was totally out of character for them. They just wanted to shield the child from knowing he or she was adopted and to protect the child from the 1950s stigma of illegitimacy.

Only the Muller, Scallaci, and Falcone immediate family members would know the truth! They were all raised to be tight lipped about family matters. Their secret would be secure.

Upon the birth of the child, Helen's family would permanently transfer all rights over to Vinny and Angelina. The new parents would also receive an amended birth certificate.

They already had names picked out. If it were a boy, they would name him Pasquale after Vinnie's father. If a girl, they would name her Giuseppina (Josephine) after Angelina's grandmother. Helen knew that it would be in the newborn's best interest to go to a loving and caring family. She was happy after meeting with Angelina and Vinny. Knowing the child would have them as parents warmed her heart!

While Angelina was staying with her aunt and uncle, she also babysat for her four-year-old cousin, Dominic, when her aunt left to work at the hospital. This would also be a way to pass the time by keeping busy and would be a good learning experience for her. Vinny would spend his days off staying with his wife and would visit her every other night during the week after work. They both would have to be patient until the birth and subsequent adoption.

During the 1950s, the United States was the world's strongest military power. Its economy was booming and the fruits of this prosperity: new cars, suburban homes, and other consumer goods were available to more people than ever before. Historians use the word "boom" to describe such things pertaining to the 1950s. For example, the "booming economy," "the booming suburbs," and, most of all, the so-called "baby boom."

The tension-filled relationship between the United States and the Soviet Union commonly known as the Cold War was another defining element of the 1950s. After WWII, Western leaders began to worry that the USSR had what one American diplomat called expansive tendencies. Moreover, they believed that the spread of communism needed to be contained by diplomacy, threats, or force. Many people in the United States worried that communists or subversives could destroy American society from within as well as from the outside.

On June 25th, 1950, the Korean War began when 75,000 soldiers of the North Korean People's Army poured across the 38th Parallel, the boundary between the Soviet-backed Democratic People's Republic to the north and the Pro-Western Republic of Korea to the south. By July, American troops had entered the war on South Korea's behalf. As far as American officials were concerned it was a war against the forces of international communism itself.

Uncle Pasquale's youngest son served in Korea with the Army and Uncle Francesco's second oldest son, served in the Marines. It was now October 1st, 1950, Helen was poised to give birth. As soon as she gave birth, her brother, Doctor Carl would contact Vinny with the news. Angelina and Vinny would now have to be patient more than ever and wait for Carl's call. Two weeks passed with no call from Carl. Then on October 16th, Vinny got the call for which they seemed to have been waiting for a lifetime!

Helen had given birth to a healthy baby boy weighing seven-pounds and measuring twenty-one inches long! The newborn was medically cleared by the good doctor, Carl. Angelina and Vinny could take their adoptive son home the following day. With this fantastic news, Vinny immediately called Angelina to let her know, and they both were extremely happy and excited. Vinny would drive to Oceanside to the home of her aunt and uncle to pick her up and then drive to the Muller house in Yonkers. Doctor Carl, who delivered the baby at his aunt's house in Westchester, would drive to his family home in Yonkers along with his aunt and the newborn baby boy.

Vinny and Angelina would also have their adoption lawyer meet them there so that they and the Muller Family could sign all the legal paperwork. It was hunting season, so Johnny Muller and his father were at their property in upstate New York. When Angelina got to hold her baby for the first time, her eyes lit up. She was in a state of euphoria, displaying the biggest smile. This was truly a magical moment for both of them! When they finished signing all the paperwork, they said their thank yous and goodbyes, and headed back to Long Island. It was such a beautiful time of the year. The leaves on the trees were on fire, with various shades of red, yellow, purple, orange, and brown.

The fall foliage was eye-catching and breathtaking. The couple could not have been any happier. Angelina would stay at her aunt and uncles' home with the new baby for one month longer. Helen would also stay with her aunt and uncle to recover from her pregnancy and the birth of the child. She would complete her high school education, then travel to Europe to live with relatives. Helen, an intelligent girl fluent in four languages, would go on to study medicine and earn her medical degree. She wanted to become a doctor like her father and brother.

Vinny spent his two-week vacation encamped with Angelina and baby, Pasquale. When his two weeks were up, he headed home and returned to work. After work, he spent his nights painting the apartment and preparing the homestead for their return. On his days off, he spent them with Angelina and baby, Pasquale. The first weeks of the baby's life were uncharted territory for Angelina, but she would have plenty of help from her mother and Aunt Rosa. The weeks passed by quickly, it was time for Angelina and little Pasquale to come home.

Vinny drove to Oceanside early on a November morning, he bought Aunt Rosa a beautiful bouquet of flowers and a lovely gold bracelet. For Uncle Vic, he got him two bottles of his favorite wine and four side-line tickets to a New York Giants football game in appreciation for all they had done for them.

It was an emotional time for Angelina, her aunt, and uncle, who all became extremely close during her stay. She would also miss her four-year-old cousin, Dominic, who she came to love like her own. After Angelina and Vinny expressed their many thank yous and gave their hugs and kisses, they said their goodbyes and headed home.

Vinny was now a member of the American Legion of the Bronx. He told his wife, "I have to make one pit stop before going home. I have to stop by the American Legion because I promised the post commander, I would show him our new baby. When they arrived, they all strolled inside the Hall and when they turned on the lights, they were greeted by all the Scallaci, Falcones, Ruggieros, and Anastasi families. Johnny, and all of Angelina's and Vinny's friends also joined in to celebrate this joyous occasion.

Angelina was completely surprised! Her husband had planned the whole thing! Angelina, who had not seen most of her family or friends in quite some time, was as overjoyed to see them as they were to see her.

Everyone got to see baby Pasquale for the first time. They brought gifts of clothes, baby toys, and other baby items. It was a Sunday.

Everyone sat down at tables and enjoyed a fabulous traditional Sunday sauce. It consisted of antipasto, meat sauce over pasta, platters of pork ribs, meatballs, and sausage. There was fresh Italian bread with which to lap up the delicious Scallaci sauce. For dessert, there were cannoli, pastries, espresso, and cordial glasses of anisette.

Baby Pasquale must have been really tired because he slept soundly in his new bassinet. All the guests enjoyed this gathering to welcome the arrival of another member to the family. Angelina could not have been more surprised and delighted to see everyone. Even her Aunt Rosa, Uncle Vic, and her young cousin, Dominic, showed up. After all the thankyous and goodbyes were exchanged once again. It was now time to bring little Pasquale to his new home on Arthur Avenue to start his life as a Scallaci.

When he was about seven months old, Angelina and Vinny realized that Pasqual was born with two different colored eyes. The left eye was **brown** and the right one **blue.** Baby Pasquale evolved from a helpless newborn to an active toddler. He grew up and changed at an astounding pace. Every month brought new and exciting developments. When Pasquale was born, he had only sparse hair on his head, but by the time he was around one year old, he sported a full head of blonde hair.

They got past the "terrible twos" where he began testing his limits with tantrums and mayhem. Young Pasquale was fully mobile now and was into everything. Angelina and Vinny showered him with love, affection, and gave him all of their attention.

Finally, in July 1953, the Korean War ended. More than 35,000 American soldiers had died, approximately 9,200 were injured, and 5,000 reported as Missing in Action. Korean War veterans will never forget their "time in hell" but for many Americans the war became known as the "forgotten war." Uncle Pasquale's son was wounded in action as was Uncle Francesco's son, who lost a leg.

On a lighter note, after seven and a half years of walking a beat and pounding the pavement on hot humid days and cold frigid nights, Vinny finally got assigned to a radio motor patrol unit (RMP), a squad car.

Vinny would now patrol the familiar streets of the South Bronx in a 1952 Ford. Johnny Muller, however, still walked a beat. Young Pasquale was starting to run, climb, and ride his tricycle. It was now September 1955. Where did the time go?

Pasquale was now a five-year-old and starting Kindergarten along with his cousin, Tony. They attended a Catholic School located on Bathgate Avenue, which they would attend all the way up to the eighth grade. In the early years of Pasquale's childhood, he kept himself occupied by playing games outside for hours with his cousins and the neighborhood children.

As time passed, he played a new and exciting game played by a few boys and a few girls, called spin the bottle. They were not afraid of catching any "Cooties;" they had the freedom to explore and play. As Pasquale grew older, the avenues of the Bronx became his playground. He would play a lot of street stickball, stoopball and wallboard with a pink rubber ball called a Spaldeen. Since Vinny's father and Uncle Salvatore's oldest son were also named Pasquale, to avoid any confusion young Pasquale was now called Patsy by family and friends alike.

Amerigo and Giovanna were getting up in years. They both were experiencing health issues. Giovanna died first. Amerigo's death followed one week later—they said from a broken heart. It was a terrible loss for the Scallaci family but knowing that they had lived a long life together and got to experience the American dream with the ever-expanding Scallaci family helped to ease the loss of the family patriarch and matriarch.

They were major contributors to the success and prosperity of the Scallaci clan. They would now rest in peace together among the rest of the Scallaci, at the family plot. Amerigo had left everything he had to his loving son, Pasquale. Uncle Salvatore's oldest son, Pasquale, and his wife, Gianna, were now the oldest living Scallaci in America. They would carry on the traditions of patriarch and matriarch.

Uncle Pasquale's youngest son, who served in Korea, opened up Frankie's Candy Store and Soda Fountain in a building his father owned on Belmont Avenue. They served the best egg creams in the Bronx! They also had a huge candy selection, a comic book and magazine section, and they sold balsa wood glider planes, (that you put together) cap guns, baseball wax packs with a slab of bubble gum, and more. There were booths where you could sit and enjoy a burger, fries, and a soda. They had two pinball machines and a jukebox for amusement, or you could sit on round red padded stools in front of a long soda counter enjoying a root-beer float or banana split. In the back of the building there was an entrance that led to a huge basement below the candy store where the Sabatino family had a bustling bookmaking operation. A bookmaker or bookie is an organization or a person that accepts and pays off bets on sporting and other events at agreed-upon odds.

In 1955, Pasquale, owner of the family grocery bought another building on Arthur Avenue and opened a new business with his cousin, Giacomo, owner of the Scallaci Butcher Shop. They named the new business, "Scallaci Chicken Market." They sold live poultry. You could select a live chicken as you pleased. It would be slaughtered, plucked, cleaned, and wrapped in a few moments. Giacomo's son, and two of his grandsons would run this new venture.

In 1956, Vinny took the New York City Police Sergeant's Exam. He passed and was promoted to patrol sergeant. That same year Rocco, younger brother of Vinny, opened up a restaurant/bar, called Rocco's. The building was vacant. It used to be an Italian restaurant, but the owner had relocated to Brooklyn. The building and property were now up for sale. With a loan from his father, Pasquale, Rocco purchased it. The Sabatino Construction Company of the Bronx where Rocco had worked for many years did a complete interior and exterior renovation on the building and landscaped the entire property.

Rocco although "pazzo" (crazy) had a good sense of humor and an engaging personality. He would greet and chat with all of his customers and became quite the Maître d. He was still unmarried, but had a younger girlfriend from the neighborhood, a pretty Italian girl, Adriana Colucci. Rocco moved out of the apartment that he shared with his parents, landing his own apartment in the old Scallaci building where his older brother, Vinny, resided.

Rocco was a big strong dude, tough as nails, and possessed a violent temper. He had a reputation on the streets as being a "leg breaker" or enforcer, who would collect loan-shark, gambling and other debts or money owed to his Uncle Pasquale and the Sabatino Crime Family. Although his father and older brother tried to tame him when he was growing up, he was a street kid who liked to fight on the mean streets of the Bronx. He loved the action and there was no changing that. During the 1950s the Sabatino crime family was also involved with hotel-casinos and lavish nightclubs in Havana, Cuba.

Shortly after Rocco opened for business, the joint became a popular place to dine for celebrities, New York's professional athletes, along with "wise guys." The Italian food served there was some of the finest in New York City. The master chef, Filippo Girardi, was famous for making delicious Southern Italian cuisine.

Vinny's best friend, Johnny Muller, was quite the gym rat and it showed. He was also a big-time naturalist who loved discovering the outdoors, hunting, and fishing in the Adirondack Mountains of upstate New York. He owned numerous guns and rifles. Vinny and Johnny both shared a love of hotrods and motorcycles. Behind the old Scallaci Building was a twelve-car garage that used to house horses and wagons. Vinny split half of the garage into one big mechanic's shop where they both performed their wrenching.

Vinny and Johnny were building a three-window 1932 Ford Deuce Coupe hotrod for Vinny. Vinny also rode a 1936 Harley-Davidson EL Model Knucklehead motorcycle. Johnny rode a 1941 Indian four-cylinder motorcycle with sidecar. Johnny finally got reassigned from foot patrol to a radio motor patrol unit. Vinny was now a sergeant and patrol supervisor. Because the brass liked Vinny, he was able to pull some strings and got Johnny assigned as his patrol partner.

It was now 1958, Vinny was 34 years old and Johnny was 33. They both had twelve years on the job and had each earned several commendation awards for meritorious service and individual acts of extraordinary bravery and valor performed in the line of duty. Do not get me wrong, they were by no means "altar boys" but did strongly believe in justice. To go along with all of his commendations received, Johnny also had several complaints against him for the use of excessive force reported to his superiors.

Vinny and Johnny finished building Vinny's '32 Ford Deuce Coupe. They stuck a hopped-up Ford flathead V-8 with Offenhauser heads and three Stromberg 97 carburetors into it. They removed its front and rear fenders along with its running boards. Vinnie's Uncle Vic from Oceanside, a master car painter sprayed it a deep black lacquer with colorful flames painted on the sides.

Now that Vinny's hotrod was complete, it was time to build Johnny's! He picked up a 1934 Ford Model 40 Deluxe Roadster.

The New York Yankees along with their two brothers of New York baseball: the Brooklyn Dodgers and the New York Giants, owned Major League baseball for much of the 1950s. All the Scallaci were big time Yankee fans and would go to their home games as often as they could.

Rock and roll dominated popular music in the latter half of the 1950s. "Doo Wop" dominated the pop charts and the Bronx's own Dion and the Belmonts were a leading American Doo Wop group. All of its members were from the Bronx. The name Belmonts was derived from the fact that two of the four singers lived on Belmont Avenue while the other two lived nearby.

Dion Francis DiMucci, or simply "Dion," was one of the most popular American rock and roll performers of the pre-British invasion era. Two of the teenaged Scallaci cousins along with some friends would harmonize on street corners in Belmont singing Doo Wop. They were actually quite good.

The end of the decade brought death in the Muller Family. Johnny's father lost his long battle with cancer. Johnny did not seem to be too upset; but Carl, who was extremely close to his father, clearly was.

They had a morning wake followed by an afternoon service and burial. Though they had never met Mr. Muller, Vinny, along with all the Scallaci family members attended the funeral out of respect for Johnny. Because the cancer in his body spread all over, they had a closed casket. Helen was in Europe attending the university, busy with exams, and would not be attending. In attendance were the Scallaci family, some of Johnny's police pals, his aunt and uncle who took care of Helen during her pregnancy, and a creepy-looking man who Johnny introduced to Vinny. His name was Otto, the family caretaker for their property in upstate New York.

Vinny felt bad for Johnny because no one else showed up, not one friend of his father's or Carl. Vinny figured Mr. Muller must have been a recluse.

"Vinny, except for my aunt and uncle that live in Westchester," Johnny said, "the rest of the relatives were back in Europe."

"Johnny," Vinny noted, "it's our honor to support you." The day ended and it had to be the most unemotional funeral Vinny had ever attended.

11

The 1960s, Awakenings

Fifty years after the Scallaci family had moved to the Bronx from Manhattan in 1910 and three generations of Italian American Scallaci later, the family had realized Uncle Natale's early dream of prosperity and a better way of life in America.

Johnny and Vinny had finally finished building Johnny's 1934 Ford Roadster with a hopped-up Ford Flathead V-8! The Roadster featured one of the first hotrods in the Bronx with a Candy Apple Red metal flake paint job. Man, did it look boss! One day, while on their lunch break, Johnny and Vinny visited Bernie's, their favorite luncheonette, where Johnny met a newly hired waitress. He felt an immediate attraction to her.

She was a good-looking Irish girl. She had blonde hair, big beautiful blue eyes, and a knockout body. Johnny was definitely shot through the heart by Cupid's arrow. Her name was Annie Nolan. Johnny started to visit her on a daily basis at the luncheonette. They soon became good friends. He then started to see her after his shift was over and they soon became an item, spending lots of time together.

She had a ten-year-old daughter, Laura, but had never married. Annie struggled to make ends meet. She was a single mom, worked long hours, and was determined to provide for her daughter. The relationship with Johnny after dating for three months was heating up.

"Annie would you and Laura like to move in with me into the

home that I share with my brother, Carl? The house is more than big enough with plenty of room for all to live comfortably."

"Sure, Johnny."

She really liked Johnny and felt truly safe with him, plus her daughter adored him.

Everything was going great for the couple. Carl and Annie got along wonderfully, as did Carl and Laura. Carl, who loved to cook, prepared their meals, then would help Laura with her homework. Carl was also a clean freak and kept the house spotless, which was no easy task, considering Johnny's habit of throwing his stuff wherever was convenient at the time. With Carl, everything had its place. He was well organized and meticulous. Annie could not believe they were brothers.

Johnny, Carl, and Annie all worked during the day. Laura was in the same grade as Patsy and was an excellent student. After living with each other for a few years, Johnny and Annie got engaged and would set a date to be married in the near future.

Shortly after noon on November 22nd, 1963, President John F. Kennedy was assassinated as he rode in a motorcade in downtown Dallas, Texas. One of President Kennedy's most famous quotes, "ask not what your country can do for you - ask what you can do for your country," challenged every American to contribute in some way to the public good.

JFK as a boy in the late 1920s, had lived in the upscale Riverdale section of the Bronx for two years. It was a sad day for the American people and the Kennedy family.

On the day President Kennedy was assassinated, Vice President Lyndon B. Johnson was sworn in as the 36th President of the United States. Maintaining security, he carried on the rapidly growing struggle to restrain communist encroachment in Vietnam.

Patsy, now thirteen years old, was finishing up eighth grade and graduating from Catholic School. Although he was an average student academically, he excelled in sports. He was a big strong kid and popular among his classmates.

Summer arrived. School was out, there was constant activity! Last summer his cousins, Sal and Tony, and his gang of friends spent their time riding their Schwinn Sting-Ray bicycles with banana seats, exploring the wooded properties owned by his grandfather. They even built a fort by the train tracks and creek where they would go to smoke cigarettes, drink beers, read dirty girlie magazines, and maybe cop a feel from one of the older neighborhood girls, or just see what kind of mischief they could get into.

Every once in a while, my parents treated us to a movie at the Whitestone Drive-In in my father's 1957 2-door Chevy Nomad to see scary movies such as "Village of the Damned," "Curse of the Werewolf," "The Two Faces of Dr. Jekyll," or "Horrors of Spider Island." After the movie, they took us across the street for ice cream at the Howard Johnsons restaurant.

We also loved going to the Savoy Movie Theatre, located on Hughes Avenue and 186th Street in our Belmont neighborhood, affectionately nicknamed "The Dumps" in honor of its rundown and shabby appearance! The Saturday-Sunday matinees were the best. We would watch a triple-feature of Sci-Fi B-Movies such as "The Creature from the Black Lagoon," "The Fly," and "The Day the Earth Stood Still" for only 35 cents!

On really hot days, my parents would take us to Orchard Beach for a day of fun n sun. One of our favorite pastimes was street stickball--we played for hours on end! Another of my favorites was helping my father and Uncle Johnny in the garage wrenching on hot-rods and motorcycles. I had become quite the little gearhead. I always looked forward to Sundays and the traditional Italian sauce my mother and grandmother prepared.

There was always something to do in the Bronx.

During this summer, "however", as we entered the ninth grade, we were interested in something different. Our teenage hormones had kicked in, we had discovered girls, and experienced sexual emotions. We spent a lot of our time trying to advance from first base to second base, then third base and possibly go all the way to home plate with our girlfriends. I would not slide-into home, so to speak until the following summer. That summer, however, we would usually come home with hickeys, which were caused by our girls sucking on our necks while making out. To avoid having to explain to our parents how we got these bruises on our necks, we would dab on some corrective concealer in the summer months. During winter, we wore turtleneck shirts and scarfs, or we would just leave them out in the open for all to see.

No matter what we did, we always had music playing on WABC by Cousin Brucie or Murray the K, on WINS.

We attended many Yankee baseball games. My grandfather sold his top-of-the-line tailormade suits to many of the Yankee players and management and obtained great tickets for any home game we desired! We loved to watch the boys of summer led by 'the Man,' Mickey Mantle and his able homerun partner, Roger Maris play.

Nightlife became increasingly important to us. We would go to parties most Friday and Saturday nights as either invitees or crashers. On other fair-weather evenings we would sneak into the drive-In, hidden inside the spacious trunk of a '57 Chevy. We always seemed to find some type of action going on in the neighborhood!

My grandfather, Pasquale, pledged a promise to his parents, Amerigo, and Giovanna, to one day visit his older brother, Vincenzo's, grave in the Meuse-Argonne American Cemetery in France. He thought that it was the right time to make good on his promise. This would be his and my grandmother, Natala's, first vacation ever. They planned to travel to France, spend a few days visiting the cemetery, pay their respects, and place flowers at his grave. From there, they would travel to Sicily, spend two weeks, then return home. They would visit the villages where they were born, stay with relatives they had not seen since they were children, and meet new relatives for the first time.

My father had always made it known to his superiors in the NYPD that he wanted to become a homicide detective. He had been on the force for sixteen years, distinguished himself, and was well liked by all of the right people. He was promoted to detective in the homicide bureau for the Borough of the Bronx.

He would be hanging up his uniform for a custom suit and tie! Thanks to his father-in-law, Nunzio Falcone, Vinny became the sharpest dresser in the bureau. His new boss, Lieutenant Greg Boucher, commander of the homicide squad, had a reputation for outstanding police work and was highly respected throughout the New York Police Department, took Vinny under his wing. He liked his new job interviewing witnesses and suspects, collecting evidence, and helping to solve homicides.

He would not see his best friend, Johnny, as often on the job, though. Johnny was still doing radio motor patrol at the 41st precinct.

One day as Johnny Muller arrived home from work after picking up Laura from a friend's house, he arrived at the Muller residence to a scene of police cars and an ambulance. He parked his car, telling Laura to stay put until he found out what was going on.

He rushed out of his vehicle and ran into his brother.

"Carl, what's happened?"

"It's Annie. There has been a terrible accident and she's gone!"

Johnny was shocked. Carl then explained to him what he thought had happened.

"The night before, Annie had told me she had the day off from work and was going to decorate the back yard with Fourth of July decorations. She must have lost her balance on the ladder she was standing on, fell and hit her head on the cobblestone patio sustaining a fatal head injury. I arrived home from work at the hospital a couple of hours before you to find Annie lying on the ground in a pool of blood by her head. I did all I could to save her, but she was unresponsive. Johnny, I am so deeply sorry."

Neither one of them were strangers to the sight of death, but this time it hit home.

Carl, who had worked before with the medical examiner, explained again to him what he thought had happened to Annie. After a brief coroner's investigation, her death was ruled as accidental.

Now, Johnny would have to explain this horrific news to Annie's thirteen-year-old daughter, Laura. He knew that was not going to be easy or pleasant. He lumbered to his car. Laura sensed by looking at Johnny that something was wrong. When Johnny opened the car door, he hugged her and told her the dreadful news of what had happened to her mother. Laura was an emotional mess. All Johnny could do was hug her and tell her how sorry he was.

He tried to assure her that everything was going to be alright.

"Laura, Carl and I will always love you and take care of you."

Carl hurried over to the parked car and also started hugging her, trying to calm her down. Carl and Laura had become extremely close.

Johnny then carried her into the house and laid her in her bed. Carl administered a sedative to calm her and induce sleep. After she fell asleep and the police cars and ambulance had left, Johnny and Carl sat in the kitchen speechless. Johnny poured them both a glass of whiskey.

This was not the first time the Muller boys experienced the death of a loved one. A freak accident at the Muller home occurred years earlier. Their mother died of a broken neck when she fell down the stairs. A coroner's report also ruled the death as accidental.

"Carl, do you find these accidental deaths on the Muller property to be just a little suspicious--not one, but death to two loved ones, both by freak accidents? When father purchased this huge house in this upscale neighborhood at way below market value, he was told the price was so cheap because the previous owner [father & husband] had murdered his entire family of six, then took his own life. I know it sounds crazy, but do you think this house is haunted and possesses some type of evil forces or evil spirits."

"No Johnny, I have never believed in the paranormal. I just see these two deaths as what they are, freak accidents."

Johnny felt grief-stricken himself, but he really felt even worse for young Laura. She only had her mother in her life for most of her childhood. Laura grew up in a dysfunctional home. Her birth father was an alcoholic and drug addict who essentially was a bum. There was constant arguing and fighting, culminating in her father abandoning Laura and her mother. She had seen her mother struggle to provide for her. Laura had never known her grandparents on either side. It was just always her and her mother. She had now finally lived in a normal environment surrounded by people that absolutely loved her and her mother. For the first time, they both felt safe and secure. Now, sadly, she was gone.

Johnny poured himself another glass of whiskey.

"Carl, I had finally found the girl of my dreams. It was the first time I ever experienced true love." He sighed in despair, "Carl, Annie was so beautiful, inside and out and now it's all gone just like that."

He knew that it was going to take a long time or perhaps these wounds would never heal for Laura and himself. He then called his best friend, Vinny, to explain to him and Angelina the bad news. After Johnny hung up the phone, Vinny and Angelina jumped into their car and raced over to the Muller home to comfort and support them in any way they could. It truly was the saddest of days. Johnny and Carl would both take time off from work and kept Laura company until she was feeling better.

Angelina, whom Laura called Aunt Ange, would also spend a lot of time with her. They were all trying their best to get on with their lives.

Some of the Scallaci had moved from Arthur Avenue to Country Club, an upscale Italian waterfront community, located in the East Bronx. The area offered peaceful streets, panoramic views of East Chester Bay, and by night the illuminating lights of the Throgs Neck Bridge twinkling in the distance like so many diamonds.

Uncle Pasquale purchased a beautiful estate, his sons and brothers and their families all bought single family homes on the water. Uncle Pasquale retired from his legal businesses and had his sons and grandsons running their daily operations. He spent most of his time at his Bella Faccia Social Club conducting Sabatino family illegal business. His brothers, owners of Scallaci Ice-Coal-Oil and Heating were semi-retired. They built the business into one of NYC's largest heating, ventilation, and air conditioning companies. They still sold and delivered bags of Scallaci Brand ice to supermarkets, beer docks, delicatessens, etc. Uncle Pasquale even started a garbage removal company: Done right Carting. Angelo Anastasi now had a Sabatino Construction Company in all five boroughs of New York

City, Long Island, and Westchester County. To keep the Sabatino name out of their legitimate companies, all Sabatino construction companies were renamed First Class Construction. Angelo also had his men build a couple of ready-mix concrete plants and were growing big in the concrete industry where you could get ready-mix concrete delivered right to the job site. This new company was called Quality Concrete.

My grandfather, Pasquale, who owned the family grocery invested his money wisely in real estate and could have also retired and relocated to an estate in Country Club but instead, he chose to continue working at the Scallaci family grocery and living on Arthur Avenue along with his wife, Natala.

On a beautiful sunny morning, over the 4th of July weekend, Johnny Muller rode his 1941 Indian four-cylinder motorcycle with sidecar over to Vinny's garage to help Vinny, assisted by thirteen-year-old Patsy do some work on his '32 Deuce Coupe. It was around 2:00 PM, and Vinny and Johnny needed to make a parts run. It was a gorgeous day, and they both decided to ride their bikes. My father kicked over his 1936 Harley-Davidson Knucklehead motorcycle and Johnny kicked over his Indian four-cylinder accompanied by me in the sidecar.

The loud rumble of the engines was music to our ears! We took off to the S & K Speed Shop located in the South Bronx, where they sold performance parts. When we got there, they parked their bikes, leaving me to watch over them while they went inside. As I was looking around, I noticed several cool looking Harley Choppers lined up in front of the Tick Tock Bar. I heard the sounds of loud music and rowdy customers emanating from inside. Then out the door barreled seven hardcore-looking bikers with beers in hand.

They staggered to the corner of the bar building and fired up a few marijuana joints that they passed around. I was a somewhat street-smart kid and knew what marijuana smelled like. These were some big, tough looking bikers, with long hair, beards, or goatees, and covered with tattoos. They wore denim jackets with cut off sleeves and several patches sewed onto the back that read Satan's Survivors on top and Bronx, N.Y.M.C." (motorcycle club) written on the bottom.

SATAN'S SURVIVORS
BRONX, NY
MC

I had heard of them, but never actually seen one before. I did not wander too far from the comfort of my Italian neighborhood. However, one day while driving with my father in the South Bronx, we passed a building that had signs on it that read Satan's Survivors Motorcycle Club with a long row of Harleys parked in front. When I asked my father about them, he cursed "That's their clubhouse. They are a violent outlaw motorcycle gang involved in numerous illegal activities. They're also extremely aggressive and dangerous; you should stay clear of them, Patsy."

While I was sitting in Johnny's side car, I noticed the biggest biker looking in my direction and pointing his finger toward me while he talked to his buddies, who were also staring at me. I murmured, "Oh man, here comes trouble." Sure enough, they all started heading toward me. As they got closer, they became even more menacing looking, then from a distance, the big one scowled at me, "Nice rides, can I sit on the Knucklehead?"

"It's my fathers, he doesn't let anyone sit on it, including me."

"I'm sure he won't mind if I sit on it."

That is just what he did.

"We don't want any trouble with you guys," I shouted, as I stepped out of the Indian's sidecar.

"My father and uncle told me to look out for the bikes and that's what I'm going to do."

The big biker who one of his buddies called Geronimo had a smaller patch sewed on the front of his jacket that read sergeant at arms, responded:

"You and what army, little man."

I was big and strong for my age and although my father taught me how to box when I was young, I was no match for even the smallest biker. So, I thought that maybe if I was polite to them, they might leave. I asked the one named Geronimo who was sitting on my father's bike to please get off. He laughed!

Then two of his buddies got on Johnny's bike, one sitting in the sidecar. At this point, I knew that they were fired up and looking for a fight with my father and Uncle Johnny. As my father was at the counter paying for his parts, Johnny walked to the front door to check on me. He noticed the ruckus that was taking place on the motorcycles through the screen door.

Without blinking an eye, Johnny pushed the screen door open so hard the screws for the hinges ripped right out of its frame and was sent flying to the street. Johnny charged out like a rhino protecting its young one. I have never seen him so pissed off and enraged.

Johnny grabbed the first biker he encountered and literally snapped his neck like a chicken.

"One down."

Geronimo got off my father's bike, reached into his jacket pocket and pulled out brass knuckles –placing them on his right hand. The rest of the bikers ran to their motorcycles and grabbed some form of weapon--axe handle, bike chain, or club. At this time, my father also heard the mayhem and ran out to the parking lot.

He yelled, "You scum messed with the wrong guys."

He joined in the fight. Johnny flew over to Geronimo and head-butted him, then proceeded to pummel his face with his giant fists until he fell to the ground like a sack of potatoes.

Geronimo never even got to use his brass knuckles. The bikers hit my father and Johnny with everything they had, but with Johnny's size and strength and my father's fighting skills the bikers were no match for them, even with all their weapons. All seven went down and did not even get up when the police and ambulances arrived. One of the bikers was found dead from his battle wounds; the other six had several broken bones each and were completely covered in blood.

Johnny definitely snapped. He turned into the Grim Reaper, intent on wreaking some serious havoc! The parking lot between the auto parts store and the Tick Tock Bar was covered in blood and littered with an assortment of weapons. Miraculously no blood landed on my father's or Johnny's bikes and neither of their bikes sustained damage. My father and Johnny were banged up and bloodied but sustained no life-threatening injuries. Johnny was stabbed in his side, and also broke his right hand, most likely on one of the biker's faces.

They would normally carry their weapons when off duty, but since they were wrenching, they left them locked up back at the garage. The bikers' friends rushed out of the bar after hearing all the sirens, because the Tic Toc Bar had a loud band, they never heard the fight going on, which was probably a good thing. There were plenty of witnesses who told the police that my father and Johnny had acted in total self-defense. Plus, they knew all the cops from the 40th Precinct working the scene. Ambulances, and there were several of them, drove the six suspects who barely survived the beating to the hospital's emergency unit and the coroner took the seventh suspect to the morgue.

Paramedics temporarily patched up Johnny and my father and

transported them to the hospital for further treatment. I joined in the fight, managing to get a few punches in and suffered a black eye in the process.

Two 40th Precinct patrol cars stayed at the scene, watching over their bikes until they were OK to get them. After spending six hours in the hospital, they got all stitched up! Johnny had a cast put on his broken right hand. Johnny had the largest hands I have ever seen. His fingers were the size of Italian sausages.

I had heard stories about how tough my father and Johnny were but now I had witnessed it first-hand.

They also got cleaned up and received treatment for cuts, abrasions, and cracked ribs and were discharged from the hospital and driven back to the crime scene. They got on their bikes and we rode home.

When we got home, my mother had a nice Italian dinner waiting for us. We explained to her what happened. She was simply happy that none of us got seriously injured. After the fine meal, my father and Johnny drank some cold brews, relaxed on the couch, and watched a classic John Wayne movie. Johnny stayed the night. I stepped across the hall to my best friend, Joey Castanza's apartment, to tell him about the exciting day we had. It was going to take some time before my father's and Johnny's battle scars healed.

The summer sadly ended! I now attended public school in the ninth grade at Theodore Roosevelt High School on Fordham Road, across the street from Fordham University. Guilia, mother of my best friend Joey Castanza, was a single mom who had just lost her job as an Italian cook when the restaurant she worked at burnt down. Joey, his sister Gina, and their mother lived across the hall from us in the old Scallaci building.

Joey's father, a Mafioso, was charged with a double homicide when Joey was eight years old. He was subsequently sentenced to death in Sing-Sing Prison located in Ossining, some thirty miles north of New York City. Because Giulia was unable to find work, the family was now struggling financially. For the first time in my life, I asked my Grandfather Pasquale for a favor to help Joey's family out. My grandfather lowered their rent, gave Joey's mother, Giulia, a job cooking in the Scallaci Family Grocery kitchen, and Joey, who was two years older than I, an after-school job. God bless my grandfather!

My grandfather had a big heart! When he saw families, he knew were struggling to make ends meet, he would help them out. He remembered the tough times the Scallaci had experienced when he was just a boy. Joey Castanza's mother and Joey were working out fine at the grocery. Giulia was an excellent cook; my grandfather was elated with her work.

The Scallaci family was well-respected and feared in the Belmont neighborhood of Little Italy. The Scallaci name was prominently affixed to several businesses and buildings.

Uncle Pasquale's side of the family were made members of the Sabatino Crime Family or were associated with it. Uncle Pasquale and his family members were flashier than my grandfather, Pasquale's, side of the family. Uncle Pasquale bought a brand-new black Cadillac every year. He owned a beautiful estate on East Chester Bay, where he moored his fifty-foot yacht. He and his sons wore expensive suits, tailor cut by my grandfather, Nunzio Falcone. They wore diamond pinky rings and always carried a huge wad of cash in their pockets. My grandfather's side were the complete opposite. All Scallaci were extremely close and 100% loyal! They would kill or die for one another without hesitation.

The first semester of high school passed quickly. Christmas was in a week. That Christmas would be the most memorable and special for me and all the Scallaci. For that year's festivities, my father rented the American Legion Hall for all Scallaci family members, their in-laws, and close friends for a Christmas reunion.

Angelo and Santo Anastasi and their families, Johnny Muller, and his now adopted daughter, Laura, along with Giulia Castanza, her son, Joey, and younger daughter, Gina, who I was now dating, all attended the festivities. The evening of Christmas Eve started out with cold temperatures followed by a severe snowstorm. Many trays and platters of assorted frutta di mare seafood were arriving from the Scallaci Family Grocery, Scallaci Wholesale Import/Export Market, Scallaci butchers and Rocco's Restaurant. The meal would be prepared and served by the happily toiling Scallaci women in the kitchen of the American Legion.

Guests arrived to the sound of the jukebox playing Christmas songs and a blazing fire in the stone fireplace. There were Christmas trees decorated with colorful lights, garland, and bulbs hanging from its branches at each end of the room. One tree was surrounded by an enormous number of presents for the children and the other tree had presents around it for the adults.

The inside and outside of the Hall were all lit up with Christmas decorations. Outside was a winter wonderland. When all the guests arrived at this wonderful occasion they were greeted with hugs and kisses, were seated at their tables, and prepared for a huge Italian Christmas dinner, feast of the "seven fishes" with an abundance of delicious seafood and a well-stocked bar.

After we all ate, my father donned the traditional Scallaci Santa Suit and handed out all the presents. First to the kids, then to the adults. My best present came from my Uncle Johnny Muller who got me a model 270 slide-action 22 caliber Winchester rifle with case, for my 14th birthday, which was October 16th and for my Christmas present. It was good to see Laura again! She looked great and told me she was happy to see me.

I exclaimed, "Laura, it's great to see you as well."

The Muller Family seemed to be getting on with their lives. I was happy for them. Uncle Pasquale, his brothers, my grandfather, and their cousin, Giacomo, all agreed that this Christmas reunion was the best one! They further suggested that Uncles; Natale, Salvatore, Giuseppe, and my great grandfather, Amerigo would certainly have agreed. There were mountains of seafood, enough to feed an army.

As the guests dressed warmly to leave, the jukebox played "I'm Dreaming of a White Christmas" performed by legendary crooner, Bing Crosby.

As it was still snowing heavily and the roads were covered with about eight inches of snow, any of the guests who lived outside the Bronx would spend the night in the Bronx with relatives. My mother's

Aunt Rosa and Uncle Vic Vitale, along with their three sons from the town of Oceanside on Long Island stayed two nights with us. What a blast we had! After our Christmas break was over, it was back to school.

Because I had a reputation as being a tough guy and my last name was Scallaci, members of the Fordham Daggers Gang asked me and my gang; Tony, Sal, and several of my neighborhood friends to pledge (join them). My gang of neighborhood friends were mostly dark-haired and dark-skinned Italians. I was the only light-skinned and blonde headed among the gang and within my family. I often wondered where my genes were derived."

The initiation into the Daggers consisted of a few days of being sucker-punched by the members. The Fordham Daggers was comprised of fourteen and fifteen-year-old kids who were always looking to prove themselves tough enough to become a member of the older Fordham Baldies Gang. The gang centered around the Little Italy section of the Bronx, East 187th Street, Belmont Avenue, and Arthur Avenue areas. Many of my older cousins entering into the ninth grade also became members of the Fordham Daggers. After they made their bones with the Daggers, they graduated to the Fordham Baldies.

The Fordham Baldies were not actually bald-headed, they were an organized gang which honestly believed that they and not the police were the true protectors of the neighborhood. If you were from the neighborhood, you felt safe walking down the street, but if you were an outsider looking for trouble you better watch out! Gang-life and street fighting were simply a rite of passage. Gang wars were typically fought over turf and girls.

Gangs were more or less divided by ethnicity, although many had a mixture of ethnic backgrounds. Italians, Irish, Blacks, and Puerto Ricans all contributed to the estimated 6,000 gang members associated with hundreds of gangs throughout the city. Rumbles became synonymous with these gangs. By the end of the week, my gang and I became members of the Daggers. At this time, I would not tell my mother or father that I joined the Dagger's Gang. I was not sure how they would react, especially my mother.

My high school years flew by. The British invasion was a phenomenon throughout the mid-1960s. Rock and Pop music acts from the United Kingdom as well as other aspects of British culture became popular in the United States. This was a significant factor which ushered in a rising counterculture on both sides of the Atlantic.

On October 16th, 1966, I turned sixteen! My cousin Sal and I visited Song Time Record Store in East Harlem to purchase Frankie Valli & The Four Seasons and Righteous Brothers records.

As we were walking down the sidewalk toward the store, we were approached by four teenagers.

One of them asked, "Do you live around here?"

"No."

"Then, what are you doing on Harlem Red Wings turf?"

"We're here to buy some records."

"Don't you have a record store in your neighborhood?"

As the kid sucker punched Sal, Sal did not see it coming. The guy also pushed him against a brick wall. He hit his head hard and fell down to the sidewalk. I quickly unleashed the Scallaci temper and grabbed the punk by his collar and belt and tossed him through a nearby car door window, breaking the glass as his head struck through it, followed by half of his body. Another hood started kicking Sal in the head with his pointy shoes while he lay helpless on the ground. I punched him hard in the throat, and he started gasping for air. I began kicking the crap out of the third guy and I sent him crashing down to the concrete. One more left. He started swinging a Garrison belt adorned with a heavy buckle on its end. He hit me three times viciously. On his fourth attempt, I grabbed it, pulled him toward me and as hard as I could I kneed him in the family jewels. He fell to the ground in a motionless lump!

When I picked Sal up off the sidewalk, his face was bloody. I threw him over my shoulder and quickly got to the car, put him in the passenger seat, took his keys, and started up the car. Sal certainly was in no shape to drive.

I quickly headed to our side of town and approached the hospital's Emergency Room. They immediately admitted Sal. I explained to the nurse what had happened. I gave her all the info on Sal that I knew and gave them the phone number so they could contact his family. As I waited in the emergency waiting room, I noticed a pay phone booth, so I called Joey Castanza, my closest friend and a high-ranking member of our gang, the Fordham Baldies.

He drove to the hospital with four other gang members. I explained to Joey and the guys what had happened. The Red Wings, a well-known and powerful Italian gang situated in East Harlem, were responsible for the savage attack. The area during the 1940s, '50s and early '60s was known as Dago Harlem, and eventually became Spanish Harlem (El Barrio). Southern Italian and Sicilians were the main groups which moved into the area and eventually became the first section of Manhattan to be referred to as Little Italy.

There had been a history of bad blood between the two rival gangs dating back to the mid-1950s. My uncle and one of Sal's older brothers arrived at the hospital. I explained to them what had happened and gave Sal's father the car keys. My uncle thanked me for looking out for him. Sal was short in stature but made up for it with "heart and guts." Pound for pound, he was one of the toughest seventeen-year-olds in the neighborhood, earning the nickname, Tasmanian Devil. After we waited for a few hours the doctor told his family and all of us that Sal had a broken nose, two cracked teeth, and a concussion. "We will be keeping Sal overnight for observation, but he should be cleared to go home tomorrow," said the doctor "He will have to take it easy for a few weeks, then he should be good as new."

"Thanks, Doc."

12

Accidental Tears

Several summers had passed. As I approached the onset of the 12th grade, I looked forward to Labor Day, as Uncle Pasquale had his annual end of the summer bash. We all had a blast; there was live music, great food, and drink. He had a huge in-ground pool, which we all enjoyed! My uncle spared no expense on his Labor Day parties. This would be my last year of high school and I would finally be done! I spent most of my spare time hanging out with my friends on the streets of the Bronx, getting our kicks, cruising in my friend Tommy Gun's '58 Chevy Impala, or hanging out at Cousin Frankie's candy store/luncheonette with our girls.

In the courtyard behind the candy store were three bocce ball courts. We would make up teams and compete against each other for the neighborhood championship!

On February 13, 1968, the Falcone and Scallaci families received shocking news about a tragic automobile accident. My grandfather, Nunzio Falcone, had taken my grandmother, Carmela, and my mother, Angelina, out for lunch at Delmonico's, a fancy Manhattan Bistro. When they finished with lunch, they got into my grandfather's Cadillac and headed toward the Bronx. A drunk driver drove his Mack Truck carrying a full load of construction debris through a red light and T-boned my grandfather's Cadillac, killing all three passengers aboard. This was a heartbreaking time for everyone and would be the saddest day and time of my life. Shock was felt by all. No one knew how to respond.

The Falcones and Scallaci were devoutly religious and held a strong faith in God's greater plan. We would have to take it one day at a time. There would be many dark days ahead as we journeyed forward through our grief. We will never truly recover from the loss of our loved ones, but we will learn to live with it. My father and I felt an empty space in our hearts. We knew we would have to move forward, building new lives without the loved ones we now mourned.

The Falcone family and my father completed all of the funeral arrangements. There would be a two-day wake at the Tarantino Funeral Home. The parlor was packed with mourners waiting in long lines to get inside to pay their respects. The mood of the day was somber. On the second night of the wake, a vigil prayer service was performed by Father Parisi. The next day, the funeral mass took place at our local Roman Catholic Church. After the church mass the caskets were carried by Falcone and Scallaci pallbearers and loaded into the waiting hearses for the journey to the cemetery in a long funeral procession. We all managed to get through the funeral. After leaving the cemetery, we all gathered at my Uncle Rocco's restaurant for a memorial luncheon.

In the week that followed this horrible tragedy, my father took a few days off from work as I did from school. A couple of weeks later, my father and I moved out of our apartment, moving next door to the second Scallaci Building. We moved in with my grandfather, Pasquale, and grandmother, Natala.

We had all grown closer than ever. We still had fond memories of our loved ones and depended upon our strong faith to endure this painful episode. All of our family and friends were supportive with encouragement and offered to help out in any way they could.

Then on April 4, 1968, the most visible spokesperson and leader of the civil rights movement, Martin Luther King Jr. was assassinated in Memphis, TN. A Baptist minister and founder of the Southern Christian Leadership Conference, King had led the civil rights movement since the mid-1950s. Using a combination of impassioned speeches and non-violent protests to fight segregation he achieved significant advances for African Americans.

Johnny Müller spent a lot of his time being a great friend to my father and a great uncle to me! Johnny took a one week vacation off from work. He took Laura, his German Shepherd, Dempsey, and me up to the Muller country home in upstate New York. I had never been there before, but knew it was located in the Northern Adirondack Mountains and that this was where Johnny did all his hunting.

Johnny thought that it would be good for me to get away from the Bronx to recover. Laura and I were off from school for Easter vacation. On the ride up, Johnny explained to me that the house stood on 800 acres that included an old hospital built in 1858 and subsequently closed in 1948. The hospital and several of its outlying buildings still stood on the property. He told me the main house was a large Victorian where the hospital superintendent and his family once resided. The main house featured a wing with six bedrooms fitted with wood burning fireplaces where the staff doctors resided. Johnny's father purchased the property in 1949.

Finally, after a 6-hour drive, we arrived at our destination, located in a heavily forested and secluded area off of a two-lane winding road.

As we turned off the road, Johnny pulled onto a cobblestone driveway adorned by large stone columns with rusty wrought iron fencing that stood about ten feet high. Around one hundred yards from the entrance, stood what appeared to be an old guard shack. Just beyond were two huge iron gates locked by a heavy-duty chain.

Johnny got out of his Jeep Wagoneer and unlocked the chain. As he swung open the gates, you could hear the squeaky sound of the rusty hinges. He got back in his Jeep and proceeded up the steep driveway until we encountered a large well-maintained Victorian style home featuring a large country style porch.

Johnny parked his vehicle. We then unloaded our gear and a couple of cardboard boxes filled with supplies and carried them into the house. The great room (living room/family room) featured elaborate woodwork. The walls had oak wainscoting. The showpieces were a huge stone fireplace with a large moose head mounted to it and a large antler chandelier hanging from the cathedral ceiling. The walls were covered with Johnny's hunting trophies. A giant black bearskin rug was lying on the hardwood floor. I thought I was at the zoo! Another one of Johnny's hobbies, taxidermy, was taught to him by his grandfather and father back in Europe when he was young.

All the Mullers were big time hunters except for Carl, who thought killing animals was barbaric. At this time, Johnny's dog, Dempsey started barking wildly. Two older-looking German Shepherds appeared. Out of nowhere, a large man with a weather-beaten face also appeared. Johnny introduced him as Otto. Johnny told me he was the caretaker for this property. Johnny knew him since they were kids growing up in Europe where Otto's father was the caretaker of the Muller Family Estate.

Otto was now the Caretaker for the current Muller Country Home. He lived in one of the old hospital's staff homes year-round. Laura explained to me, "The dogs are named, Blitzkrieg, the male and Schatzi, the female. They are the parents of Johnny's dog, Dempsey."

Schatzi had given birth to a litter of eight puppies three months ago. Otto bred these pedigree German Shepherds with champion bloodlines, and he would train and sell them as guard dogs. His family had been breeding and training such dogs since the early 1900s back in Europe.

Otto showed me to my quarters on the second floor; situated between Laura's and Johnny's rooms. He also helped bring up all of our gear. Laura knew Otto well and had been to the Muller Country Home many times before. While Johnny was getting settled in, Laura gave me a tour of the house. When we were done, Johnny, Laura, Dempsey, and I took a stroll on the property.

As we marched up the steep cobblestone driveway, Johnny pointed out some of the outbuildings and told me that when the hospital was operational the property was a working farm that grew its own crops and housed dairy and beef cows, goats, pigs and chickens in the two silo-equipped barns."

Next to the barn stood the horse stables. Adjacent to them, Johnny explained was the maintenance building, which housed all the farm equipment and tools used to maintain the property. He told me the property once operated its own power plant, water system, bakery, laundry, and staff housing. The facility functioned almost completely independently from the rest of society. The property was once self-sufficient with even its own small fire department and police force. The three-level hospital building was built from hand-cut stone and was designed in a brooding Gothic architecture.

Johnny told Laura and I the old Hospital Building was strictly off limits to everyone because it was in total disrepair and considered dangerous and unsafe to access.

There were several more buildings: a coal burning power plant building and a coal boiler furnace building with massive brick smokestacks. Johnny told me the power plant was no longer operational.

The main house, Otto's house, the two barns, and several of the other outbuildings were now connected to the county's power plant. The property had several fields and meadows that were once used for farming and pastures for the livestock to graze on. They are still viable today. The rest of the property was thickly forested with sugar maple and eastern white pine and was enhanced by a babbling brook running through the property.

After we passed most of the outbuildings and hiked up the steep cobblestone driveway, the pavement gave way to a dirt road. There we observed a herd of white-tailed deer grazing in a meadow, with a majestic sunset and endless tall evergreens as a backdrop. What a picture-perfect moment! We also encountered several chipmunks scurrying across the dirt road, which seemed to go on forever up the mountainside.

It was becoming dark out, so we turned around and returned home. We had sampled only a portion of the tremendous property's beauty, but we had a whole week to explore. On the way back, I saw another large building in the distance that I had missed on the way up. Johnny told me it was an old ice-house used to store ice cut out of the pond and the nearby lake during winter. The ice was stored in the ice-house for the warmer months before electricity and refrigeration were invented."

When we got back to the house, Otto and Laura prepared a delicious venison steak dinner served with homegrown Adirondack potatoes and corn. Otto was quite the chef, as was Laura, who learned how to cook from Johnny's brother, Carl, an excellent chef in his own right.

After dinner, Johnny demonstrated to me how to build a fire in the great room fireplace. We all played card games until midnight. We had a big day planned for tomorrow, so it was time to hit the rack. Before we headed to bed, Johnny wanted to show me something, so we headed out to the back porch and he told me, "Look up at the sky." I did and viewed the most spectacular array of stars I have seen in my life. It was black as coal outside and frigid as well.

Johnny told me, "The winter season comes early and leaves late up here.

Spring, summer, and fall are also truly breathtaking in the Adirondacks, but have shorter seasons."

We headed up to our rooms. It was a little brisk, so I lit a fire in my own fireplace! The fresh mountain air knocked me out; I enjoyed the best sleep I have had in a "very" long time!

Morning arrived and Otto cooked us a big country breakfast. Even though Otto was not particularly friendly, he was multi-talented. He could fish, hunt, farm crops, raise livestock, repair anything, do taxi-dermy, butcher meat, breed dogs, and the list goes on.

He ran the Muller property efficiently; nothing went to waste. Otto had two young farmhands to help him with daily chores--Jake and his cousin, Jocko. They had their own rooms in Otto's house. They were away for the holidays, spending time with their families in the Finger Lakes region of western New York for Easter. They would return in a few days.

After finishing breakfast, I collected my .22-caliber rifle that Johnny had given me for Christmas when I was 14. Johnny collected some of his rifles and handguns. We meandered over to a small outdoor range that Otto had built years earlier. Johnny, who was an expert marksman, let me shoot a variety of weapons at targets. We also used double barrel over-and-under shotguns for some skeet shooting. Surprisingly, Laura was also a good shot. Johnny had started teaching her when she was just ten years old. We practiced for a good part of the day and most every day we were there.

There was also a large pond on the property where we fished for brook trout. Johnny and Laura taught me how to catch, clean, and cook the tasty fish! Johnny also had horses, which we rode through the mountain trails. This was the first time I had ever ridden a horse or experienced country life. This was truly God's country! The views were magnificent. I was a "city boy" and had never observed such pristine beauty before.

I now understood why Johnny and Laura visited here as often as they did. One of the trails led us to a river, with gushing water and a beautiful waterfall. Johnny told me the water was still quite cold from the winter snow melt. This summer, however, when it warmed up was when we would enjoy the waterfall slide and the clear deep swimming holes. Cold crystal-clear water was cascading over the rocks, through the mountain valley.

Laura told me it empties into the nearby freshwater lake.

We got off our horses and tied them up to a hitching post Otto had constructed. We then did a little exploring. Johnny stumbled upon a large snake and captured it!

"Patsy, watch out for this kind because it's a Timber Rattler."

He showed me its rattle and venomous fangs, then released it back into the wild.

Over the years, arrowheads, pottery fragments, and other Indian artifacts had been found on the property. Legend had it that the Algonquin natives and the Mohawk Nation once used these grounds for hunting and travel.

At night, we would go frogging with flashlights for bullfrogs at the pond or we would travel into town for ice cream and to play a game of miniature golf.

Johnny was like an Indian, he could certainly live off the land, forage for food, hunt, fish, or gather plant matter. We also fished at the lake a couple of times for lake trout. Johnny kept his fishing boat at a friend's waterfront cabin on the nearby pristine lake. The week was full of daily adventure. It was so peaceful and tranquil there. I thought it was the most beautiful place on earth, even though it is the only place I have been to outside of the Bronx.

Today was our last day in paradise. Johnny told me, "I have a surprise for you."

He took me into a building I had not yet visited. When we got inside, I saw several German Shepherd puppies in fenced pens. He told me this was their kennel building and that I could pick out one of the puppies for myself. "I already got the OK from your father and grandfather," said Johnny.

I could not have been more excited. They were all so damn cute, but one puppy in particular caught my eye. He had big paws and his ears were standing up. When I opened the gate to the dogs' pen, he immediately ran over to me, gave me his paw, and started licking my hand. This was the dog for me. Johnny noted, "good choice." I named him Bruiser. I still cannot believe it. The week was one of the best I had ever had and now this! I owned Dempsey's little brother!

"He can sleep with you tonight if you want."

"Hell, yeah."

Sadly, this night was our last. Johnny invited some friends and neighbors over for a barbecue cooked by Otto. Jake and Jocko, just back from their trip home for Easter joined in the festivities. Johnny and Otto loved to drink beer! With all the guests joining in, about fifteen cases of cold Genesee Cream Ale met their demise. Laura and I knocked-off our fair share.

What a fantastic barbecue, complete with plenty of food, beer, and a whole lot of Johnny's lumberjack friends joining the festivities. He even had the small town's sheriff and doctor in attendance. Johnny taught me how to throw an axe at a target. We engaged in a competition with the lumberjacks to see which of us could land the axe in the bullseye! We left early the next morning as Johnny wanted to get on the road to beat the traffic. Our one week of peace and tranquility had come to an end. Now back to the concrete jungle otherwise known as the Bronx!

Although I did miss my family and friends and the aromas of my grandmother's Italian cuisine cooking on the stove, I experienced a wonderful time up in God's country. Laura and I definitely bonded with each other as we both shared the pain of losing our mothers at such a young age. We would always have that in common.

When we got back to the Bronx, we stopped by the Scallaci Family Grocery. I could not wait to see my father and grandfather and to show them my new puppy, Bruiser. Johnny, Laura, and Dempsey stayed for a while. When they were getting ready to leave, I shook Johnny's hand and thanked him for everything. I hugged and kissed Laura, telling her:

"I had the best time and I can't wait to do it again."

"You're welcome anytime, Patsy."

We all exchanged our goodbyes and they headed back to Yonkers.

"Ah, home sweet home! The next day, I visited with relatives and several of my neighborhood friends. Soon, I would head back to school to finish my last two months before graduating. I had just received the news that Buster Cappelletti, another good friend of mine was killed at the battle of Khe Sanh in South Vietnam. My closest friend, Joey Castanza, had joined the Army and was leaving that day for eight weeks of Basic Training held at the Army Base at Fort Dix, New Jersey.

"Fallen Soldier Memorial- Battlefield Cross"

My father and Giulia were taking him. Since Joey's father was sentenced to Sing Sing prison where he was executed in the electric chair, when Joey was just a boy my father took the kid under his wing and treated him like a son. Joey would be going through a transformation from civilian life to military life, saying goodbye to his civilian clothes and greaser hairstyle. He was a big strong guy, physically fit and tough as nails so he would have no problem with Basic Training. But I was going to miss him and was sorry to see him leave as were so many others from the neighborhood.

Joey did what he felt was the right thing to do. He was not drafted, he enlisted. I was still dating his younger sister, Gina, and it had been four years now. It was the middle of June when I received a letter from Joey telling me he just graduated from Boot Camp and that all was well with him.

He wrote me, "You won't recognize the new Joey with my army fatigues and crew cut. Now that Basic Training is done at Fort Dix, my next stop will be Fort Polk, Louisiana for another eight weeks of intense Advanced Infantry Training or AIT, in preparation for war in the jungles of Southeast Asia."

"Anything new and exciting, Patsy?" I wrote back to him and told him, "Joey, you aren't missing a thing, but I am finally graduating high school in less than a week."

He wrote back, "Congratulations, little brother, and as soon as I finish training, I will be coming home on a thirty-day pass. Tell my family and yours that I send my love and tell all our friends I say hello. See you soon. Take care, Joey."

It had finally arrived, the day I had been waiting for, for most of my life—graduation day. I was finally done with school! My friends and I did some serious celebrating. I must have gone to ten graduation parties in a week's time. When I was done with all the celebrating, my grandfather and father surprised me with a custom bad-ass '55 Chevy Bel Air two-door post sedan for my graduation present. This was the best present, by far, that I could ever have wished for. My father knew that I was a big fan of this year and model Chevy.

My old man's friend, Sal Fischetti, an excellent mechanic and a legendary East Coast hotrod customizer built me a '55 Chevy Custom Bel-Air with a solid lifter 427 cubic inch motor with three 2-barrel carburetors (tri-power), and aluminum heads mated to a Muncie four-speed transmission, with a Hurst shifter and white shift knob. He took the engine and transmission out of a 1967 Corvette with rear total damage and low mileage. He also added ladder bars and installed a Ford 9-inch rear end. This ride had all the bells and whistles! It was rust-free, straight as an arrow, and finished with a stunning custom deep-deep black lacquer paint job. The interior was fitted with a kick-ass 8-track stereo. I personally added white fuzzy dice and two small "Woody Woodpecker" cigar smoking decals on the rear side windows. It even had a Sun tachometer mounted on the steering column and a set of four SS Crager Mag Wheels with Mickey Thompson tires.

This car was cherry in every way. The sound of the big block 427 with power steering and power front disc brakes was the ultimate in sheer neck-snapping overkill. I knew that I would be going through a lot of rear tires burning rubber.

As my father and Uncle Johnny Muller had planned, they both retired after twenty-two years of faithful service to the New York Police Department (NYPD). Their police family and the Scallaci family had each thrown them retirement parties. It was a beautiful send-off for their distinguished and dedicated service to the New York City Police Department. Even though he retired from his police career, my father took a couple of days off to take care of some business. He then began to work full-time at the Scallaci Family Grocery.

Laura had also graduated from high school, subsequently Johnny and she moved upstate full-time to the Muller country home in the Adirondack Mountains. He would take some time off before decid-ing on his next adventure. Doctor Carl Muller remained living in the Muller home in Yonkers and is still working at his job as Chief Physician of Orthopedic Surgery at the hospital.

I obtained a new job as a junior mechanic at Sal Fischetti's A-1 Automotive Repair Shop and Custom Hotrod Builders of the Bronx.

I worked with Sal and his younger brothers, Carmine and Mario, all third-generation master mechanics. I was learning from the best and getting a variety of experience on all different makes and models of cars. I loved wrenching and being a grease monkey.

My sweetheart, Gina, and I had to make the hardest decision yet in our young lives. With Gina going away to a four-year college in the fall and law school after that, we had quite different plans for our futures. After much thought and pain, we both decided that it was best to end our relationship.

I was going to be an auto mechanic until I was old enough to become a New York City police officer and would continue to live in the Belmont section of the Bronx. Gina, conversely, a good student desired to obtain a law degree, pursue her professional career with plans to live in a house on the ocean on Long Island.

We always held a place in our hearts for one another. Hell, we lived across the hall from each other since we were four years old! We started Kindergarten together and had been in a relationship since the ninth grade. She will always be like family to me. I know I felt an emptiness in my heart, and I am sure she felt the same way too. Gina, a beautiful Italian girl with long brown hair, big brown eyes, and olive colored skin was special to me. We lost our virginity to each other; she was voluptuous at 5-foot-7-inches tall and would have no problem at all meeting someone else.

Summer arrived, we all earned our driver's licenses and owned hot rod or muscle cars! The best thing to do was illegal street racing on public roads such as Hutchinson River Parkway, Pelham Parkway in the Bronx, or the Connecting Highway in Queens. We would race for pink slips. Two racers would put their cars on the line by offering their registration slips as winnings. The victor of the resulting race won the opponent's car. My '55 Chevy was certainly fast, but you never knew if the other guy's car was faster. Besides, if I did happen to lose my '55, my old man would kick my ass.

I enjoyed watching my friends race and every once in a while, I would compete just for bragging rights. So far, I was undefeated, but knew there were faster cars out there. We also enjoyed cruising the streets for chicks or hanging out at the White Castles hamburger joint, where all the other hot rods and muscle cars hung out. On the weekends, if the weather was nice, my cousins, Sal and Tony, a couple of friends, along with my dog, Bruiser, and I, would cruise down to Long Island to visit my cousins, Leo, and Pauly Vitale in Oceanside. We would fill our coolers with Pabst Blue Ribbon Beer, (PBR) on ice and then follow Leo to the beach. He drove a cherry 1961 Black 2-door Chevy Impala Super Sport with red interior, 4-speed, bucket seats, and a 409 engine. My Uncle Vic and his younger brother, Bruno, owned a successful auto repair/body shop in Island Park, one town over from their home. We would cruise to Long Beach to swim, catch some rays, listen to music, and socialize with all the chicks walking the boardwalk in their hot bikinis. And if we got lucky, we would spend time "under the Boardwalk" with them! On Saturday nights, we would all go to Freeport Stadium to watch the stock car races and to watch my Uncle Vic, who everyone called Sonny drive his midget-racer.

13

Homecoming

It was the 20th of August and my best friend, Joey Castanza, arrived home today on a thirty-day pass from the Army. My old man, Giulia, Gina, and I drove to John F Kennedy (JFK) Airport in Queens to pick him up. We were all excited to see him! He had been away for over four months. We arrived at the airport and waited at the terminal for his plane to land. When it did, we searched the faces coming off the plane. There were several soldiers walking down the ramp, we knew it was not going to be easy for us to recognize him. Most of the soldiers were wearing shiny new uniforms and had crew cuts. They all looked alike--strong, and proud indeed!

Joey actually found us. As soon as he spotted us, he ran toward where we were standing and greeted us with big hugs and kisses. What an exciting moment we all shared together! We were as happy to see him as he was to see all of us. It felt strange to see Joey without his jet-black, slicked back greasy hair! His goatee was gone, as were his black leather jacket, T-shirt with pack of Lucky Strikes rolled up his sleeve, and his Garrison belt with buckle on the side. He now looked clean cut and distinguished in his uniform, but it goes to show you that you cannot take the greaser out of the soldier; he still had a fresh wooden toothpick in his mouth.

Joey had always been a lean, mean fighting machine, and one of the toughest kids from the neighborhood. He was one badass dude, but his army training had sculpted him into a chiseled piece of steel. I have known Joey since he moved across the Hall from me when I was four and he was six years of age. We became lifelong best friends. I have always looked up to him as my older brother, who I respected and loved. He in turn, told me, "you are the little brother I never had, but always wanted."

We walked to my father's station wagon located in Parking Lot B, threw Joey's gear into the car, and drove off to the Bronx. Joey earned a thirty-day pass and wanted to spend the entire time with us!

Joey explained: "On September 19th, my new orders are to report to Oakland Army Base in California. From there, I will be shipped out to Vietnam."

"Then, we better make it a special thirty days, Joey."

"I'm all for that."

"How was Basic and Advanced Infantry Training?"

"I enjoyed the rigorous Infantry Training at Tigerland, an area filled with dense jungle-like vegetation where commanders prepared their units for battle in Vietnam. I brought you home a present, Patsy."

He opened up his duffel bag and pulled out a brand-new pair of black leather Army Boots and blurted:

"I hope they're the right size. "

"They are thanks."

I took off my old ratty pair of engineer boots and put on my new pair. They fit perfectly, with some room for growth. We caught up on what happened while he was gone. I could tell that the old man was immensely proud of Joey.

When we arrived in the Bronx, my father pulled into the parking lot of the American Legion Hall where he now held the office of post commander.

"Joey and Patsy, I need a hand moving a large piece of furniture. It should only take a few minutes."

"Of course, Mr. Scallaci, we're glad to help."

"Thanks, guys."

As we entered, the old man turned on the lights. Over 100 people shouted, "Surprise."

Joey was surprised for sure! All of the Scallaci, Castanzas, Giulia's side of the family, Uncle Johnny and Laura, friends, and neighbors who knew Joey were in attendance.

The place was all decorated with red, white, and blue streamers which read, "God Bless America!" The jukebox was playing Soldier Boy, by the Shirelles. There was a huge open bar that Joey's friends guided him toward for a toast of Jack Daniels and a cold Pabst Blue Ribbon.

Joey was a popular neighborhood kid. This was Joey's night! We all enjoyed a fun and wonderful time and were happy to have Joey home for another 29 days. Before Joey left for the Army, he started dating a hot Italian girl, Gabriella, who always had feelings for handsome Joey. They hooked up at his party and rekindled their romance. We spent a lot of our nights cruising in my '55 Chevy, which he loved. We attended a few parties and even got into a couple of brawls with some out-of-towners looking for trouble.

The summer turned out to be fabulous! Even though I worked Monday through Friday, I still had weeknights and weekends to have some fun. Boy, did we! It seems we had an unlimited supply of energy! As usual, Uncle Pasquale had his end of the summer Labor Day bash and this year's was the best one yet! The next day my father, Giulia, Joey, and Gabriella drove Gina upstate to start her first year of college. I did not go because I had to work. I was sorry to see Gina go, but I knew that with her school and street smarts combined with her gorgeous looks, she was going places and would someday make a great lawyer!

Although I dated a few different girls casually over the summer and had loads of fun, I thought it would be a good time to stay single. I wanted to focus on my job and learn to be a good mechanic. I just could not believe that instead of going back to school this fall, I would be working full-time, and probably would be for the rest of my life.

My cousin, Sal, planned on enlisting with the United States Navy, after the summer was over. He just left for Boot Camp at Great Lakes, Chicago. My cousin, Tony, knocked-up his girlfriend, and they planned for a middle of November wedding.

My good friend, Jimmy "Bats" De Angelis died last week when he flipped his car racing for "pinks." We had sadly just celebrated his eighteenth birthday. Although Joey and I spent a lot of time together, he also spent a lot of time with his girlfriend. They were now in a serious relationship.

As a group, we all attended the Lowe's Paradise a few times to see films such as Midnight Cowboy, Butch Cassidy and the Sundance Kid and the Wild Bunch. We also enjoyed spending time at our local bar, the "Velvet Touch Lounge", playing pool and rocking to the jukebox! Downstairs in the basement, we played dice and poker for cash! Joey told me, "that besides missing his family, friends, and the Bronx, he also missed his mother's homemade Italian cooking."

Joey's thirty-day pass expired! Time flew by and before I knew it, my father, Giulia, Gabriella, and I were heading to LaGuardia airport also in Queens, but this time to drop Joey off for his flight to Oakland. It was sad to see him leave and I think I spoke for everyone in the car. When we got to the airport, the parking lot was full, so my old man double parked in front of the terminal. Joey told everyone that he loved them and not to worry. With that movie star smile of his he mused, "I'll be fine and will see you all one year from now."

Giulia and Gabriella got out of the car, both of them gave Joey big hugs and kisses. You could see the tears running down their faces, but they managed to hold it together. They told Joey that they loved him and to write home often.

Now it was the old man's and my turn to hug and kiss Joey, say our goodbyes, tell him we loved him, and how immensely proud of him we were for serving his country. The old man then exclaimed, "Joey, remember what I taught you and Patsy when you were kids. 'Eye of the Tiger' never surrenders, never gives up and never says die - win lose or draw and always try your best to keep a positive attitude, and a cool head, even in the worst of situations. Keep your head down and kick some ass."

Joey headed into the terminal. We all got into the station wagon and headed home to the Bronx. The car ride home was a quiet and a sad moment for each of us. But in the weeks that followed, we got back to our daily routines.

My eighteenth birthday was on October 16th, but with everything that was going on it was just another day for me. I was finally legal to drink alcohol, even though I had been drinking beers on occasion since the seventh grade. I received my first letter from Joey today! He told me: "I arrived at Oakland Army Base, then a few days later I was bussed to Travis Air Force Base. From there, I was shipped out with the soldiers I had trained with on a Continental commercial flight to 'Tan Son Nhut Air Base' in South Vietnam.

"From there, I was driven to the Cu Chi Replacement Company for the 25th Infantry Division where I was sent to my new unit, Company A, Fourth Battalion, Ninth Regiment 25th Infantry Division. The Division earned the nickname "Tropic Lightning". They tell me there are two seasons here, dry, and wet. Everything is fine, the guys in my unit were cool. This place is the ultimate adrenaline rush! I love you, brother. Take care and say hello to everybody."

It was an eventful fall; I was looking forward to my cousin, Tony's, wedding the next Sunday. He was marrying his childhood sweetheart from the neighborhood, Tina Cartalano. The day arrived; the wedding was extraordinary! I was so happy again to see all my relatives minus my cousin, Sal. He was away doing his naval training and hopefully staying out of trouble. This was a most happy occasion; all of our neighborhood friends were there. I was happy for Tony and Tina ("TNT").

Tony was such a great guy and always loyal to the end. Out of all the guys in the gang, he was the most levelheaded. Tony and his bride would move into the old Scallaci building. His wife wasn't due to give birth until June of '69. The holidays came and went. It was my first Thanksgiving and Christmas spent without my mother or my Falcone grandparents, so I had my sad moments. We spent Christmas at our apartment with my Scallaci grandparents, my father, Uncle Rocco, along with his girlfriend, Uncle Johnny Muller, Laura, Giulia, and Gina Castanza. Gina was home from college for the holidays. All in all, we had a festive time! As usual, my grandmother's and Giulia's cooking was Four-Star.

It was now a new year--1969 arrived, ushering in the end of the wild '60s. It was a cold winter, I kept busy working inside at A-1 Automotive. It was now February 13th, I would be taking the New York Police Department's entrance exam the following day. Even if I passed all the requirements, I could not be hired onto the Force until my 21st birthday. The NYPD gave the Entrance Exam only once every four years. The big day arrived, and I took the written, physical fitness, and psychological exams.

I was told I would receive the results of the exam in about six-months via a post in the Civil Service Newspaper: The Chief. I was filled with anticipation and could not wait for the results to come out!

March crept in. My cousin Sal, a Naval seaman, shipped out to Vietnam. He was attached to a crew which manned a Patrol Boat Riverine (PBR) used to stop and search river traffic in areas such as the Mekong Delta. Sal, the Tasmanian Devil was definitely in his element being on the water. He was another proud American who was serving his country. My buddy and co-worker, Irish, enlisted in the Marines and was off to Basic Training at Paris Island, South Carolina. I was not drafted, but did want to enlist in the Army, but my father told me that because I was his only child, he did not want me to.

Toward the middle of March, my father had to drive to the decaying South Bronx to pick up some paperwork at the 41st Precinct. While there, he ran into his old police sergeant, now a retired NYPD Captain. They got to talking and it turns out he started a security guard company called Above All, Security.

"My son recently completed the NYPD Entrance Exam," my dad reported, "and is waiting for the results to come out to see if he has passed or failed. If he passed, as he was only eighteen years old, he will have to wait three more years to be hired."

"Vinny, would your son like a job as a security officer, while he waits to turn twenty-one?"

"I don't know, but I'll ask him."

With that said, he gave my father his business card and told him to give him a call if interested.

Anyway, my father was telling me the story:

"Are you interested in the job?"

"I don't know, let me sleep on it, I'll give you an answer tomorrow."

The next morning, my grandfather, father, and I sat down, ate breakfast cooked by my grandmother, and discussed the possibility of becoming a security guard.

"I thought about what I wanted to do. I enjoyed working for Sal and have learned a lot, but my future is in law enforcement. Until I turn twenty-one, being a rent a cop will be time well spent affording me some insight into law enforcement."

"The time you spent working on cars was well worth it too, Patsy."

He always believed like all Scallaci that, the more you know, the more you are worth. With that said, my father phoned the guy and told him, "My son wants to know when he can start."

Firstly, I had to submit to an FBI background check to see if I had any serious convictions or felonies. I did not and easily passed the background check.

Secondly, I was required to take a course to get my Security Guard Certification and lastly, take another course on firearm safety and handling. Upon completion of the requirements, I received my permit to carry a weapon. Shortly after, I started my new job!

The summer had arrived, and this would be a working summer for me. I was working the night shift full-time Monday through Friday as a security guard and part time Monday through Friday afternoons at the Scallaci Family Grocery. I did, thank God, have weekends off.

My grandfather and father always told me. "It takes money to make money, so work really hard and save your money," which I did.

So, now that I had saved my money all these years, I heard about a great deal on a 1965 Harley-Davidson, FL Electra Glide. I checked it out, and it was in brand new condition. The guy selling it, Joey Meatballs, needed cash fast to pay off his bookie before someone showed up to rough him up. He was selling the motorcycle real cheap to make a quick sale. I had the cash and I knew it was a great bargain, so I bought it.

When I showed it to my grandfather and father the old man asked me:

"What did you pay for it?"

I told him and he shook my hand.

"You got a great deal! We are proud of you, son, You got yourself a beautiful bike at a really good price." The motorcycle was the final year of the Panhead motor and the first year of the big twin Harley engines to be equipped with electric starters.

Now, I had a *1965 Harley* to cruise around with for the summer. My cousin, Tony and his wife, Tina, welcomed a healthy baby boy, John Anthony Scallaci.

"As you get older, time seems to go by a lot faster," at least that is what my old man told me, but I would have to agree with him.

The summer of '69 neared its end. My old friend, Irish, was home on leave from the Marines before shipping out to Vietnam. It was August 28th. All of our friends got together and took Irish out to the Lowe's Paradise Movie Theater to see Easy Rider. After that, they all traveled to the Velvet Touch Lounge for a night of drinking. I made it to the movie but had to take a rain check on the partying because I had to be at work by midnight.

The following night was Friday and that was the night a shooting trans-pired on my job. I shot and possibly killed an unarmed suspect. I finally got home from the 50th Precinct Station House sometime late Saturday afternoon. I was so tired from the night's excitement that I fell into a deep sleep. When my grandfather and father returned home after closing the store, they woke me up. It was still storming out. My grandmother was home from church now and the first thing she says to me was:

"Patsy, for dinner tonight I cooked you one of your favorite meals, Eggplant Parmesan, pasta with Marinara sauce and artichokes."

"God bless you, Nonna."

My father told me:

"I heard from one of the 50th Precinct Detectives I am friends with."

He told my father that the Bronx District Attorney ordered the 50th Precinct Detective Squad to keep my case open and to proceed with the investigation. I will keep you informed on any new progress."

My father explained to me: "I have my own plan. You will take time off from your job until your situation is completely straightened out. Pack enough clothes to live on for two to three months and anything else you might need and come Monday you and Bruiser are heading upstate to the Muller country homestead. You will stay there until you are 100% cleared of any wrongdoing."

The old man was pissed. He knew the source of this bullshit was flowing down from New York State Senator and former Bronx District Attorney, William H Cunningham, who he had always despised and thought corrupt.

My father was going to take some time off from work at the family grocery and start his own investigation into what had happened. He also told me, "There is no way this incident is going to keep you from becoming a New York City Police Officer."

My father then called Uncle Johnny to explain my situation. He was eager to have me for as long as it took. He also volunteered to aid in the investigation, but my father told him, "Thanks, if I need you, I'll call."

My father also called my employer and his former boss:

"Patsy will be taking a leave of absence from work until this whole affair is cleared up."

"He should take all the time needed. My security firm also wants this matter put to rest. I am pleased that you are running your own investigation. If I can assist in any way, call me."

On Sunday night, I picked my buddy Irish up and we met some friends down at the Velvet Touch for a get together. We called him Irish as his father's family were from Ireland, while his mother's family hailed from Trapani, Sicily (located near Palermo). After about six beers, I tired. It was time to leave, it was midnight and I had some serious traveling to do in the morning. I hugged and kissed Irish, one of my closest friends, and said goodbye to everyone. I told Irish, "Keep your head down and get some for me." I knew that I probably would not get back in time to say goodbye to him before he shipped out, when his leave was up.

As I plodded through the parking lot toward my car, it hit me. I realized that this might be the last time I got to see one of my oldest neighborhood friends. We grew up together in the early 1950s and had experienced all of the tumult of the1960s together. There was a definite possibility of his death occurring--I did not even want to go there. Joey, my cousin Sal, are now all serving in Vietnam along with some other neighborhood pals and Irish would soon be joining them. God bless the men and women who have served their country and those who still do.

In my young life, I have lost family members and a few friends who I loved dearly. My grandfather and father both tried to teach me at a young age that death was a part of life and that no matter what, life must go on. They told me that death can take anyone, at any age, or at any time, so enjoy life, or as my grandfather would say in broken English, "Any day above ground is a good day."

I got into my car and headed home to get a good night's sleep. Monday morning beckoned; I said my goodbyes to family.

My father chuckled: "Have a safe trip and not to worry about the investigation. Your old man is on the job once again. Say hello to Johnny and Laura and tell them the Scallaci family misses them, and we send our love."

"I'll do it, Dad."

"And no racing!"

"OK, Pop, no racing!"

I loaded my gear into my car. My father, grandfather, and grandmother told me to be careful and that they loved me.

I told them, "I love you right back."

"Patsy, do you need any bread (money)?"

"No thanks, Dad, I'm good.

"I'll keep you informed on any progress with the case."

"Thank you for everything, Pop."

With that, Bruiser and I got into my car and drove to A-1 Automotive to fill up on high-test. With the directions my father gave me in hand, I headed up north to the picturesque Adirondack Mountains. It was roughly a six-hour drive from the Bronx to the Muller country home. This was the first time I was taking my '55 on a long trip. The car ran like a top! I will admit that I was a little concerned that the car might overheat, so as a precaution, I brought two containers of mixed antifreeze, just in case.

When Sal built the '55 and souped it up, he told me, "I replaced the stock radiator with a high performance one." Happily, I did not have any problem with overheating. My gas mileage sucked though! After driving what seemed like forever, I finally encountered the old cobblestone driveway of the Muller country homestead. I drove up the driveway as far as I could before I had to stop at the old iron gates to the property, and, of course, the chain was locked.

My father told me when I left, that he was going to call Johnny and give him a rough estimate of the time of my arrival. I looked at my watch, I beat my father's prediction of arrival time by thirty minutes! I figured Johnny had to be nearby. I then heard the sound of a chainsaw echoing from the storage barn, I honked my horn. After six honks from my car's loud horn, I noticed Johnny heading my way.

He was looking as gigantic as ever and proudly sporting his favorite cowboy hat. He unlocked the chain and pushed open the ten-foot-high rusty gates. It was great to see my Uncle Johnny, whom I had not seen in over three months. He, of course, gave me a giant bear hug, lifting me off the ground while shaking my hand with his large vice-grip-like mitt.

We were both extremely happy to see one another. Johnny locked the gate after I pulled in and followed my car up to the house. When we got to the porch, he told me, "I was just cutting up logs and splitting them for next year's winter. Your '55 Chevy looks boss. You can park her in the storage barn next to Jake's car."

"Thanks, Uncle Johnny, I'll do that."

I let Bruiser out of the car and filled his bowl with some cool mountain water. He slurped it down, then got a whiff of Johnny's dog, Dempsey's, scent and behaved wildly with anticipation. Dempsey came running, they both ran off and hooked up with Schatzi and Blitzkrieg. They enjoyed their family reunion!

While they played, I unloaded my gear.

"Johnny, am I in the same room that I stayed in last time?"

"Hell, yeah, that's your room for life."

"Thanks, I love that room."

After lugging all my gear up to my room, I parked my wheels in the storage barn next to Jake's ride. He had a 1967 Chevelle Super Sport (SS) with a beautiful Marina Blue paint job with dark blue painted brake drums, four classic Keystone Mag wheels, and a set of red line tires. Man, what a beauty!

After I parked my car and checked Jake's car over, I returned to the house. Johnny was sitting on a rocking chair on the porch, with his cooler full of ice-cold bottles of Genesee Cream Ale. I sat down next to him and he handed me a cold one.

14

The Adirondacks; Peace and Tranquility

I could not believe my rapture as I sat on Johnny's porch drinking a cold one, breathing in the fresh Adirondack mountain air. We caught up on old times and what was new in our lives.

Adirondack Lake Vista

Johnny said, "Patsy, a few months before Laura's graduation and before moving up here full time, I had an opportunity to purchase the Old George's Tavern/Grill. You were there last time you visited. It is located on the water's edge of the pristine crystal-clear lake, abutted against seventy-five wooded acres, adorned by three-thousand feet of beautiful waterfront shoreline. George died at the ripe old age of 94 years."

"Ok, Johnny, what more can you tell me about the property?"

"The old building was built by George's father, the original proprietor in 1880. Since then, it has served as the town's local watering hole and gathering place. It even had a four-lane bowling alley! The place had seen better days, the rustic structure aged by the winter's savagery. Upon George's death, the property and buildings were put up for sale. I had always had a vision of building a Four Seasons Resort, so I purchased it. A full reclamation was to be our next adventure."

"How's the local labor pool?"

"I hired an architect and had my lumberjack friends log the forest where we are going to build. I then assembled a large crew of local tradesmen to knock down the old structures and build new ones. My crew was building a rustic twenty-five-unit motel with parking lot, eight two-bedroom log cabins, and four three-bedroom log cabins. All the cabins to be adorned with stone-faced wood-burning fireplaces and covered porches featuring spectacular secluded shoreline vistas."

"Do you have a name for the resort in mind?"

"Yes, we named the resort, Swede's Lake and Mountain Four Season Resort. A rustic bar/restaurant was also built on the water's edge! Both the bar/restaurant and the office are now up and running. Phase One now completed! When fully concluded, we hope it will become a Wilderness Wonderland for any outdoorsman. That is what we have been up to over the last few months. Laura works there as does Otto, who's in charge of overseeing all construction."

The "Swede" was Johnny's nickname, everyone called him that because he was born in Sweden. I thought a good name for the resort might have been Paul Bunyan's Four-Season Resort, as Johnny always reminded me of the legendary giant lumberjack. I was happy for Johnny and Laura! I knew how much they loved the Adirondacks and how happy it made them to share this beautiful paradise with others.

My father told me, "Johnny's father's family in Europe had great wealth, and when his father died, he received a large inheritance. Along with his police pension and wheeling and dealing all his life, he has sufficient money to build his resort, with plenty more leftover."

"Johnny, is Laura working?"

"Yes, she knows you're here and is leaving work early."

As we were bullshitting and knocking down several cold ones, Laura pulled into the parking lot. She drove up in her 1958 Chevy Corvette with a shiny red paint job and white coves. I remember when we were both twelve years old, she showed me a model of a 1958 red Corvette with white coves, and she told me that this was her favorite car and that hopefully one day she would own the real deal. Johnny, who enjoyed spoiling his adopted daughter, bought this stunning car for her high school graduation present. She got out of the car, ran over to me, hugged, and kissed me, and exclaimed "It's great to see you, it's been such a long time."

I have always had an eye for pretty women, but Laura was choice! She could have been a successful model if she wanted to, she had it all. On a scale from one to ten, she was an eleven! She told me, "I'll be right back." She went upstairs to her room to change out of her work clothes into something more comfortable. While she was changing, I checked out her ride. The car was equipped with power windows, a 283 cubic-inch motor with mechanical fuel injection, and a four-speed transmission. The car was in cherry condition, inside and out!

Johnny told me:

"I'm heading up to the hunting cabin tomorrow morning to get it ready for the fall hunting season. Do you want to take a ride with me, Patsy? I have some repairs to make, so we'll be staying overnight."

"Sure, that sounds good. What time are we leaving?"

"About six AM."

"I'll be ready."

Laura returned wearing something more comfortable. Damn, she looked amazing! Laura had beautiful long blonde hair, big blue eyes, perfect pearly white teeth, long legs, and a body to die for. She threw me a heavy-made red hooded sweatshirt with, "The Swedes Lake and Mountain Resort" written in white letters on top accompanied by a white outline of a Twelve-Point Buck. Underneath that, read Adirondacks, NY. I thanked her with a giant hug and kiss. Any excuse to get close to her! I told her, "I'll be right back," hurried upstairs to my room and grabbed a box, and then ran back down telling her:

"Laura, I brought your favorite cannoli from Giorgio's Italian bakery."

"Thanks, Patsy."

"I checked first to make sure they survived the trip up from the Bronx; they did."

"I have to go to the storage barn to load up the truck with tools and materials to take with us for the morning's trip."

"Do you need my help, Johnny?"

"Jake, Jocko, or the new kid should be done for the day mending fences. I'll have one of them give me a hand but thanks for asking."

When Johnny left, Laura and I caught up on what was new and exciting in our lives.

I explained to her what had happened on my job and that my father thought it best for me to leave the Bronx, while he conducts his own investigation. I also told her about my '55 Chevy Bel Air that my grandfather and father got me for my high school graduation present and of the 1965 Harley-Davidson Panhead Motorcycle I picked up. Laura was totally into hotrods, muscle cars, motorcycles, and everything else I liked, thanks to Johnny's influence. Laura was more of a flower child (hippie chick) than the tough talking neighborhood street chicks I grew up with. Laura and some of her friends even attended the musical festival at Woodstock. Do not get me wrong, Laura was tough, she received her black belt in Karate and could definitely handle herself. We could not have gotten along any better growing up together!

She spoke of her father's new project, Swede's Lake and Mountain Resort.

"For many years now, it had been a dream of my Father and I, now it was becoming a reality. We are extremely excited and motivated to make this the place for your Four-Season Adventure and Getaway."

"I love the name of the resort, Laura. Do you enjoy working there?"

"Patsy, I am an assistant manager in training and learning on the job. My manager is a great teacher, with over twenty-five years of experience working at one of the largest resorts on beautiful Lake George. Her mother and grandmother were getting older and she wanted to work closer to home, so she left her job to work part-time at Swede's. When all the construction is completed, she would work full-time."

"How are the construction projects progressing?"

"The only structures that are currently fully operational are the bar/restaurant and the office. The construction of the twenty-five-unit motel with parking lot, twelve log cabins, sandy beach, in-ground-pool, and docks are still being built. All construction is set to be finished for the Summer Season of 1970."

"Kathy, my manager, is such a sweet and beautiful person inside and out."

I was thinking, "That's exactly how I would have described Laura."

"We just have so many ideas and plans to make this resort the place to vacation at, all-year round."

"Patsy, show me your '55 Chevy."

We walked to the barn, Laura checked my car over and told me, "What a thing of beauty. It looks totally righteous!"

"Hop in, Laura."

Johnny was in the barn loading up his truck with help from Jake and the new guy. Johnny threw me a keychain with two keys on it. He yelled to me:

"The bigger key is the house key and the smaller one is for the gate chain, and that is your set to keep."

"Thanks, big man."

I started the beast up. The big block 427 sounded mean, powerful, and loud with its Hooker headers and cherry bomb mufflers. I was glad we were in the storage barn and not the livestock barn because all of the animals would definitely have been spooked by the thunderous rumble! We all felt the vibration.

"Be careful and don't be too long, I'm taking both of you out to dinner tonight."

"No problem, Uncle Johnny," I said as we drove toward the gate.

I opened it and took Laura for a cruise down the long and winding road.

"I love the leather diamond tuck-n-roll interior; it's really groovy Patsy! I'll let you know when we're coming to the straight section of the road."

She did, I looked around and noticed no one was in sight, not in front of or behind me. I came to a complete stop.

"Laura, hold on tight."

I smoked the tires laying down some serious rubber! Then I accelerated through the gears for over a quarter mile, giving Laura a taste of how powerful this beast was.

"Wow, Patsy, I thought my Corvette was fast!"

We navigated a U-turn, cruised past all the smoke and the smell of burnt rubber, and headed back to the barn.

"Your car was out of sight."

"Did you have a fun ride?"

"Yes, it was a gas."

We exited the car. Jake strutted over with the new guy and introduced us. His name was Jimmy, a local kid. We all shook hands.

"We're impressed with your ride; you have one mean machine."

"Jake, your '67 Chevelle is not too shabby either. How does she run?"

"It has the original 396 big block motor still in it. I just gave it a tune-up, but it is still running really rough. I can't figure out why."

"If you'd like I can take a look at it for you when I get back from our trip to the hunting cabin."

"That would be great, I'll leave the doors unlocked with the keys in the ignition. Thanks Patsy, I really appreciate this."

"No sweat. Goodbye."

Both of us headed to the house. Johnny had left the barn before us and was already showered and getting dressed.

"Do what you got to do and meet me on the porch in a half hour or less."

"Ok, Dad, will do."

"We are going out to the finest restaurant in town, Swede's!"

"It's the only restaurant in town, Dad."

We took showers and got dressed. I was ready in fifteen minutes - Laura was ready in twenty. Not bad for a girl! She kept it simple; she did not wear makeup and dressed casually; she definitely was no mirror warmer. We joined Johnny on the porch, got into his Jeep and headed for the restaurant. It was about a twenty-minute drive through the cascading mountains. Right before we entered town, I noticed a large log structure sitting on the lake's shoreline. We pulled into the parking lot and parked. The log building was magnificent! We could see the majestic views of the lake, mountains and the towering eastern white pine trees surrounding the construction site.

We walked into the new restaurant. It looked totally different from the old George's Tavern and Grill. The place was a lot bigger and was constructed using knotty pine tongue and groove for the interior and exposed post and beam for the cathedral ceiling. The focal point was a massive double-sided stone wood-burning fireplace. The interior featured a wall of windows with tables and chairs set up to take in the spectacular views. A large bar showcasing a few of Johnny's prized hunting trophies mounted above, completed the splendid decor.

I could hardly contain myself, "Wow, this place has sure come a long way from George's Tavern & Grill."

They laughed, "It sure has!"

The Maître D greeted us and showed us to a table right by the wall of windows. We reveled at the dusk setting over the gorgeous lake and mountain range--a definite million-dollar view.

"This is the same alluring lake that I dock my boat at, and we fished on the last time I took you up here. It doesn't get any better than this!"

"You're right about that, Johnny, this place is spectacular."

The waitress engaged us right away. Johnny ordered three Gennys, with frozen glass mugs.

"I recommend you try the Porterhouse steak."

"Sounds good to me."

I was starving. Laura and Johnny already knew what they wanted, so we ordered.

Johnny excused himself to check on a few things. He got up and engaged the Maître D, and they had a brief chat. He then scooted over to the bar to talk with the bartender. His last stop was the kitchen. While Johnny was gone, Laura and I had our own chat:

"My father was most proud of the fact that this whole project was creating jobs for the local townspeople and upon completion, would bring additional revenue to the small town's few businesses."

"I'm not surprised; Johnny has always been generous."

"If you were a local who lived in the Adirondacks year-round, not just the summer months, you had to be a jack-of-all-trades to earn a living, as most of the available jobs were seasonal. You had to do whatever it took to put food on the table."

"The townspeople must appreciate what your father is doing."

"They do! My father is using only local tradesmen for the entire construction and landscaping projects. His goal is to keep the locals working and the town prospering."

"Is the town prospering, Laura?"

"It's fairly quiet now, Patsy, but come Friday and Saturday this place gets hopping with both locals and out-of-towners!"

Johnny exited the kitchen with the waitress following right behind carrying a large tray of food. Johnny and I ordered the 27-ounce, Laura the Rainbow trout. I could not believe the enormity of the Porterhouse.

I bet I know who put this entrée on the dinner menu! This meal was not created for someone with limited appetite in mind. Laura wanted me to try some of her fish. I managed to find room in my stomach for a morsel. It was mouthwatering!

"Johnny, this Porterhouse is the biggest and best tasting steak I ever ate."

"Patsy, I told you it was a good choice. I hired a four-star chef."

He was not lying! When I glanced at the menu, I noticed the prices were inexpensive compared to New York City prices.

"Are you ready for dessert?"

"Are you kidding?"

I heard Johnny say he was stuffed, which I had never heard him say before. I know I was filled to the max. We all enjoyed a delicious meal and a nice relaxing evening. When we left and walked outside, it was pitch black out. On the side of the road, by the parking lot driveway was a huge lit up neon sign. It was bright and colorful and read: "Swede's Lake and Mountain Resort & Four-Star Restaurant & Bar."

On our drive home, we smelled a familiar odor. I looked at Johnny and he looked at me; we both laughed. I knew that the stink was not one of Johnny's rancid beer farts; rather it was the smell of a fresh roadkill skunk.

"Thanks for taking us out to dinner."

"Anytime, it was my pleasure."

When we got home, Johnny changed into his sweat suit and scurried down to the basement gym that Otto and he built. Johnny had been working out religiously since he was a teenager. I know I must have spoken it a hundred times before and I am not exaggerating when I claim that Johnny was the largest and strongest man I have ever seen, either in person or in a magazine. Since his retirement he put on some twenty pounds, so he looked bigger than ever.

After relaxing for a bit, Laura and I grabbed two flashlights and took a nice long walk up the cobblestone driveway. As we continued our walk, Laura spotted a family of raccoons climbing a tree and a bobcat running across the dirt road. This place was home to all kinds of wildlife.

After a good night's sleep, Johnny and I got up early, had breakfast, walked over to the storage barn, and got into Johnny's truck, beginning our journey to the cabin. I had not been to his hunting cabin before. The drive on the mountain dirt road that ran through Johnny's property was certainly a bumpy one.

"It was an old logging road, Patsy."

"The panoramic views are breathtaking."

When we got there, we carried the food and gear we packed for our overnight stay into the cabin. We opened all the windows to air it out. This was a real old-fashioned log cabin. It had a small kitchen, a decent-size living room/dining room with a wood burning stove, and a bunk room with several bunk beds, and another wood burning stove. I think Johnny was obsessed with fire. Every structure that he owned had multiple fireplaces or wood burning stoves.

"Patsy, it can get quite frigid up here and these stoves are the only source of heat."

The kitchen sink has running water, but in winter, the water is shut off to prevent the pipes from freezing, and there is no bathroom--only an outhouse outside.

"Does it have a television?"

"No, but it does offer a lovely view of the sky!"

The property housed a gasoline powered generator shed supplying electricity, a small barn with horse stalls, and a corral. The cabin also had a small covered porch.

Johnny then showed me the generator shed. With one pull, the generator started right up. It ran like a top! Now, with electricity, the first thing Johnny did was plug in his portable eight-track player and put in a Percy Sledge tape, that played one of his favorite songs— When a Man Loves a Woman.

"Are you ready to get to work?"

"Yes, Uncle Johnny, I am."

We started unloading the truck bed, which was over-filled with tools, a pair of wooden horses, lumber, nails, and split firewood. We had also towed a trailer behind the truck loaded with bales of hay, which we stored in the barn. When we were done unloading everything, we got to work on Johnny's list of repairs to attend.

We had breakfast before we left, so we skipped lunch and snacked on a bag full of Johnny's homemade smoked venison jerky to carry us through until dinner. We worked hard and finished all of our tasks as darkness approached. We loaded the truck back up with all of the tools we took with us and the debris from the repairs. When we entered the cabin, it was starting to get a little chilly out, so Johnny lit a fire in the wood burning stove.

Johnny cooked us dinner and we ate at the dining room table. After we got done, since he cooked, I got to clean up. Johnny headed to the refrigerator and took out two ice cold Gennys. Oh yeah, I forgot to mention that a case of Genesee Cream Ale was part of our overnight supplies. He opened the bottles and handed me a cold one. We toasted to a good day's work.

"Now the cabin is ready for the fall hunting season, Patsy!"

"It sure seems that way."

We both walked out onto the front porch, sat in the Adirondack chairs, and bull shitted. Johnny lit up a cigar and I lit up a Lucky Strike.

"I thought your old man told me you were quitting."

"I am for the New Year."

"We'll see come January. Well, I hope you do. My father was a heavy cigarette smoker for years, which the doctors and Carl diagnosed as the cause of his throat cancer. If you have to smoke, do what your grandfather, father, and I do and only have an occasional cigar."

"I'll need to call my old man when I get back, to check in with him and see how his investigation is going."

"Yes, I bet he'll be glad to hear from us country folk!"

After a few more beers, we hurried inside to get warm. Johnny wanted to check his two-way radio out. He used it to communicate with the ranger station or sheriff's office to get weather reports or in case of an emergency. The cabin was located in a remote area. There was no one around for many miles. The radio could work off electricity or battery backup. Otto also had a radio set up in his house.

Johnny powered it up, selected the frequency, and contacted Otto for a radio check. Otto and Johnny communicated back and forth. What struck me as odd was that they were speaking in German. I did not even know Johnny knew German. When he completed the radio check, we drank a couple of more beers. Johnny and I were now ready to hit the rack. He struck a fire in the bunk room, grabbed a flashlight, and turned off all the lights. He showed me where the kill-switch was that Otto had ingeniously engineered to shut down the generator from inside the cabin.

Though Otto had an extremely anti-social attitude, when it applied to mechanical and electrical knowledge, he was a genius.

"Patsy, do not open the refrigerator until tomorrow morning when we get up, it will keep everything cold through the night."

"Absolutely, Johnny."

We brought two sleeping bags and pillows for our comfort. Johnny shut off the flashlight, we said our good nights, and crashed. We got up early and Johnny cooked us breakfast. We cleaned up, closed down, locked up the cabin, barn, and generator shed. Then we got into his truck and headed back to the homestead. Again, the ride home was a bumpy one, but at least my ass did not get as sore as the time we rode the horses!

When we got back, Johnny dropped me off and he drove to work at Swede's. I walked to the storage barn, grabbed my toolbox out of my trunk, and walked over to Jake's car to find out why his Chevelle was running rough. Jake had left the doors unlocked and keys in the ignition.

First thing I did was to pop open his hood and start up the engine to listen to how it ran. I could tell right away the engine was idling rough. I began adjusting the idle mixture screws on the four-barrel carburetor, with no noticeable effect. Upon further inspection, I heard a hissing noise. I found out where it was coming from. The problem turned out to be a vacuum leak. I replaced the cracked hose. The Chevelle idled fine now! I also adjusted the valves to their factory set clearances and cleaned and tuned his carburetor. After finishing with the repair and adjustments, I was confident I had fixed Jake's problem. I did not test drive it though. He would have to do that after he got done with work. When I was cleaning his carburetor, I ran out of cleaner, Jake had told me he kept some automotive supplies in his trunk. So, I opened his trunk and sure enough there was a can of carburetor cleaner. I also noticed Jake had some WW II Nazi memorabilia stored in a box. I assumed he collected old military items.

With that problem solved, looking around I spotted four separate canvassed tarps covering what I believed to be some type of vehicles. I was curious, wondering what was underneath them. I pulled one off. Under the first cover lay Johnny's 1934 Ford Roadster! It still looked cherry. Under the second cover, there was a 1910 Ford Model T. After carefully putting the canvas tarps back on the two cars, I removed canvas number three to reveal a soft blanket underneath. I realized that this car must be special, and it was. It was a luxurious 1936 Mercedes-Benz 500 K Spezial Roadster in absolutely flawless condition. I immediately covered the car.

Underneath the last canvas was Johnny's 1941 four-cylinder Indian Motorcycle with sidecar and two Ski-Doo snowmobiles. I covered them back up. All the covers were back exactly how they were before. Now that I caught the curiosity bug, I looked around and realized just how big a space this barn was. There were antiques everywhere. I was extremely interested in history and nostalgic items. I never particularly liked school, but enjoyed social studies, gym, woodshop, and auto mechanic classes.

The walls of the barn were littered with relics from the early 1800s through the mid-1900s. There was a ladder that led to an enormous loft. I instinctively climbed up and explored. Some of the fascinating artifacts were over a hundred years old. There were oil lanterns, old snow skis and fishing rods, steel animal traps, an assortment of chains, two-man tree saws, wooden block and tackle systems, a pile of burlap sacks, wooden crates, wooden barrels, wooden chests, etc.

I noticed a few old signs leaning against the wall. I could make out the words on the outside sign! It was wooden with black lettering painted on a white background with a black border. It read, County Poor House & Poor Farm and at the bottom, in smaller letters it read, EST. (established) 1835. As I separated the three signs, I noticed that the second one was a larger wooden sign and was more ornate than the first one. I looked at it and it read, Serenity Falls Insane Asylum. On the bottom it read EST. 1858. The third sign was porcelain and it read Stillwater Mental Hospital.

I did not think much of it at the time.

I remember Johnny telling me the property once housed an old hospital, built sometime in the 1850s.

When I finished examining, I put everything back exactly how I found it, among the thousands of cobwebs.

15

The Cemetery Plot Thickens

Since I was totally filthy by now, I walked back to the house and took a nice long hot shower. When I got done, I put on clean clothes and walked back to the barn. Jake, Jocko, and Jimmy were there; they had just finished work for the day.

I never realized before how tall Jocko was, I stood six feet three inches tall, he was noticeably taller than I and covered in illustrative tattoos; he also rode a Harley-Davidson motorcycle.

"Jake, I think I found why your engine was running so rough. Start it up."

"Wow, it now has a much smoother idle."

He opened the passenger door and mumbled, "Get in." Jake pulled out of the barn and opened the gate. We headed down the long cobblestone driveway and onto the winding country road. When Jake got to the straight stretch of the road, he shifted into third, then fourth gear, putting the pedal to the metal. The Chevelle took off like a bat out of hell. We were really bookin!

When Jake reached the end of the straight section of the road, he exclaimed:

"Man, Patsy, I don't know what you did to this engine, but since I've owned this car it has never run so smoothly. Now it really screams."

"I found a vacuum leak. Adjusted your valves and cleaned and tuned your carburetor."

"Thanks so much, now my friends can't say to me my car is all show and no go."

Jake turned around, headed back to the farm, and dropped me off at the house. I sat and waited on the porch for Johnny and Laura to get home from work.

I grabbed a cold brew from the fridge and put six more on ice in Johnny's cooler in anticipation for when they got home. They pulled into the parking lot fifteen minutes later, I handed them both a cold brew, which they thanked me for.

"How was your day, Patsy?"

"I worked on Jake's car."

"Good, did you have any luck finding the problem?"

"I did, and Jake was extremely happy with the way it's running."

I knew this news would make Johnny happy. Johnny and Otto had been busy at the resort and had not had the time to work on it.

They had been working seven days a week. Now that Otto was working at the resort full-time, Jake was his foreman on the farm running its daily operation.

"How was your day, Johnny?"

"Busy! We're trying to get as much done on the construction as possible before the snow arrives."

"That makes sense."

"Patsy, do you want to earn some money working construction at the resort? You can start this Monday morning."

"Sure, you know I relish physical labor and working with my hands. When I was growing up, I would work with my Uncle Rocco on the weekends doing all different types of construction projects."

"I want to build a barn for entertainment and a place to host craft fairs and holiday events. You would be part of a crew of local tradesmen. Otto will be your foreman."

"Sounds good to me."

"Otto is making his famous venison sauerbraten, (German Pot

Roast) tonight. The meat has been marinating for five days and will be served with side dishes of red cabbage and potato dumplings. Jake, Jocko, and Jimmy will be joining us."

I'm looking forward to that, I love venison!"

The dinner Otto prepared was excellent! After dinner, I called my father to say hello and check in.

"How is the investigation going, Pop?"

"I was just going to call you. I have great news for you, they just posted the results - you passed the NYPD Entrance Exam, congratulations!"

"Cool, I've been waiting patiently for six months now; I am one happy dude!"

"I tracked down Billy Cunningham's old partner who was with him during his prior arrest for grand theft auto."

The guy had this to say about his old friend:

"Billy and I had a falling out over some money that he owed me, so we were not friends anymore. I heard about Billy's death; the news did not come as a surprise. With Billy's lifestyle it was just a matter of when. A few months ago, I heard Billy was hanging out with members of the Satan Survivors Motorcycle Club. He became a prospect for the club and was part of a crew that stole expensive sports cars."

"I also explained the entire situation to Uncle Pasquale. I told him the reason the Bronx DA's Office was still pursuing Billy Cunningham's shooting was because of his father, Senator William H. Cunningham, and his close ties with the Bronx DA. Two days later, Uncle Pasquale called and gave me a contact name and phone number to call to get some information on the Cunninghams."

"It turns out this guy's wife has known Cunningham's wife since childhood. They are still best friends, talking to each other on a daily basis.

"Uncle Pasquale's friend didn't like William H. Cunningham either! He was a snob who thought his shit didn't stink. Billy was always in trouble. He was the youngest of three boys. His two older brothers were successful lawyers working in their father's law firm. Billy Boy was the black sheep of the family, a motorcycling rebel, and a real dirt bag. With his father's connections and law firm representing him, they always seemed to get him out of it."

"That is interesting, Pop. What else did Uncle Pasquale's friend say?"

"Billy's father aspired to one day become President of the United States. His son was an anchor, always pulling him down. After years of bailing his ass out of trouble, combined with his son's lack of motivation for his future, his laziness, and poor attitude he had enough and kicked him out of the house. The senator had his reputation to think about--for the first time Billy would have to stand on his own two feet.

"The guy even heard the Senator had paid Billy $5,000 to change his last name.

"Now that I found out Billy's troubles, I am going to track down Billy's last partner, Chains, who was with Billy on the night of his shooting death. I think he might be an associate or a full-patch member of the Satan's Survivors' Motorcycle Club.

"Thanks, Pop. I appreciate your efforts."

"Don't worry about anything, Patsy; we'll figure this whole thing out. I'll keep you updated on any additional progress."

"Is grandpa there?"

"Yes, here he is."

"I love you, Gramps, tell Nonna I say hello and that I love her too."

He put my father back on the phone.

"How's your vacation going?"

"Starting this Monday, I will be working for Johnny, doing construction at the resort."

"Good for you, it will keep your mind busy, plus you can earn some scratch. Tell Johnny thanks for everything." With that we said our goodbyes and we both hung up.

"Patsy, I'm off from work on Sunday; would you like to go horseback riding?"

"Sure, Laura!"

"Good, there's something I want to show you."

On Friday and Saturday, I worked on my car. I did some minor adjustments, changed my oil and filter, washed, and waxed, and totally detailed my ride, inside and out. The small town did not have an Auto Parts Store, but the old Jager Brother's General Store had an automotive section carrying basic items needed to maintain your vehicle. The old rustic wooden building was huge and carried a little bit of everything. It had a grocery section, hunting and fishing, hardware, liquor, tools, gardening, kids' water toys, children's toys, souvenirs, candy, clothes, boots, ski equipment and so much more.

Jager's also served as the local gas station with two pumps, one out front for automobiles and another on a dock behind the building on the lake. You could pull your boat up, fill up your tank, purchase bait and tackle, snacks, or cold beverages. This was the 'everything' store in this small town. It had been in business since 1875 and was located next to Swede's Resort.

I knew Johnny and Laura missed having home-cooked Italian meals, so I thought I would surprise them! The products I purchased were not of the Italian quality that you would get at the Scallaci Family Grocery, but they would have to suffice.

When I finished working on my '55, I walked to the house, took a shower, put on some clean clothes, and got to work preparing dinner. As soon as I had finished, Johnny and Laura walked through the door to the delicious aromas of my sauce simmering. Meatballs, pork ribs, and sausage, were browned and added to the mix. They were both excited to taste it! They hustled upstairs to wash up and change clothes. I threw my pasta into another large pot of salted boiling water, cooking it al-dente or fully cooked, but still firm to the bite. By the time I drained the spaghetti, Johnny and Laura were already seated at the table, perfect timing!

We sat down, and I shouted, "mangiamo," Italian for let's eat! I shared a bottle of red wine with Laura. Johnny had his customary ice-cold mug of Genesee Cream Ale. We all enjoyed our dinner; I was even impressed with the way it turned out. Johnny's kitchen was well-stocked, he had all the other ingredients I needed, including fresh vegetables to make a great salad. Because there were so many good cooks in the Scallaci family, I really did not get the chance to cook very often, but I did get to watch and learn from the best. For dessert, Laura and I finished the cannoli left over from Giorgio's Italian bakery.

After we ate our dinner and cleaned up, Laura and I stayed home playing cards and watching the boob tube. Johnny took a shower, put on some nice threads, and drove back to Swede's, for a Saturday night out with live entertainment. Laura and I stayed up to around midnight. We were both beat, so we crashed out. Johnny was still out partying and having fun. After a good night's sleep, I got up about 8:00. It was Laura's only day off, so I did not wake her; she slept to about ten.

Johnny either got up early before me and left the house or he never came home. Laura told me, "He usually stays over at his girlfriend's house on Saturday nights."

"What? I didn't even know he had a girlfriend!"

"My manager at the resort, Kathy, and my father have been dating for about two months now. I am happy for him."

Johnny had not been in a serious relationship since Laura's mother, Annie died. I was overjoyed that he found someone!

This day, Laura and I planned to go horseback riding. Since I got up first and had to wait for Laura to awaken, I thought it would be nice to make her my first big country breakfast. I prepared farm-fresh scrambled eggs, home fries, bacon, sausage, toast, and flapjacks smothered in pure Adirondack maple syrup. By the time we got finished eating, cleaning up, washing, and getting dressed, it was time to go for our ride.

Laura, Bruiser, and I headed to the stable next to the livestock barn and saddled up our horses. I would ride the Pinto, 'Cochise,' the same horse I rode last time. I felt like Little Joe from Bonanza. Laura rode her beautiful Quarter horse, 'Star.'

"I want to show you something I discovered just recently while out riding."

"Sounds like fun, Laura."

We traveled the trail for a short while when Laura pointed to something alongside the dirt road we were on. All I noticed were thick brush and dense forest. Laura stopped her horse and dismounted. She approached the location she had pointed at.

Lying beneath the brush appeared to be some type of stone marker. She got back up on her horse and at that precise point guided Star through the brush. Using both her hands and with lots of help from her trusty steed's head, she parted the thick brush. I followed right behind her. I would never have noticed this path. It was naturally camouflaged. Once we trekked through the heavy brush, I saw what appeared to be an old trail carved through the woods.

It was like entering a portal that led to the unknown! We quickly found ourselves surrounded on all sides by towering trees. About ten minutes up the trail, just after crossing over a small brook, the trees suddenly opened into a clearing. We entered what appeared to be an old graveyard. There was something particularly unusual about this graveyard--there were no gravestones. Instead, the cemetery was rimmed with grey numbered, metal T-shaped markers. There were literally hundreds of these markers. This cemetery was one of the most haunting graveyards I had ever seen.

Beyond the feeling of isolation, the cold anonymity of the endless rows of numbered markers sent a shiver down my spine!

"Patsy, they serve as a perpetual reminder that in death, as in life, these people were considered not even worthy of a name or date of birth. They represented nuisances to be numbered and hidden away in obscurity. Here they shall remain forever anonymous."

"Why bury people with numbers instead of names?"

"Because they were never meant to be remembered, this is the castaway graveyard of the old hospital."

I noticed that there were nine gravesites located in their own little area, away from the others. They had wooden markers with no names - just numbered one through nine. I felt the hair on my neck stand up and goosebumps on my arms. This place was certainly spooky! We explored the area, stumbling upon an old out-building with two wide steel doors rusted shut. We did not find any outside lock, but the doors would not budge. The whole area was overgrown with vegetation.

"I haven't told anyone else about my discovery."

"I agree, Laura, let's keep this secret strictly between us for now."

I then relayed to her about the three old signs that I found up in the storage barn. We both expressed a feeling that the two finds could be somehow connected. I think Bruiser also found this place to be quite eerie, he would not stop barking.

"Laura, let's get out of here; this place gives me the creeps."

"I feel the same."

We got back up on our horses and headed back on the narrow and overgrown trail. As soon as we exited the thick brush and got back on the main trail, Bruiser calmed down and stopped barking. The ride home was alarmingly quiet. We did not know what to make of this. By now, we kind of knew that this was no ordinary hospital. We also knew we would have to further investigate and do some research on this matter.

By the time we got back to the stable, it was dusk, and my ass was once again sore. It felt really good to get out of my saddle. We took care of our horses, put them in their stalls, and endured the walk to the house. Johnny and Otto were barbecuing some steaks for dinner. Jake, Jocko, and Jimmy who all lived in the old staff quarters along with

Otto, were sitting on the porch sucking down some cold brewskies before dinner. Laura and I sat down and joined them.

"How was your ride? "

"Fine Jake."

Johnny yelled to us, "Dinner's on." We all sat down at the dining room table. The steak was delicious as were the potatoes, turnips, green beans, and corn on the cob, all of which were grown on the Muller farm.

When we all finished this hearty meal, our company stayed for a while then left. Laura and I sat on the porch and tried to figure out how we could find out more information about the history of this property.

"I'll start by asking my boss, Kathy," said Laura. "She is the fifth generation of her family to be born and raised in this area of the Adirondacks. She has to know something!"

"Sounds like a person to ask."

We talked for a while, then watched the boob tube, and headed to bed early. Tomorrow morning would be my first day of work at the resort and I wanted to get a good night's sleep. We all got up early the next morning and had breakfast. I rode to the resort in Otto's 1951 Dodge Power Wagon and Laura rode in Johnny's pickup truck. When we arrived, there were multitudes of workers waiting for us. The larger crew of tradesmen were building the motel and cabins, the new crew, which I would be working with, was hired to build the barn. Otto already had the site that the new barn would be built on all marked out.

After Otto showed us what he wanted done, we started clearing the area of vegetation and helped the local lumberjacks cut down the towering eastern white pine trees. We did as much as we could by hand, then the bulldozer and backhoe took over, removing rocks and debris and leveling the site. The trees we cut down were transported to the local mill to be cut into lumber and used in constructing the barn. We took a late lunch.

Laura and I enjoyed lunch by the lake's shoreline!

"I spoke to my boss and asked her if she knew the history of the old Poor House and Insane Asylum occupying the Muller homestead and farm's property."

"What did she say?"

She said, "I was told many stories by family members when I was a young girl. My great great-grandmother was a staff member at the hospital and started working there when it first opened. My grandmother, a graduate of the Bellevue Hospital School of Nursing of New York City, became a staff nurse working in the Insane Ward at the turn of the century. Laura, you could talk to my grandmother after work if you want to."

"That would be great but, Kathy, please keep this conversation strictly between us."

"Laura," I said, "I want to go with you to hear what your bosses' grandmother has to say."

She agreed.

We both returned to work. After we were finished for the day, Laura asked her father:

"Can you ride home with Otto? I need to borrow your truck. Patsy and I are going shopping at the general store to buy some Halloween decorations for the restaurant and office."

"Sure, no problem."

Laura had never lied to her father before, but she felt this little white lie was harmless, but necessary to keep our secret. Johnny and Otto left for home. Laura and I would follow Kathy to her mother's house, where her grandmother also lived. Laura explained to me that Kathy had her own house. She was once married to a local lumberjack who was killed in a logging accident early in their marriage. They never had children, nor did Kathy ever remarry, but her and Johnny were now in a relationship.

"I'm glad for her and Johnny."

"Patsy, you look like a smaller version of Johnny."

"Thanks, Kathy, I will take that as a compliment."

Laura was right, she was an attractive woman. She appeared physically fit and seemed like a nice person. It was a short ride to her mother's house. When we got there, Kathy introduced me to her mother, Cynthia, and grandmother, Rita. Laura already knew her family and hugged and kissed them hello. We all sat in the living room. Kathy had already called her mother from work to tell her that Laura and her friend would be coming by after work. She said, they wanted to find out some information from grandma about the old hospital located on Laura's property.

Her grandmother started off by telling us:

"My grandmother began working there when the hospital first opened in the late 1850s. My grandfather told me that before they built the hospital around the 1830s, it was a County Poor House/Poor Farm. A childhood friend of my grandfather's uncle was appointed as keeper of the Poor House. He managed the residence and farm. Poorhouses or poor farms were county- or town-run residencies where paupers--mainly elderly and disabled–were supported at public expense. It also served as a dumping ground for the outcasts of society. Orphans and widows lived alongside the severely mentally handicapped and criminals, all of whom were known as inmates."

"Can you tell us more?"

"Of course, it was a working farm which produced at least some of the produce, grain, and livestock they consumed. The residents were expected to provide labor to the extent that their health would allow. They worked really hard in the fields and provided housekeeping and care for other residents. Their rules were strict. Accommodations were minimal. Inmates lived a structured life consisting of small meals and cramped and dirty living conditions. In this particular poor house there was no smoking, drinking, cursing, or recreational activities of any kind. Violation of these rules was punishable by solitary confinement with only bread and water for nourishment."

"What do you recall about the hospital's construction?"

"During the early1850s, construction began on a one-hundred and fifty bed hospital facility with several more outbuildings built as well. Four hundred acres of property were added to the four-hundred acres that the county poor house already occupied, for a total of eight-hundred acres. The new hospital opened up sometime around the late 1850s and was called Serenity Falls Insane Asylum. My grandmother became a staff member there. My mother also served as a staff member there sometime during the 1880s."

"Why were people committed?"

"Some of the reasons for admission into asylums in the late 1800s included suppression of menses, masturbation, hysteria, nymphomania, idiocy, lunacy, dementia, melancholia, epilepsy, exposure while in the Army, greediness, over-study of religion, laziness, and other psychological maladies."

"How were the inmates treated?"

Patient Scrawl

The most frightening revelation for those in the asylum was that their lives would be spent in veritable rat traps. It was easy to get in, but nearly impossible to get out! Because so little was known about mental illness, there was great prejudice against inmates. Some family members even viewed their demented kin as evidence of sin and regarded them as being possessed by some evil entity. My grandmother recalled that in the late 1850s when she worked there, most of the hospital staff did not treat the patients with a kind and affirming hand. Quite the opposite happened! Patients were subjected to horrendous cruelty, experimentation, neglect, and humiliation. All of which was entirely socially acceptable at the time."

"Frightening! How were the conditions?"

"After I graduated nursing school, I started working there in the early 1900s. The hospital had overcrowded conditions where patients slept in their own feces and urine. Some were even sexually assaulted by the staff or other patients. Hundreds of patients were allowed to roam the facility naked. I recall patients as aimlessly wandering the halls or vacantly staring at the walls. The hospital was understaffed, undersized, under-funded, and overpopulated. It became a dumping ground for people with developmental disabilities and society's undesirables."

"That's so sad. Were other types of treatments conducted?"

The mental hospital's aggressive methods of treatment ranged from insulin coma therapy, use of strait jackets, electroshock therapy, ice baths, ice cold showers, to full-scale lobotomies. After physician, Walter Freeman, performed the United States' first transorbital lobotomy in 1936, many large psychiatric hospitals utilized the procedure, affixing a metal pick into the corner of each eye-socket, hammering it through the thin bone there with a mallet, and moving it back and forth, severing the connections to the prefrontal cortex in the frontal lobes of the brain. This new procedure became known as the "icepick" lobotomy, using it to treat everything from daydreaming and backaches to delusions and major depression.

"Shocking! Is there any memory which stands out?"

"There were several murders committed inside its walls. I can tell you so many horror stories that took place when I worked there, but we do not have that kind of time. One of my most horrific memories took place in 1935, when a mentally deranged and brutally violent patient escaped from the facility and murdered an entire family of five. It took place right in this very neighborhood that our family lived in. The patient stole a meat cleaver from the hospital's kitchen, escaped, and used it to hack up a mother, father, and three young children as they slept. I was happy when they closed down the mental hospital; it truly was a looney bin!"

"Thank you for sharing all that with us."

"You are very welcome, Laura."

We said our goodbyes and headed home, but first we had to stop off at Jager's General Store to get some Halloween decorations. We were both shocked by the appalling stories she had shared. Now I knew why Johnny always wanted the entrance gates locked, to keep out thrill and curiosity seekers!

"Patsy, I want to explore the old hospital building. I know my father told us that it was strictly off limits to everyone, but was the reason because it was unsafe or is, he trying to hide something?"

"I don't know, Laura. We don't want to disobey his order, but we do want to get inside the old asylum."

"The best time to do it, Patsy, is when he goes small-game hunting during the second week of October. My father, Otto, and Jake would leave on a Friday after work and head to the hunting cabin, returning early Monday morning. Friday is payday, Jocko and Jimmy go to the resort office to get paid. From there, they usually go to the bar at Swede's, staying until at least midnight or later."

"I agree, Laura. This will give us plenty of time to explore the place. We just have to be patient and wait a few weeks."

Two weeks passed by, and we made great progress on the barn construction. During this time, I received a phone call from my father telling me that he had news for me regarding my case.

"Patsy, Billy Cunningham's partner, 'Chains,' who was with him on the night you shot and killed Billy was busted by the NYPD for drug dealing. If found guilty, he was looking at spending a long time behind bars. To help his situation he admitted to the police that he was with Billy the night of the shooting. He told them, Billy, another guy who was the driver, and himself went to the Fieldston Complex in Riverdale to steal Billy's father's 1969 Ferrari Daytona."

"Pop, that's great news. Is there more?"

"Yes, Chains spoke further: 'Because of the blackout and heavy thunder, we thought it would be the perfect time. Billy was the lookout, while I used a Slim Jim to pry open the car door. During the robbery, Billy noticed a security guard making his rounds watching them from behind a cement column. When the security guard emerged from behind the column to confront us, Billy put his hand at his pants waist and pulled out his .32-caliber chrome-plated semi-automatic pistol."

"That's exactly how I remember it, Pop."

"There's more from his statement, son."

"The security guard removed his handgun from its holster and fired three times in self-defense. Billy went down! The security guard then took cover behind the column. I quickly grabbed Billy's flashlight and weapon and ran as fast as I could to a waiting car outside the parking lot. We hightailed it out of there!"

"With Chain's confession, the district attorney's investigation squad closed the case. You are 100% clear of any wrongdoing. It was determined by the DA's investigation squad to be a self-defense shooting."

"That's the best news I've ever gotten!"

"You can come home anytime you want."

"Thanks for all your hard work."

"That's what family does."

"I miss you, grandpa, Nonna, and the rest of the Scallaci family, but I want to stay a little bit longer to help finish the barn."

"I understand, there is more great news - Joey Castanza returned home from his one-year tour in Vietnam the other day and can't wait to see you!"

I was happy as a pig in shit!

16

Exploration Destination

The Secret Passageway

"I will keep in touch, Pop. Tell Joey I will see him soon. I love you."

What a cheerful phone call. I was so happy to get that monkey off my back! It was nice to know the incident was not going to affect my becoming a New York City Policeman. Hearing the news about Joey being home was icing on the cake.

Time passed quickly, and it was now Friday October 10th. The cool fall weather descended upon us. It was quite chilly out; the leaves were turning the beautiful colors that only autumn foliage will bear. The mountains were ablaze in a symphony of color. Today was a big day for Laura and me. We had waited patiently for tonight to finally arrive. After work, we were going to explore the old asylum!

Johnny, Otto, and Jake left work early for their weekend hunting trip. They would not return until Monday. Laura and I had just finished work for the day at the resort. As we were leaving, Jocko and Jimmy pulled into the parking lot in Jimmies 64 GTO. It was payday and like clockwork the boys were looking forward to their Friday night out. We got into Laura's Corvette and headed home. When we arrived, we changed out of our work clothes and into something more durable. I wore my leather jacket, straight-legged black jeans with my black Chuck Taylor Converse All-Star high-top sneakers. Laura wore her Keds, bell-bottomed jeans, and a denim jacket. We were now ready for action!

We grabbed three of Johnny's brightest flashlights, one for each of us, and a spare for backup. We walked over to the storage barn to grab a hammer, pry bar, and a forty-foot wooden extension ladder. During the week, I went on a scouting mission at the old hospital building to see if I could locate some type of access into the facility. All of the basement and first floor doors and windows were boarded up. In addition, most of the windows on the second floor were barred as well, except for three adjacent windows.

With the help of the extension ladder that we got from the barn, we attempted to gain access through one of the three unbarred windows. I adjusted the heavy wooden ladder to reach just under the bottom of the first window. Hoping it was unlocked, I climbed the ladder and tried opening the window. It would not budge, it was locked.

Undaunted, I continued onto the second window. No dice, it was also locked. If worse came to worse, I could break one of the small panes of glass located by the window lock, and then unlock it from the outside.

I was amazed--the second and third floors did not show any broken glass or damaged windows even though they were over 100 years old.

I positioned the ladder under the third and final window, climbed up, and tried to open it. Using all my strength, the window sash actually moved slightly. I knew it was not locked; it was simply stuck from years of inactivity. I positioned my prybar, used the hammer, and was able to get the window up enough to get my hands underneath it. Again, with all my might, I lifted the sash and got it up high enough for us to slip through. It was tight for me, but I managed to squeeze underneath the window and gain access.

I motioned to Laura to come up. She did and slipped underneath the window sash with no problem at all. Both of us were inside! The sun was setting as we turned on our flashlights and looked down the darkened hallway. The ceiling was crumbling. The floor was sagging and littered with old paper documents. As we started exploring the area, we entered what appeared to be the central part of the hospital. It must have been the administration section, there were desks, filing cabinets, and several offices. Everything was covered in a thick layer of coated dust.

We started exploring the hallways and rooms. They were cluttered with old rusty wheelchairs, gurneys, medical beds, and decaying medical equipment. We came across padded cells used to prevent patients from hurting themselves. We exercised extreme caution navigating these rooms! There were two wings connected to the central part of the hospital, with signs indicating which psychiatric ward you were in. This wing contained the children and female wards. The opposite wing contained the male wards. At the end of the female and male wings were the wards for the criminally insane.

Reserved for J.J.J.

There was plenty of chipped paint on the walls and the old structure emitted a nauseating musty smell. The patient rooms were fitted with barred windows and rusty bedframes. Each room contained a large metal door with small observation windows affixed with wire mesh between the glass that staff would use to observe patients. There were creepy wall-art and frenzied writing on some of the walls. Patients wrote messages such as, "my idea of fun is killing everyone." Another message read, "help me, I'm being held here against my will" and "please forgive me, let me out." Others read, "it was more fun in Hell," and "you are here because the outside world rejects you."

I was thinking about all the pain buried in these walls. If they could talk, what a tale they would weave.

All of a sudden, we were startled by a loud noise that sounded like a door being slammed shut!

Laura yelled, "What was that?"

"I don't know," I said, "but this building is old and probably quite drafty. The night is extremely windy and could have played a part in the haunting noise."

I did not want to tell Laura what I also thought it could have possibly been. I did not want to frighten her any more than she already was.

"Patsy, I have an overwhelming wave of sadness and feel a haunting and disturbing presence."

"There's nothing to be afraid of, Laura, just stay close to me."

As we navigated through the creaky dark halls of this abandoned asylum, we saw many more rooms; nurses' station, X-Ray room, bathrooms with showers and washing tables, doctors' and nurses' lounge, waiting rooms, music room, a barber shop, dining halls, a dentist's office, a pharmacy, laboratory, and operating rooms complete with lab equipment, old medical devices, medicines, and hypodermic needles.

During the time waiting for this day to come, Laura conducted extensive research on old insane asylums and mental hospitals from the mid-1800s to the mid -1900s. She became quite knowledgeable on the distasteful subject. Laura learned that the hospital was a remnant of a darker medical past, when the diseased and undesirables were placed far from civilization. We ambled our way to the attic where we stumbled upon hundreds of dusty old suitcases brought by patients upon their admittance to the hospital. Some patients resided at the asylum for decades and those who died there were buried in the hospital cemetery.

If no family claimed a patient's belongings, the staff stored them in the attic. Walking the decaying hallways of the asylum gave me a raw and real perspective of psychological and medical treatment of the era. After we finished exploring the attic, we took the stairs down to the first floor, where the main lobby was at the front entrance of the facility. The staircases, though decaying, were quite elaborate. The first floor housed a small gymnasium, chapel, auditorium, and sitting rooms.

After we got done exploring the first floor, we took the stairs down to the last place left to investigate, the basement. The basement was huge and dungeon-like. The first part of the basement contained the hospital's laundry area, a large kitchen and a staff dining room. We started to explore the rest of the basement, encountering several bathtubs.

"Patsy, they were probably used for hydrotherapy, where patients would be immersed in an ice-cold tub of water, with only their heads exposed."

We noticed shackles attached to the walls, restraint chairs, isolation cages, seclusion cells, cabinets full of strait jackets and restraints, therapy rooms and operating rooms.

"Obviously, Patsy, the treatment of inmates in early lunatic asylums was sometimes brutal and focused on containment and restraint."

"Geez, Laura, I feel so sorry for these poor souls."

Looking around, I noticed a pair of wooden double doors with a sign above that read, Morgue. We entered to see a wall filled with body coolers, which once held the corpses of patients. With their iron doors opened, we noticed a large sink area, autopsy tables, embalming tables, gurneys, medical equipment, cupboards, cabinets, several pine coffins stacked on top of one another, and numbered grave markers lying in a corner. There was an old decrepit incinerator furnace, which Laura surmised was most likely used to cremate body parts. In the back part of the morgue, I saw a ramp leading to a pair of heavy-duty metal doors.

The doors were locked from the inside by two 2" x 4" iron drop bars resting on brackets fastened to the wall. One at the top, the other one at the bottom of the door. The brackets mounted to the wall had holes drilled in them for padlocks, ensuring one could not remove the drop bars unless the padlocks were removed. With some manly force, I pulled the two drop bars out of their brackets!

I opened the doors to find a wide brick-lined tunnel staring at me. On one side of the tunnel floor lay a pair of rail tracks running as far as our flashlights would allow us to survey.

The tunnel also contained steam pipes, water pipes, and electrical conduits that must have carried heat, water, and electricity throughout all the buildings when the hospital was operational. The tunnel was dark, dirty, and dingy. All of a sudden, it grew bright! To our surprise, the tunnel was lined with a string of lights hanging from the ceiling, which had strangely illuminated. As if this place was not spooky enough!

It turned out that Laura had backed into a switch located on the wall and inadvertently turned the lights on. Johnny had once mentioned that the old hospital had no electricity since its 1948 closure. For some strange reason, the tunnel lighting must now be connected to the county's power grid. As we stepped through the tunnel, we encountered an old steel cart sitting on the track, with a full load of coal still inside it. We also noticed some skylights built into the tunnel, which helped to enhance air flow ventilation and to provide sunlight.

We also discovered skeletal remains of small animals scattered throughout the tunnel.

"What the hell has gone on down here, Laura?"

"I don't know, Patsy, let's keep moving!"

About fifty yards into the tunnel, it branched off to the left to another brick-lined tunnel which the rail tracks veered into. There was a sign above the tunnel that read, Access to Boiler Building, Power Plant, & Coal Storage. We decided to go straight and stay on the main tunnel that led to who knew where? Around 150 yards later, we reached another stone ramp that took us up to some sort of a tool room. Within the tool room, we observed various types of shovels, pickaxes, mattocks, sledgehammers, lining its walls. This room had no windows, but it did have a set of metal doors with iron drop bars and bar brackets mounted to the wall similar to the previous ones we encountered.

Once again, I used some brute force to remove the 2" x 4" bars. When I got them out, I kicked open the rusty doors, only to be staring at the same creepy and overgrown cemetery we had visited over a month ago.

"Patsy, this is the cemetery of the dead insane."

"You're right!"

Walking outside, we discovered the room that was connected to the end of the tunnel was the outbuilding we previously attempted to gain access to!

The doors would not budge; we thought they were rusted shut. We had inadvertently discovered how the inmates or patients who died at the old mental institution were transported to the cemetery!

"Laura, they probably used the rusty gurneys now sitting in the morgue to move the corpses from the morgue to the cemetery without the other patients being aware."

"That makes sense."

We closed, locked up the doors, and headed back through the tunnel to the morgue.

"I wonder what really happened here, Laura?"

"Patsy, the details of the types of procedures performed in this insane asylum and others are beyond shocking."

Learning that this building was in use during some of the darkest days of psychiatric care made our minds wander and wonder what dark deeds occurred within these halls and rooms. It took just two signatures to have a person condemned to a psychiatric ward. This period was truly a time when an understanding of mental illness was desperately lacking.

We returned to the morgue. I shut the tunnel lights switch off and buttoned up the steel double doors. For curiosity sake, I tried the morgue's light switch. Much to my surprise, the room illuminated. I then went one step further and turned on the sink's faucet. An even bigger surprise occurred; there was hot and cold running water. We had no idea why.

We shut the lights off and exited the eerie place. Around the

J.J.J.

corner, we encountered a set of wooden double doors. The sign above these doors read Operating Room. We tried to open them, but the room must have been locked from the inside, but why? None of the other rooms' doors we discovered were locked in such a manner. I tried to kick the doors in, with no affect. These doors were constructed of solid oak and had no outside handles. There was not even the slightest movement when I body-slammed the doors. This truly was a mystery!

It was getting late and we were filthy. It was time to leave! We returned to the second floor, heading to the open window. Just for the hell of it, I tried a few light switches, but none functioned. We even tried to turn on some of the bathroom sinks. There was no running water either. We both looked at each other.

Laura frowned. "Why did the tunnel and morgue have electricity and the latter have hot and cold running water?"

"I don't know - this is truly mystifying!"

We exited via the window. Laura climbed down the ladder first- followed closely by me. I closed the window behind me and swiftly moved down. We were thankful to be out of such a haunting and creepy place!

We lowered the ladder, took it down and returned it, along with the tools to the storage barn. We headed back to the house and took long hot showers. I got done first and put on some clean clothes. I went to the kitchen to fill the cooler with ice and beer. Bruiser and I walked out to the rear porch, sat down on one of the rocking chairs, popped open a cold brew, lit up a Lucky Strike and tried to make sense of all that we had witnessed.

It was a cool night out, and the night's sky sported a full moon. Laura got done with her shower and joined me on the porch. Man-oh-man, did she look bewildered! I cracked open a cold one and handed it to her. She fired up a fat joint and joked, "It helps me to relax - I definitely need to chill after our haunting night-tour."

I had tried smoking grass once with one of my friends but did not like the high and decided to just stick with my beers. I had no problem with it as far as anyone else partaking. I had the attitude of different strokes for different folks.

"Patsy, I get most everything we experienced today, but there are a few questions that I don't have answers for. Like why did the morgue have electricity and hot and cold running water? Also, why was the tunnel that led to the cemetery lined with lights? Why were the doors to the operating room in the basement around the corner from the morgue the only ones in the entire hospital that were locked?"

"I feel the same way, "I wish I had the answers."

We could not ask Johnny because we were not even supposed to be in that building in the first place. We sat on the porch for a few hours, drank beer, and racked our brains trying to identify answers to our newfound puzzle!

We developed a few different theories, but we wanted the facts! By now, we both had a nice buzz going on.

"Patsy, besides the days when my mother and your mother died, this day was one of the saddest days of my life."

"Why is that?"

"Because of the shocking horrors and suffering endured by the poor souls imprisoned between the walls of this way-out venue and at similar facilities. They're scary because they force us to confront the simple fact that our brains could turn on us at any moment and turn us into entirely different people."

"That sounds heavy. Makes you think, doesn't it?"

"Patsy, please hold me."

I did, kissing her gently on her cheek. She responded by kissing me on the lips. That kiss led to a more intimate and passionate French kiss. The romantic nature of our encounter quickly escalated.

When we finally came up for air:

"I've been wanting to do that for years."

"I wish I would have known that Laura, because I felt the same way about you."

As it was getting late, the temperature plunged. We entered and sat on the couch in the great room. We lit a fire in the huge stone fireplace, snuggled up to one another and picked up where we had left off. I could not believe this was really happening. It was a dream come true!

After a session of heavy petting, Laura whispered:

"I know of a place where we can go to get even warmer."

She grabbed my hand. I did not hesitate. I jumped right up! She led me upstairs to her pad and built a blazing fire in her fireplace.

She whispered, "I am still a virgin, Patsy."

"Wow!"

I could not believe this was real. I had to pinch myself to make sure this was really happening and not just a dream.

"Several of my previous boyfriends have tried over the years to go all the way, but I am saving myself for a boy I truly love, and that boy is you."

My eyes lit up with excitement!

For years now, I had thought she was the sweetest and most beautiful girl I had ever known. "Man was I excited!

I was totally infatuated with her. She put on a Beatles album. I was never one to kiss and tell, so I will leave it up to your imagination to guess what transpired next. This was one of my happiest days ever! I ended up spending the night and shared Laura's comfortable big brass bed. We slept until about 9:00 AM, woke up, fooled around, and went back to sleep, finally waking up at around 11:00 AM.

We got out of bed and headed down to the kitchen, where Laura prepared a delicious brunch. I was still on cloud-nine over last night and probably would not be coming down anytime soon! Just thinking about it lit me up like fireworks on the 4th of July, or a pinball machine on tilt! After we finished eating and cleaning up, we showered, and got dressed. We were ready to start our day.

"Don't ask me why, Patsy, but I want to go back to Johnny's father's study."

"OK, I'm with you."

She took me to a room and told me, "This was his study where he kept an extensive library."

The door was locked. Johnny had kept it locked and intact after his father died to preserve his father's memory. Laura knew where he kept the key. This is the library/study where she conducted all of her research on insane asylums and mental hospitals.

"Johnny's father must have been interested in mental illness, as he had several books on that very topic."

"I can see that Laura."

This is the first time I had been in the study. When Laura did her research, Johnny and I were working late on building the new barn. Since we still needed to find the answers to the questions we had about the old asylum, Laura thought with all the old books she hadn't gone through yet, perhaps one of them might give us some type of clue as to what has occurred here. We both got to work, going through four walls of floor to ceiling bookshelves of the huge study. The study had elaborate woodwork, an ornate antique desk, and a beautiful river rock fireplace. Many of the book titles we viewed pertained to war, medicine, history, philosophy, anatomy, and other intellectual concepts. I was greatly surprised to see the sheer volume of those written in German.

"Why all the German books, Laura?"

"I don't know. Add that to the pile of unanswered questions."

Johnny's father must have spent a great deal of his time in this room reading and thinking. I never saw Johnny read any books other than Field and Stream, Playboy, or Hot Rod magazines. And he usually just looked at the pictures. I did not know exactly what we were looking for, but we felt we had to do something - anything!

We spent quite some time reading the titles of the books. I was like Johnny, I only looked at the same type of magazines as he did, plus Mad Magazine. I had even read the Godfather during quiet hours at work. I was certainly no bookworm. I finally arrived at the last section of the majestic book-lined study when a Hallelujah moment struck me!

I started at the bottom and worked my way up. When I got to the middle of the bookshelf, I noticed a spine of a book that caught my eye. The title read, "History of Eugenics" printed in red with a black X underneath. It appeared as if someone drew the black X on it. I pulled the book off the shelf … just like that, the bookcase swung out like a door being opened! I immediately looked at Laura and she at me. We were both in total shock! I must have triggered some type of mechanism when I pulled out the book.

"This is exciting and maybe dangerous, Patsy."

We immediately entered into the formerly secret and now revealed passageway. It was dark, but at the beginning of the opening on the wall, I could see the faint hint of a light switch. I flipped it on, a ceiling light illuminated. The space was about the size of a closet. The passageway led to a stone staircase descending to a basement. I asked Laura to grab two good flashlights and told her, "Here we go again." I waited for her return. We then completed the slow walk down the stairs. This time we took Bruiser, my loyal canine sidekick and faithful bodyguard with us!

I cannot speak for Laura, but I clearly felt my body tighten, adrenaline rush, and blood pressure skyrocket. I felt that something harmful or evil had happened down here! After all, a hidden bookshelf door led us to this cold and creepy basement. When we got to the bottom of the stairs, I could see another light switch on the wall. I tried it and we had light. Now the whole basement was lit up. It was a small space fortified by stone walls and no windows. In the middle of the wall that was parallel to the stairs, I could see a framed picture hanging, but from this angle I could not make out what it was. We headed to it and gave it a look!

To my utter disdain, it was a painting of Adolf Hitler giving his famous salute and probably saying "sieg heil." What the hell did this mean?

"Come here, Patsy."

"I'm coming."

I ambled over to the other side of the stairway. On that side were two distinct flags hanging. One flag was red, with a white circle in the middle displaying a black Swastika. The other flag was black, with two grey lightning bolts with flat ends instead of the more common pointy ends. I knew enough about World War II symbols to identify the one with the Swastika as the flag of the Nazi Party. The other flag appeared to represent the elite Corps of the "SS" of Nazi Germany.

I had studied WWII in history class, plus I had first-hand knowledge from the old man's war souvenirs. He had brought back many such mementos with him from the war, in which the United States and its allies had kicked the Nazis' asses.

Laura pointed to another set of heavy metal doors similar to the ones we used to access the morgue's tunnel and the hospital cemetery. The doors were locked from the inside of the basement by the same type of iron 2" x 4" drop bars and brackets we had run into during our initial investigation. Again, using some brute strength and after wrestling with them for a while, I finally got the bars out. I was glad I work out because these were the toughest ones I had encountered.

We pushed open the doors, found a light switch on the wall and turned it on. The lights came on. At this point, it was not even a surprise when the lights illuminated. There was a landing that led to a stone ramp. We headed down the ramp, arriving at another brick-lined tunnel equipped with a wall mounted light switch. I flipped the switch, illuminating our pathway. We wandered the tunnel for about 100 yards, where we were greeted by another set of metal doors.

We removed the two drop bars. These two released a lot easier than the previous two. I opened these doors and switched on the lights. We were now inside a 10-foot-long hallway that led us to a set of wooden doors, which we approached and opened. These double doors swung open both ways. We located the light switch and turned those lights on. We were in total disbelief, as this room was extremely bright and strikingly clean. I felt a déjà vu moment at the level of cleanliness and order, but my memory failed me. Had I previously encountered a similar environment?

I could tell this space was renovated and updated. There was an operating table, equipped with a set of operating lights hanging above the center of the room. Upon further inspection, we observed a long array of newer floor and wall cabinets. The walls and ceiling had a fresher coat of paint on them.

We opened all of the doors and the drawers of the cabinets. They were stocked with updated medical supplies. As I was rifling through one of the drawers, I came across a notebook. Its cover read, New York City Police Academy. Underneath that title, it read, Class of 1946. I opened the inside cover revealing, Recruit John J. Muller written in pen. All of the pages inside the book were blank. I did not show this to or tell Laura about it. I thought it was better to keep this information to myself for now. I did, however, take the notebook with me. I stuffed it in my pants waist and pulled my T-shirt over it.

We further noticed medical instruments laid out neatly on a metal tray lying on the counter. This room was well lit and featured a large stainless-steel sink area. I turned the faucet, releasing both hot and cold running water. Upon further investigation, we discovered two holding cells and two sets of shackles chained to the wall and in the nearby corner of the room stacked neatly were several different types of children's toys still in their boxes. On the other side of the room were a bedroom with two single beds, a bathroom, and shower. Walking past the operating table, I noticed what appeared to be a large blood stain on the floor. The sanguine outline intrigued me. For some reason unbeknownst to me, I broke out in a cold sweat.

I then set my sights on another set of double wooden doors featuring a newer looking drop bar setup than all the previous ones. These double doors were easier to open. When walking out through these doors, the surroundings looked strangely familiar to me. Laura recalled, "That's because this is the basement of the old asylum." As we continued walking around the corner, we revisited the double doors of the morgue, which we had visited last night.

"Laura, these solid oak wooden doors that we couldn't open last night are the very same doors that just led us out of the updated operating room."

"I think you're right. This is strange indeed."

This whole mystery was becoming more and more complicated by the minute. We retraced our steps, shutting off all of the lights, and locking the doors.

We finally returned to the study. I reinserted the book I had removed and pushed it back into its original place, closing the opening to the secret passageway. Now, everything we had touched or opened was back to normal. Laura locked the study door and put the key back where Johnny had originally hidden it. I went to the ice box and grabbed some brews. We headed outside to the porch to discuss our latest encounters.

Laura said, "This whole experience has been so surreal!"

"I agree. Now we have to figure out what all this means and what we should do next."

We could not believe or did not want to believe that Johnny was somehow mixed up in all of this, but the mounting evidence pointed in his direction. He did tell us the structure was just an old hospital and that the whole building was strictly off limits to all because it was unsafe and in total disrepair.

Was he just telling us this to keep us out?

The facility, although decaying, seemed structurally sound to me. Johnny also never mentioned that the hospital had its own cemetery. Johnny had mentioned that the old hospital building was without electricity and running water. He also routinely locked the rusty old entrance gates to keep curiosity seekers out. Or was his real motivation to stop anybody from finding something out? He also locked his father's study. In addition, I had heard Johnny and Otto speaking to each other on the two-way radio in German.

The biggest piece of incriminating evidence, however, pertained to finding the New York City Police Academy notebook with Johnny's name printed on the inside of the cover. There were just too many coincidences! Something was amiss.

17

Barks No More

Was Johnny a murderous psychopath?

I knew he possessed an explosive temper and became extremely violent at the drop of a hat. But then again, he could also be a gentle giant to anyone. Laura and I were confused, we were just amateur detectives. This situation was totally out of our league. We needed someone who was a professional investigator. There was no one better for the job than the old man!

I called him right away and, luckily, he happened to be home.

"Hi Pop, Laura and I need your help!"

I explained the entire story to him.

"I'll drive up tomorrow," my father told me, "and confront Johnny on Monday when he returns from his hunting trip. I'll call Johnny's older brother, Carl, to relay the news and see if he wants to take the ride up."

He called me back later that day noting:

"I spoke to Carl, told him your entire story, and he agreed to take the ride up. I'll pick him up tomorrow morning, and we should arrive sometime in the afternoon."

We said our goodbyes and hung up. I then looked into Laura's eyes and could see that she was extremely distraught and totally bummed-out.

Johnny, her adopted father, was her life. She worshipped the ground he walked on and loved him like he was her real father.

"Don't worry, Laura. My father will put all the pieces of this puzzle together. He also told me not to jump to any conclusions."

Over the past couple of days, we had endured a rollercoaster of emotions. Laura hugged and kissed me, she felt better knowing that my father and her beloved Uncle Carl were making the trip to the Muller farm. Evening approached and we both were hungry. We sat at the kitchen table and pigged-out on leftovers for dinner. We spent the night hanging out in Laura's room listening to her records, drinking wine, and enjoying a game of Twister. Her room had a black light and some cool psychedelic posters on the walls. We shared a romantic evening together. We decided with all that was going on, we would keep our burgeoning romance a secret for now.

My old man and Uncle Carl should arrive tomorrow afternoon. Johnny, Otto, and Jake would be returning from their hunting trip the following morning. We would be spending our last night together for a while. We made the best of it. We would also have Sunday morning to spend together. We agreed to return to being just close friends until this mystery was solved.

I have to say that this was the best night ever! It truly was a fantasy come true. We arose from bed around 10:00 AM and started our day. My father and Laura's Uncle Carl would be here within a few hours. We ate, took showers, and jumped back in her bed one last time before getting dressed. We sat on the porch awaiting their imminent arrival.

It was a cloudy, cold, and miserable morning. We rocked in our chairs and chatted awhile. We heard a powerful-sounding car pulling up to the chain-locked gates. The driver of the vehicle started beeping the horn. Laura and I walked over to the gates to see what they wanted. As we got closer, I identified the make and model of the car. It was a brand new black 1969 Dodge Charger RT. A man then stepped out of the driver side. He sported a big black pompadour hairstyle and goatee. As we stepped closer, I realized it was my father.

I threw away my cigarette and ran over to him, giving him a big hug and kiss.

"I didn't recognize you at first glance. You're driving an unfamiliar car and sporting a new goatee." He then gave me a soft slap on the side of my head. "You're still smoking?"

Carl, riding shotgun stepped out of the vehicle and said, "Hello."

Laura ran over to him and gave him a big hug and a kiss. I shook Carl's small hand, noting the precision of his recent manicure.

"Long time no see; how have you been?"

"Better now that I am here, Patsy."

Laura and I could not have been happier to see both of them. I opened the lock and swung open the creaky gates. My father and Carl got back in the car and drove to the parking area in front of the house.

"Nice ride, Pop."

"It's the first brand new car I have ever owned, and I love it. This baby has a 426 Street-Hemi engine with, a four-speed transmission. It really goes. I picked it up just last week."

Laura and I carried their belongings up to their rooms. We then all sat in the great room and caught up on what was happening.

"Patsy, all is well in the Bronx. Grandpa, Nonna, Uncle Rocco and all the other Scallaci say hello and send their love. All your friends have been asking for you. Joey wants you to call him. He has been keeping busy making up for lost time, spending it with his girlfriend. Other than that, everything has been pretty quiet. Oh yeah, your friend Frankie Scalero's father, Allie Boy, was found shot to death the other day in his Cadillac. In addition, the FBI is investigating Senator William H. Cunningham's ties to organized crime."

"Have you two made any new discoveries?"

"Yes, Carl, we have."

We conveyed everything we had experienced.

Carl sat silently for a few moments, then responded. "I recall that the old hospital property had a history of once being a poor house/ poor farm, the hospital being an insane asylum, and more recently a mental hospital. When my father purchased the property, we heard rumors that the old facility was haunted, but I do not believe in the paranormal, so I never gave it much thought. I also remember that the hospital had underground tunnels that connected most of the buildings, but I never explored them.

"I have never heard about a secret passageway in my father's study, though. I did not know that the mental hospital had its own cemetery. Back then though, it was common practice for insane asylums to have their own cemeteries."

My father and Carl were hungry from their trip, so we decided to have a late lunch before Laura, and I showed them the secret passageway.

"Carl, what do you know about Otto?"

"As far as any affiliation with Nazis go, Otto had been a soldier in one of Germany's elite Waffen SS units during World War II, but that was thirty years ago. Let's eat and then you can show us what you discovered."

Giulia Castanza sent my father up with a tray of lasagna, cooked fresh this morning. She was a fine Italian cook and all of her meals were delicious, but her lasagna was the best I ever had, and I have consumed a lot of people's lasagna in my soon-to-be nineteen years (ha,ha).

She also brewed a gallon of her thick minestrone soup, loaded with vegetables, beans and pasta, which we would have for lunch along with some fresh Italian bread she sent up. We would save the lasagna for tonight's dinner! Laura and I enjoyed a late breakfast and really were not very hungry. My father ate two big bowls. Carl could not finish his first bowl; he ate like a bird. He must have weighed no more than 130 pounds, dripping wet.

After lunch, Laura and I cleaned up and we all went to the great room to give my father and Carl some time to relax. We were all anxious to get started with our expedition! A short time later Laura got the key from Johnny's hiding spot. We accompanied her to Carl and Johnny's father's study. We took three flashlights and Bruiser along with us.

"I have not been inside this study since my father passed away," said Carl.

I could see him getting a little teary-eyed.

"This is some-sized study with quite an impressive library, Carl."

"You're right about that, Vinny."

I walked over to the special book with the black "X" and said:

"This was the book that when pulled, triggers some sort of mechanism which allows the bookshelf to open like a door."

The old man read the title of the book, The History of Eugenics. He then pulled the book out of the shelf. Sure enough, the bookshelf opened just like we told them. I knew from my biology studies in high school that Eugenics was—the science of improving a human population by controlled breeding to increase the occurrence of desirable heritable characteristics.

"What a strange topic; why was this book among the collection?"

Laura turned on the light, illuminating the small space with the stairway leading down to the dark and dingy basement. Laura and Bruiser led the way, followed by my father, Carl, then me bringing up the rear. When Laura got to the bottom, she reached for the wall and turned on the basement lights. She turned to the right side and pointed to the wall where a picture hung. She headed over to it and showed my father and Carl the painting.

"The oil painting of Adolf Hitler appears to be of high-quality and original."

Laura then proceeded to the other side of the basement and showed them the two flags that were hanging from the wall.

My father checked them out:

"These flags are the real deal! You were right about the one flag being the flag of the Nazi party and the other one being the flag of the SS."

Laura then embraced the heavy-duty metal doors. My father helped her pry off the two iron drop bars--they loosened a helluva lot easier than yesterday. She opened them and turned on the lights, proceeded down the landing to the ramp, then to the tunnel entrance. She explained to them that this tunnel led to the old mental hospital basement. She turned on the wall switch and the string of lights lit up the brick-lined tunnel. She led on, stating,

"This is where the mystery gets even more complicated."

We followed her lead to the end of the tunnel, navigating the ramp to another set of metal double doors. Once again, the old man and Laura removed the two iron drop bars, opening the doors. She turned on the lights and we all advanced down the hallway that led us to the set of wooden doors, which Laura swung open. She shouted, "Brace yourself" and turned on the lights. The room was bright and uncommonly clean, nearly sterile. I could see the startled look on their faces.

I showed them the new shiny stainless-steel sink with functioning hot and cold running water and all the newer looking medical supplies in the wall and the base-cabinets. Carl examined the medical instruments laid out on the tray and the other seemingly modern medical equipment. I showed them what I thought to be a large bloodstain along the side of the operating table. They further inspected the two holding cells and the shackles chained to the wall. I led them to the small bedroom with bathroom and shower.

"All of this medical equipment appeared as state of the art, manufactured long after the hospital had shut its doors."

"I agree, Carl."

Laura told them:

"You are now standing inside of the updated operating room located in the basement of the old asylum. Follow me." As she approached the other set of solid oak doors fitted with a newer drop bar setup, she removed them and pushed open the doors. As she led us to the enormous basement, we turned our flashlights on. As we stepped around the corner, Laura pointed to a sign above another set of wooden doors that read, Morgue.

We followed her and Bruiser inside. Again, Laura turned on the lights and we gave them the tour. We showed them the body coolers, the old incinerator furnace, old rusty gurneys, embalming and autopsy tables, two stacks of pine coffins, along with the numbered grave markers. I showed them the old sink that had hot and cold running water and explained to them that Johnny told us the old hospital building did not have electricity or running water. We also told them we checked out all the floors of the facility and found there was no electricity or running water anywhere, except for these two rooms in the basement.

After my father and Carl gave the morgue a thorough perusal, we moved on down the ramp toward another set of heavy metal doors. We removed the two drop bars and opened them to view another brick-lined tunnel. Laura turned on the tunnel lights.

"This tunnel led to the cemetery and about fifty yards up, it branched off to the utility buildings. The rails were once used for hauling coal."

"Patsy, this tunnel is a lot larger than the other one, probably to accommodate the rail tracks, steam pipes, water pipes and electrical conduit."

We next passed the old coal cart. A little further up, we stumbled upon the tunnel that veered off to the left, along with the pair of rail tracks routed to the utility buildings. Further up, we reached the up ramp that led us to the cemetery's outbuilding and the final set of heavy-duty metal doors. My father and Laura once again removed both drop bars. They kicked open the doors to view the unkept and overgrown cemetery accentuated by row after row of numbered markers.

I took the old man and Carl to what I found to be most curious! There were nine gravesites lying in their own separate area. They were adorned with wooden-post grave markers numbered one through nine, instead of the old metal markers that were used for the rest.

"This section of the cemetery is a lot less overgrown than the rest of it." My father stated. "the gravesites look to be more recent."

"I agree, Pop."

After further investigation, the old man muttered, "Let's head back." We turned off all the lights, locked all doors, and returned to the study. We put everything back the way we had found it. Laura locked the door and put the key back in its place.

We were all now pretty grungy, so we took turns taking showers and put on clean clothes. When we all were ready, we met in the great room to discuss the situation. The temperature was dropping, so I lit a blazing fire. There was never a shortage of firewood on this property. Johnny made sure of that; he loved to split wood year-round.

"What do you make of all this, Pop?"

"There has definitely been more recent activity going on since the closure of the hospital. Exactly what, I cannot yet say until I confront Johnny."

"Carl, what do you think?"

"Come to think of it, Otto has always been a fanatic of Nazi ideology. Johnny idolized the older Otto growing up. He taught Johnny how to hunt, fish and to live off the land. He also had some medical training before the war and served as a medic for his infantry unit during the war. Could it be possible Otto had corrupted Johnny's mind, making him susceptible to the Nazi ideology that he so strongly embraced?"

I also told them that I found a box in Jake's car's trunk that contained Nazi memorabilia and that Jocko wore a Nazi helmet when he rode his motorcycle. I conveyed to my old man the possibility that both of them could also be mixed up in this.

"I don't know but be careful not to jump to any conclusions. Hopefully, we will find out more tomorrow night. We need to come up with a plan for tomorrow evening! That is when I will confront Johnny and Otto. Laura, what type of bounty did they go hunting for?"

"Small game like turkey, cottontail rabbits, snowshoe hare, squirrel, pheasants and other gamebirds."

"Good!"

"Carl, if they shot some pheasants, you could make Johnny's favorite, your delicious German pheasant stew and roasted pheasant. This way Johnny and Otto will be more relaxed."

"I'll be happy to cook dinner!"

When the old man finished speaking, he entered the kitchen, put the tray of lasagna that Giulia had made for us into the oven, and set the heat for tonight's dinner.

I followed him, I had something else I wanted to show him. He followed me to my room where I showed him Johnny's old Police Academy notebook.

"I found it in one of the cabinet drawers in the updated operating room in the old hospital basement. I have not spoken about or showed it to anyone else. "

"Good, keep this between us."

He looked the binding over, then opened it.

"Johnny's name printed on the inside cover is in his own handwriting? I have the very same book from my days at the Academy, now stored away in a box of mementoes inside a closet in our apartment. The pages are blank; I will hang onto this for now, Patsy.

The lasagna was ready, and everyone sat in the spacious dining room. The lasagna was out of this world! Giulia even sent dessert, a dozen homemade cannoli, which Laura and I had no problem polishing off!

After dinner, dessert, and cleaning up, my father, Laura, and I played cards. Carl, who brought a book, read quietly.

Laura and I both had to work tomorrow. The old man and Carl were exhausted from the trip up. We all hit the rack early. Laura and I left for work the next morning. My father and Carl were up waiting for Johnny, Otto, and Jake to return from their hunting trip. I was working with a small crew now, finishing up the new barn. Laura's crew was finishing up decorating the resort with scary Halloween decorations and were waiting on us to hand over the finished barn so they could decorate it as well.

A few hours into the job, Johnny, my old man, and Carl pulled into the Swede's parking lot. Johnny had returned from his hunting trip an hour after we left for work.

"I was totally surprised and happy to see Vinny and Carl waiting for me on the porch."

"Johnny gave us the grand tour of his Adirondack Shangri-La, Patsy."

"How was your trip, Johnny?"

"Great. All combined, we got four turkeys, eight pheasant, two cotton tail rabbits, one snowshoe hare, and six squirrels to add to the freezer chest, and we hope to be adding to it as soon as the big game season opens! Otto and Jake are back at the farm, butchering our kill right now. Carl is going to make my favorite meal for dinner tonight, German pheasant stew and roast pheasant. You are going to love it! The barn is looking really good."

"We should be finished in a day or two. "

"Great!"

I stared at Johnny. As huge and intimidating as he looked, he had always treated me with love and kindness, like my real uncle. I could not and did not want to even think that he had a dark side to him and could possibly be involved in cold-blooded murder."

I had seen Johnny's rage and witnessed death by his own two hands when he killed that outlaw biker, but that was in self-defense. I sure hoped for Laura's sake that I was right.

My father and Johnny had always had each other's backs. They were best friends for sure, but even more like brothers, just like Joey Castanza and me!

I believed the special bond they shared could never be broken. I returned to work and told them all, "I'll see you guys later."

Johnny, who had not yet seen Laura, hurried off to find her. He took the old man and Carl to the resort's restaurant, home of the big country breakfast and lumberjack special.

When they finished their breakfast, they drove back to the farm. Johnny and my old man sat on the porch and caught up on old times. They spent the rest of the morning and all afternoon reminiscing and were still bullshitting on the porch when we got home from work. When Carl got back from breakfast, he got busy in the kitchen preparing dinner. Otto had brought over the pheasant that Jake and he had just plucked and cleaned for tonight.

Carl told my father: "Otto and I spoke for a while. I wanted to see if I could find out any information pertaining to what might be going on here without his becoming suspicious."

"With no luck."

Carl normally marinated the pheasant for three or four days, but this time he only had eight hours to work his magic, consequently he spent the entire day in the kitchen!

Laura and I were extremely anxious to find out the truth about what was going on here. I am sure the old man and Carl were as well. All we wanted was to get to the bottom of this mystery. Hopefully, we would within about an hour. Laura and I washed up, got dressed, and joined Johnny, my father and Otto, seated in the great room, chatting by a nice warm fire. Carl was finishing up in the kitchen.

"Jake, Jimmy, and Jocko won't be joining us for dinner tonight. Carl thought that it would be nice to just have a quiet dinner with old friends.

"That will work, Johnny."

My dog, Bruiser, and his older brother, Dempsey, were sprawled out next to each other on the bear-skin rug.

Johnny asked Laura and I if we could start a fire in the dining room's fireplace.

"You bet!"

I was happy with this request. I knew it would give us five minutes of alone time! Although we were in love, we did not know what our future together held or what we were going to find out tonight about Johnny. After we set the fire, Carl yelled out to us, "Set the table."

We then helped Carl bring all the delicious-looking food that he prepared for us and laid it out on the large dining room table. Once we were done with that, Carl called Johnny, my father, and Otto to the dinner table. Johnny, Otto, and Carl sat on one side of the table, my father sat across from Johnny, I sat across from Otto and Laura sat across from Carl, our backs to the far wall.

Johnny's dog, Dempsey, must have smelled the aromas of pheasant because he entered the dining room and started barking at Johnny.

Johnny laughed! "He loves pheasant as much as I do."

He picked a good-sized chunk of pheasant up from the platter and threw it to Dempsey. Carl started to say, "Don't waste the delicacy on the mutt," but it was too late.

18

Shock Therapy

We started to fill our bowls with delicious German pheasant stew, which served as an appetizer before the main course of roast pheasant. Carl left for the kitchen to get one of his now-ready side dishes.

Within a few minutes, Dempsey began panting heavily and vomited. Johnny jumped out of his chair and ran to Dempsey's aid. He opened Dempsey's jaw, searching for a lodged bone or other airway obstruction. By now, poor Dempsey was trembling uncontrollably and drooling. Otto began to assist Johnny, immediately checking Dempsey over.

"These symptoms could possibly indicate a heart problem, Johnny."

They both felt completely helpless, sensing the seriousness of the situation.

"Carl, get in here now!"

Carl entered quickly from the kitchen to see what all the commotion was about.

As he approached, Dempsey collapsed to the floor. Carl listened to Dempsey's heart and checked to see if he was breathing properly.

"I'm so sorry, Johnny, Dempsey is gone."

Johnny was shocked.

"He was such a healthy dog to become this ill so suddenly!"

Then, my father yelled out: "Do not eat the pheasant!"

To our utter astonishment and disbelief, Carl reached under his apron and pulled a German Luger and shot at Johnny twice! The first bullet missed, the second did not!

Before Carl could get a third shot off, my father, with his .38-caliber Snub-Nose pistol at the ready, shot Carl right between the eyes, dropping him to the floor. Otto, then pulled a German Luger out of his pants waist. With that, I instinctively aimed my father's WWII .45 semi-automatic pistol, which I had concealed under my flannel shirt and shot Otto in his shooting arm. He immediately dropped his gun.

My father pointed his weapon at Otto, and commanded, "Lay on the floor face down and put both your hands behind your head."

The old man had come prepared! He proceeded to handcuff Otto behind his back.

"Do not move an inch, Otto."

The horrific scene Laura had just witnessed of her father being shot by her much-adored Uncle Carl and then getting shot in the head himself shocked her to the bone.

She started freaking out. I tried to calm her down, then we both went to Johnny's aid.

"Johnny, are you OK?"

"I'm alright, the bullet caught me in the shoulder."

With this news, Laura calmed down.

Johnny yelled out: "What the Hell just happened?"

My father said, "Call the town's sheriff, tell him to call for a doctor and an ambulance."

My old man checked to see if Carl had a pulse, he did not. Johnny appeared more upset that his beloved, dog, Dempsey, was dead than about his own brother, whose lifeless body lay on the floor.

"Watch Otto while I check on Johnny."

"Don't touch anything."

"Johnny, are you OK?"

"Yeah, again, I'm OK."

"Your good friends, the sheriff and doctor are on their way."

Twenty minutes later, someone banged on the front door. I handed Laura my 45.

"Keep an eye on Otto, I'll get the door."

I opened the door. The sheriff, his two deputies, and the town's only doctor were there.

"Take us to where Johnny is."

I did. The doctor immediately checked his wound.

"Johnny, today must be your lucky day."

"I don't feel very lucky, Doc."

"Because of the location the bullet entered your shoulder, it passed without hitting any major organs, blood vessels, or bones, and exited cleanly out your back."

"Can Johnny be moved?"

"Johnny, do you feel well enough to walk?"

"Yeah, I think so."

The doctor then checked on Carl's status; whose limp body lay silently on the floor.

"We have a D.O.A. Call the hospital and have the coroner come out here."

The sheriff did and he also notified the state police. The doctor attended to Johnny's wound and examined Otto's.

"It's almost the same exact wound as Johnny's except in the upper arm. No major damage and a clean exit."

The doctor cleaned and bandaged it.

The sheriff told his deputies, "Escort the suspect out of the house and into the patrol car. Stay with him until the state police relieve you."

"Where are the weapons?"

My father relinquished the .38 snub nose revolver he used to shoot Johnny's brother and handed it over to the sheriff. The .45 which wounded Otto was turned over as well. Both firearms were bagged as evidence.

"My name is Vincent Scallaci, a long-time friend of Johnny. I am a retired New York City Homicide Detective Sergeant."

The sheriff shook the old man's hand.

"I'm Richie. Johnny has always spoken very highly of you and with the utmost respect."

"This is my son, Patsy, and of course you know Laura."

The ambulance and coroner showed up first. Two paramedics tried to help Johnny to the ambulance, but a little shove from Johnny almost knocked them off their feet. They headed to the town's small hospital, a thirty-minute drive from here. Twenty minutes later, the state police showed up. Their investigators immediately took control of the crime scene.

The sheriff told them, "This gentleman's name is Vincent Scallaci, a retired NYPD homicide Detective Sergeant who shot and killed one of the suspects."

He handed them our bagged weapons.

"This is his son, Patsy; he shot and wounded the other suspect."

"Once this whole mess is sorted out, you will both get your weapons back."

My father, Laura, and I sat in the great room. My father explained to the lead investigator, Bobby, and his partner, Tommy, the sheriff the entire story that led up to the shooting. He left no detail out!

Laura and I also filled them in on our experiences. The other crime scene investigators were going through the crime scene, with a fine-toothed comb. When Bobby and his partner were done talking with us, they joined everyone in the dining room. We stayed in the great room along with the sheriff. The CSIs (crime scene investigators) took numerous photos, etched sketches, gathered all the evidence and bagged and tagged all of the food. They put poor Dempsey's carcass in a body bag in anticipation of an autopsy. They bagged Carl's German Luger , his two spent casings, along with Otto's unfired German Luger.

They recovered Carl's spent 9 MM rounds and my .45 caliber round that were lodged in the thick hardwood panels of the dining room walls. They also located my spent .45 caliber casing. The investigators also conducted a thorough search of Carl's room and searched for evidence in the kitchen where Carl had prepared dinner. Carl's body was transferred into a body bag, placed on a gurney, rolled into the coroner's station wagon, and taken to the hospital morgue where an autopsy would be performed. After spending several hours gathering all the evidence and completing a thorough premise search, the lead investigator approached us.

"Johnny will be staying overnight at the hospital. We will talk to him when we leave here and hopefully, he can shed some light on this case. Two uniformed New York State Police Troopers relieving the sheriff's deputies will be taking the surviving suspect, Otto, to the hospital for additional medical treatment. Then we will be taking him to headquarters for an interrogation after which, he will be placed in our jail. I will be back sometime tomorrow morning with a team of investigators, the town sheriff, and his deputies to perform a thorough search of the property. We will ask Johnny for his permission to search his premises when we talk to him at the hospital. If he says yes, then we won't need to get a warrant."

It was difficult to make any sense of what just happened. I knew it was a lot for Laura and Johnny to take in all at once. I was not worried for Johnny because he was just as mentally tough as he was physically.

"We will know more tomorrow when they talk to Johnny and hopefully Otto will talk when they interrogate him."

Now that the state police, the sheriff, and his deputies had finished with the crime scene, the lead investigator gave us the OK to clean it up.

The old man and I did a thorough cleanup of the dining room and kitchen.

"We never did get to eat dinner, Pop!"

"Probably a good thing, Patsy, as I believe Carl, of all people, poisoned the pheasant. Because of Dempsey, we are all still standing." The old man told Laura and I that he knew all along that there was no way Johnny could be involved in something so immoral but kept his thoughts to himself.

We were hungry, so Laura prepared us tuna fish sandwiches. It was late when we were done.

"The sheriff and the New York State investigators will return at first light, so we should try to get some sleep."

I cannot speak for Laura or my father, but I got zero sleep. I tossed and turned all night long, thinking about the night's tragic events.

Just as promised, the place crawled with law enforcement officers early the next morning. We were all ready for them! Bobby, the lead investigator told us:

"We spoke with Johnny at the hospital and got his permission to search the entire property."

We started off by showing them the secret passageway in the study. We pulled out the book that had the black "X" and the bookshelf opened. We took the stairs down to the basement. My father pointed out the authentic Nazi artifacts, which they bagged and tagged.

We took them to the heavy metal double doors and trekked the ramp to the tunnel. The old man explained to the investigators,

"This tunnel leads to the old mental hospital's basement."

When we arrived at the updated operating room, Bobby told Laura and I not to touch anything.

They snapped numerous photos and inspected everything thoroughly; bagging and tagging all evidence found. Bobby left the three investigators there to finish up. The rest of us headed over to the morgue where they all looked it over, from top to bottom. The investigators finished in the updated operating room and now were inspecting the morgue.

Bobby, his partner, the sheriff, a deputy, my father, Laura, and I took the tunnel that led to the cemetery. We showed them the tunnel that branched off enroute to the utility buildings, while informing them that we had not explored in that direction. When we reached the double doors of the tool shed, we opened them to reveal a sweeping view of the eerie overgrown graveyard.

The old man showed them the nine grave sites he felt were suspicious.

"They have newer grave markers than the hundreds of other graves and they also look to be more recently dug. They had their own little area that was a lot less overgrown than the rest of the cemetery."

The investigators spent some time at this location.

Bobby asked, "Is there any kind of road access to the cemetery?"

Laura pointed in the direction to the trail's entrance into the graveyard.

"There is a dirt road that has an access path through the brush, leading you to a trail that brings you here."

"Good! Not now, but maybe tomorrow, could you take us to the location?"

"No problem."

"Thanks for your help."

The sheriff then had his deputy escort us back to the house. The investigators and sheriff wanted to explore the other tunnel with the tracks that veered off toward the utility buildings. Upon returning through the tunnel and arriving at the morgue, we found the investigators were no longer there.

The sheriff's deputy said, "They accompanied the other sheriff's deputy to explore the rest of the basement and the remaining floors of the old hospital building."

When we returned to the house, Johnny and his girlfriend, Kathy, were sitting in the great room. We were all excited to see him up and about! Laura must have hugged him for five minutes.

We had to tell her, "Let your father sit and rest."

"The hospital wanted to keep me a bit longer, but I told them I felt fine and checked myself out. The doctor told me to take it easy and to keep my wound clean--I need to have my dressing changed daily. The doctor said if there's no problem, come back to see him in two weeks and he'd remove the stitches."

In response to Kathy's obvious concern, Johnny added, "I feel a little sore, but other than that I feel strong."

Under my breath I mumbled, "No shit!"

At Johnny's request, my father reiterated everything we knew about what was going on to Johnny even though the New York State Police investigators had filled him in last night at the hospital. Johnny looked at all of us.

"Vinny, here's what I know."

"OK, Johnny, go ahead."

"Everything that happened last night took me totally by surprise. I had no clue that Carl and Otto were involved in something so sinister. Carl was born in Germany, and his real name was Heinrich Von Mueller. When he was twelve years old, his birth mother died. My father, a prominent doctor, needed some time away to recover and took a job at a hospital in Sweden."

"What happened to Heinrich next, Johnny?"

"Heinrich remained in Germany under the care of family members on the von Mueller Estate. He enjoyed an education from the finest schools that money could buy. Meanwhile, at the hospital in Sweden, where our father worked, he met a young nurse. They fell in love and got married. That young nurse was my mother! She gave birth to me and my younger sister, Helga. When I was a young boy, our family left Sweden and moved to the Von Mueller Estate in Germany. My father's parents were getting up in age, so he wanted to spend their final years with them. My father took a job teaching medicine at the University of Frankfurt and my half-brother, Heinrich, attended the University of Munich.

"During my years spent at the Estate, I learned how to hunt, fish, and the art of taxidermy. When Heinrich and Otto reached their teens, my father, my uncles, Heinrich, Otto's father, Otto, and his brothers joined the National Socialist German Workers Party, which was the Nazi Party, a far-right political organization."

"The Nazi Party, really?"

"Yes, Vinny."

"Please, continue Johnny."

"Heinrich got his degree in Anthropology from the University of Munich and continued on to medical school at Frankfurt University, where my father was a professor and department chair. After Heinrich received his medical degree, he continued on to study under Otmar Freiherr von Verschuel, a human biologist, geneticist, and trail blazing eugenicist. At the end of 1938, my German grandparents both died. My mother's parents were back in Sweden. She had not seen them in many years and was homesick. In 1939, my father was commissioned a colonel in the German Army Medical Corps and Heinrich as a first lieutenant also in the army medical corps."

"What happened to you and Helga?"

My mother told my father, "I'm taking Helga and Helmut to Sweden to spend time with their grandparents."

My father agreed that it was a smart idea. Tensions in Europe were high, Adolf Hitler and the German Army were threatening to invade Poland."

After my mother, my sister, and I left Germany, they did invade Poland, launching World War Two.

"We would not be reunited with my father or Heinrich until the end of the war. We lived with my Scandinavian grandparents, direct descendants of noble Vikings. When World War Two was coming to an end, and with my father's money and connections, Heinrich was able to escape from Poland and my father from Berlin. Both found refuge in Sweden. We were once again reunited as a family!"

"What do you remember about your German grandparents?"

"My father's parents were born of wealthy families."

"My paternal grandmother, daughter of German immigrants, was born in the United States. My grandfather, at age eighteen, left Germany to study at a prestigious American University. During that time, my grandparents met, married, and gave birth to a baby boy, my father. Several years later, my grandparents moved back to Germany. As my father was born in the United States, he attained dual citizenship, as did his children.

"We lived with our Scandinavian maternal grandparents for one month. My father then had all our passport names altered. My mother's first name changed from Catherine to Marilyn. My father's from Siegfried to Robert. Heinrich's new name was Carl. My sister, Helga, was now Helen and my name changed from Helmut to John. Our last name transitioned from Von Mueller to Muller."

"That is an incredible story, Johnny. How did your family get to America?"

"Our father sought to leave Sweden, his plan was to travel and eventually settle down in America, where his sister and her husband lived. Our first stop on our voyage took us to South America. We lived there for a five-month period in Bariloche, Argentina. While we were living there, Heinrich was involved in a severe car wreck. He became a patient at a Buenos Aires hospital for several months, undergoing several surgeries. When we left Argentina, our next stop was Brazil, where we stayed for two weeks with my father's relatives. From there, we migrated to America! We settled in Yonkers, New York in Westchester County, just north of the Bronx, and not far from my father's sister's home."

"Do you recall much about Helen?"

"My father inherited great wealth and retired as a physician. Carl obtained a position as a physician at a Bronx hospital. My sister, Helen, attended public school. When she was ready to go to college, my father sent her to a prestigious university in Europe. She got her undergraduate degree and proceeded on to medical school. She received her MD and became a prominent doctor. Carl kept in touch with her over the years. She never returned to America. In June of 1946, I began training at the New York City Police Academy. I became a cop, but you know that already. I apologize to all of you for never telling you this information. I didn't want to be deceitful in any way."

"That's a lot to hold secret."

"My father drilled it into our heads not to discuss our past with anyone! All I knew was that my father and brother served in the German Army Medical Corps during World War Two. If anyone else found out this information, there could be trouble for the family! This was relayed to our extended family as well. We left our past behind and embarked on our new lives. If asked, we would tell people that we immigrated from Sweden."

The state investigators, the sheriff, and his deputy returned a few hours later. They were happy to see Johnny back home as well!

Bobby explained that the state police were obtaining the necessary legal authority for permission to have all nine gravesites exhumed.

Bobby, his partner, and the sheriff felt that the gravesites had been dug sometime after the facility had closed.

"We want to complete a medical investigation," he declared, "and conduct an identity investigation on the remains."

"Bobby, perhaps your superiors should contact the NYPD and the Yonkers Police Department concerning the details of this investigation."

Johnny gave them Carl's address in Yonkers.

"Otto lives in the old staff quarters on this property along with three other employees. You have my permission to search their premises for any clues or evidence."

"Thank you, Johnny and Vinny, for all of your help."

"Laura, can you lead my team and me to the location off the dirt road of the trail leading to the cemetery tomorrow morning."

"Yes, of course."

Laura and I provided them access to Otto's residence. They searched the residence and questioned Jake, Jimmy, and Jocko, who were all found not to be involved in any of this.

When the investigators split up to check the rest of the hospital's basement earlier, they unearthed another brick-lined tunnel leading from the basement of the old hospital. The trail ended at a set of heavy-duty metal doors locked by two iron 2 x 4 drop bars on the other side. While they were searching Otto's basement, they encountered those double doors. They opened them, revealing the tunnel that led from the hospital. After they were done, they said their goodbyes and told us they would see us all the next morning.

The following morning, state police investigators, several uniformed police officers, the town sheriff, his two deputies, and several personnel from the NY State Medical Examiner's office pulled into the property accompanied by a bulldozer, backhoe, and three flatbed 4-wheel drive trucks. The detective told Johnny and the old man:

"My superiors contacted the NYPD and Yonkers PD and explained the whole situation to them. The NYPD dispatched two experienced detectives and the Yonkers Police sent two of their detectives with a warrant to search Carl's residence. "Vinny, when your name was mentioned, the NYPD brass had only high praise for you and agreed that you are surely considered to be one of New York's finest! Depending on how the search goes at Carl's residence, there is a possibility the detectives could be heading up here to assist in the investigation."

"Laura, are you ready to take us to the dirt road?"

"Yes, I am."

My father, Laura, and I boarded Johnny's truck and led the caravan of vehicles to the spot off the dirt road. Johnny wanted to join us, but my old man talked him out of it.

"Johnny, all the bouncing around in the truck will reopen your wound."

He was hardheaded but reluctantly took my father's advice and agreed to remain behind. When we got to the spot off the dirt road, we showed the bulldozer operator, following right behind us the thick brush off the side of the dirt road that needed to be cleared, permitting access to the overgrown trail that led to the spooky cemetery.

The bulldozer operator cleared the thick brush, carving a road to the overgrown trail. He then cleared it. Now, instead of a trail, we had a road leading to the graveyard. When we got to the nine gravesites, and before we got started, my father thought it best that Laura does not witness this.

"Laura, take Johnny's truck and head back home to keep your father company."

"OK, Uncle Vinny, I'll be happy to do that."

After she left, they began the meticulous task of exhuming one corpse at a time.

19

Bloodline Broken

It took all day, but we finally concluded the exhumations. We witnessed the various stages of each corpse's decomposition, while inhaling the putrid stench of death. The scene was truly gruesome; we all wore ghastly looks on our faces that day. Of the nine gravesites exhumed, eight contained children's corpses, and one adult.

When the dig team finished loading the trucks, they followed the sheriff's deputy's patrol car leading the way, joined by a state police patrol car following in the rear, and headed to the hospital. A large tent had been set up outside the small hospital's morgue. The tent would be used as a staging area where medical examiners performed autopsies on the nine corpses. My father and I caught a ride back to the house with Bobby and his partner. When we arrived at the house, we were greeted by two New York Police Department Detectives who had worked with the old man when he was with the Bronx Homicide Bureau.

What a surprise for my father! They hugged and shook hands. They were NYPD detectives sent up to assist state police investigators. They were accompanied by two detectives from the Yonkers PD. I knew Jack Nulty, one of the NYPD detectives.

"Vinny, what are the odds of running into you guys way up here in the boonies?"

The old man laughed. The two detectives from Yonkers barreled their way to the door and shook my father's hand. He also knew both of them from the job.

"Hello Jack, long time no see."

My father then introduced everyone.

Jack told Bobby, the man in charge of the investigation, his partner, three other state investigators, the sheriff, and us, that we arrived at Johnny's house about an hour ago.

The NYPD and Yonkers detectives all knew Johnny, the "Swede" from the job as well, but then again who did not know the big guy? After amenities, we all took our seats in the great room and listened to what Jack, Senior and Lead Investigator for the Homicide Division for the Borough of the Bronx had to say:

"Johnny filled us in on what had happened here the other night. He told me that Vinny Scallaci was also up here. He'll be involved in the investigation as Johnny takes it easy for a while, doctors' orders!"

"I have good news to share involving this case."

"Firstly, I need to talk to Vinny Scallaci in private for a moment."

"Sure."

They headed off toward the kitchen.

"Vinny, we have uncovered evidence that is going to blow this case wide open. This evidence will be great for the case, but heartbreaking for Laura and Johnny. What I am about to say will be extremely shocking to Johnny and his daughter. How should we handle it?"

"Jack, no matter how painful this news might be to Johnny, he must know everything. However, I do not want Laura to hear what you have to say. I will take care of her."

"Vinny, I'm concerned about Johnny's temper and rage. I just don't know how he will react."

"Johnny has maintained himself thus far. At the hospital, the sheriff explained Johnny's temper issues to the doctor. He wrote him a prescription for medication to control his anger. Johnny was told they were antibiotics for his wounds. Plus, there are eleven of us here, which should be more than enough to restrain him if we had to."

When they returned from their private meeting, we were eager to hear Jack's updates. As soon as they entered the great room, the first thing the old man did was to hand me a $50 bill.

"Take Laura out for dinner and drinks."

"No problem."

Laura was in her room.

"There has been a change of plans, Laura; You and Patsy have fun and don't come back too early."

"Don't worry, we won't."

We grabbed our coats, my keys, and hurried out the door.

My father would tell me the next day what Jack had to say:

"This morning, my partner and I, escorted by two detectives from the Yonkers PD obtained a warrant to search Doctor Carl Muller's Yonkers residence. While searching for evidence, we located Carl's personal journals, hidden under a loose piece of flooring, covered over by a throw-rug. In one of the meticulously maintained journals, Carl chronicled detailed records including names, dates, and ages of eleven human beings he had murdered."

He looked directly at Johnny.

"What I am about to tell you will be shocking, especially for you, Johnny!"

My father told me, "I sat next to my best friend to provide him moral support."

Jack continued on to say:

"Carl's second murder occurred in 1950. He murdered his younger sister, Helen's high school teacher, Antonio Russo. He was the man who got the 16-year-old pregnant. He would not acknowledge or take any responsibility for the welfare of the child. Carl killed him by putting a lethal dose of cyanide into his coffee. They had met to discuss Helen's illegitimate pregnancy. He took the dead body to the Muller property in upstate New York in his Volkswagen bus and performed his first medical experiments on United States soil."

"When he was finished, he had Otto bury what was left of him in grave number one in the old hospital cemetery."

"Johnny, brace yourself. Carl's first murder occurred in 1949. His first victim was his stepmother, Johnny's birth mother."

As Jack was explaining, he glanced at Johnny for any reaction. He could see that his face had blossomed red.

"Jack, this nightmare just keeps on getting worse and worse."

"Carl wrote, "'I didn't plan this to happen, but after years of arguing and fighting with her, one day, during a major altercation, I snapped. I pushed her down the top of the long stairs. She fell and broke her neck. My family and the coroner thought it was a terrible freak accident. Everyone reasoned she must have lost her footing and fell down the stairs. She was buried in the family plot in Yonkers'.'"

Jack continued:

"Then in 1951, Carl murdered his first set of twins – two eight-year-old brothers, victims number three and four."

"It seems Doctor Carl performed charity work on his days off from his job. He volunteered his time and provided medical services at Westchester County and New York City Children's Orphanages. These orphanages were overcrowded, newly arrived orphans could go unseen or they simply disappeared from the premises with a promise of candy or a bunch of toy presents from the good doctor. He would take them for a trip to the mountains, where he and Otto would poison them to death with his favorite weapon of choice. He put cyanide in their food, then used their dead bodies for his evil medical experiments. Or he might leave them alive for a while and do horrible experiments.

"Once Carl completed removal of organs such as the heart, lungs, liver, stomach, and kidneys, he would remove the brain from the cranium and take tissue samples. Otto would then inter the children in gravesites number two and three. Carl struck again in 1955. He abducted twin eleven-year old brothers. He fed them a nice lunch, ice cream for dessert, and took them on a vacation to the country, where they opened gifts of trucks or other toys. These twins became victims number five and six. When Carl got done dissecting them for his twisted medical experiments, Otto would bury them in gravesites Four and Five.

"In 1961, Carl kidnapped and murdered his third set of twins. A nine-year-old brother and sister became his seventh and eighth victims. They were eventually interred at grave sites number Six and Seven. Carl's next murder occurred June 22nd, 1963."

Johnny's eyes widened in rage; he knew that date well!

"Carl murdered Annie Nolan, Johnny's fiancé and Laura's mother, and victim number nine."

Johnny's face festered beet-red, veins popped out on his forehead. "OMG," he bellowed.

"Johnny, are you alright?"

"Hell, no Vinny, but continue, Jack," he muttered through clenched teeth.

Carl wrote: "I had the routines and schedules of everyone that lived in the Muller house in Yonkers down to a science. On that particular day I knew my brother Johnny worked until 3:00 PM and then would pick Laura up from her friend's house. Annie worked until 4:00 PM. On that day, I finished work at 12:00 noon and arrived home from the hospital at around 12:30. When I entered the house, I called Otto and we discussed plans for my next abduction. While I spoke with Otto, Annie strolled through the kitchen. Her arrival took me totally by surprise!"

"Otto, hold on for a second."

"Hi Carl."

"Hi Annie, I thought you had to work today."

I was supposed to, but my boss told me that I have been putting in a lot of hours and working really hard, so he decided to give me the day off.

"I didn't see your car."

"Oh, I dropped it off at the service station for repairs. One of the mechanics drove me home."

"Carl goes on to write, 'Annie told me she had just come down from the attic where she found the box of Fourth of July decorations for the back of the house. She then continued on her way to decorate."

"Otto, I don't know if she overheard any of our conversation."

"I hope not, it would mean the end of us."

"You're right, I'll call you back early next week."

He writes further," I thought about it for a few minutes then proceeded outside. Annie stood on a ladder, putting up the decorations. I did not want to kill her but could not take the chance that she might have overheard us talking. She just happened to be in the wrong place at the wrong time. I knew there was just one thing to do, I pushed Annie's ladder over. She fell on the hard cobblestone patio, splitting her head wide open. I checked her pulse and to see if she was breathing. She was dead."

Shortly thereafter, he contacted the Yonkers PD. He knew the medical examiner and explained:

"I returned home around 1:30 and found Annie motionless. I tried everything I could do to bring her back, but it was too late. I believed she was putting up 4th of July decorations and lost her balance, tipped over the ladder, striking her head on the hard-stone surface."

After performing a cursory examination only, the medical examiner ruled it an accidental death by falling.

"Carl noted, we gave Annie a proper Christian burial. She was laid to rest in a beautiful plot, in a peaceful cemetery."

When Jack finished, Johnny got up off the couch, neared the wall and punched several holes through the plaster. He probably would have punched several more holes but my old man along with the rest of the "army" were able to restrain him.

Johnny released an overwhelming roar of anguish.

After things had calmed down, everyone took a seat and once again Jack spoke:

Carl wrote, "because of this unplanned killing, I decided to take a break. I thought it best to take some time off from murder. In April of 1965, I got the itch to murder once again. I abducted another set of twins, a 6-year-old brother and sister."

Jack added:

"They would be his last victims, number ten and eleven, and the end of his evil reign. He treated these poor children like lab rats. Otto buried their remains in gravesites number eight and nine. Carl goes on to write, "Unfortunately, my younger brother, Johnny, planned to retire from the police force in 1968. He has spent many of his weekends at our farm, in preparation for moving up there full-time. Otto and I concluded it was no longer safe for us."

Johnny still upset, stood up.

"I know all of you are good cops. I've never before asked a fellow cop to cover up or alter any kind of evidence, but today I am asking you to remove Carl's handwritten entry that explained his cold-blooded murder of my fiancé, Annie, birth mother of my daughter, Laura."

"Please continue, Johnny."

"Thanks, Jack."

"I ask you all not for myself, but for my daughter's well-being. She has suffered enough! This information would crush her. I am not only asking all of you, I am begging all of you, for Laura's sake. "

"Johnny, please, go outside and wait on the porch so that I can speak privately to all of the law enforcement officers in this room."

"OK, Vinny."

Johnny got up and exited. My old man spoke on Johnny's behalf:

"Does it really matter if Carl is guilty of ten murders or eleven? Either way, he will still be considered and judged as a mass murderer! I can honestly say that I have never known a finer person or a better cop than Johnny Muller in my entire life. I have never seen or heard of a cop who spilled more of his own blood or that of criminals' on the job than him."

That raised a subdued laugh from everyone.

"Johnny has been shot and stabbed in the line of duty and has given the city of New York 110% on a daily basis for twenty-two years. He kept the streets of the South Bronx safe for so many, which we all know is no easy task. I think all of you will agree with me when I say it is time to give back this simple favor to a cop's cop. Yes, we are both retired and all of you are not, but even if I were still on the job, I would do this for him. Johnny and his daughter, Laura, have been through

Hell over this whole inferno. Annie Nolan's death back in 1963, was ruled an accidental death by a state certified medical examiner and I believe that's the way it should remain."

My father told me: "I then sat down, and the sheriff, a dear friend of Johnny's got up and spoke to everyone in the room."

"I also agree one-hundred percent with what Vinny had to say."

Jack Nulty chimed in:

"It wouldn't be difficult to just lose the page containing the entry about Annie Nolan. The pages are not numbered or anything like that. We would be giving Annie's daughter, Laura, a chance at leading a productive life, full of peace and happiness."

Bobby, the lead investigator for the state police on this case spoke up next:

"If Carl's entry about Annie Nolan's murder should somehow disappear, it certainly would accomplish more good than bad. We would eliminate a lot of pain and misery in a young woman's life. If everyone in this room agrees with what has just been spoken, raise your hand."

They all raised their hands.

"OK, then it's final! Everything that has been talked about or done in this room, stays in this room!"

Everyone agreed. With that, the old man exited and got Johnny.

Bobby summarized:

"Johnny, we took a vote - the vote was unanimous in your favor."

Johnny was as satisfied as anyone could be under these dire circumstances and as close to tears as a tough-as-nails cop could ever be.

"Everyone in this room agreed that whatever was said or done was never to be mentioned again."

"Thanks, Bobby."

"Johnny, we are all so very sorry that you and Laura have gone through this painful turmoil."

Johnny and the old man thanked everyone in the room individually.

"Johnny, I am sorry I was the one who had to be the bearer of this horrific news."

"Jack, you were just doing your job."

When Johnny got done saying all his thank yous, he and my old man ambled outside and sat on the porch.

My father told me, "They left the detectives alone to do what they had to do."

As he exited, Bobby informed us:

"So far, Otto has not been cooperating with the investigation at all, but now we have solid evidence that he was Carl's accomplice in this murder conspiracy. I have a feeling he will be changing his tune once he hears the evidence incriminating him. We'll see you guys tomorrow."

Bobby and Tommy left along with the other three state Investigators and the sheriff.

Johnny and the old man walked back inside toward the warm fire. The NYPD, along with the other detectives, were putting their coats on and getting ready to leave when Johnny spoke:

"Where are you guys headed?"

"We are going to find a place to eat and a motel. Johnny, do you know of any?"

"Nonsense, you guys are staying here. We have plenty of spare bedrooms, and you can stay as long as you need to."

Johnny convinced them to stay without much effort.

"Do you like steak?"

"Yes!"

His chef grilled six Porterhouse steak dinners to go and one of his employees delivered them to the house.

"Johnny, this piece of steak was the biggest and finest tasting piece of meat we have ever eaten!"

Besides Johnny and the old man, of course, Jack was the only one to finish the entire meal.

After dinner, they gathered in the great room, drank some beers, and reminisced about the old days on the job.

"Vinny, do you have a minute? I'd like to speak with you."

"Sure, Jack."

"Let's go out onto the porch."

"Vinny, Carl kept several other journals."

"Really, what was in the journals?"

"Carl wrote of his sixteen-year-old sister, Helen's pregnancy, which he supervised. He administered weekly injections over the course of her nine-month term. Carl referred to the injections as 'Aryan Nutrients.' On October 16, 1950, she gave birth to a set of identical male twins. The first-born was subsequently adopted by close friends of his brother, Johnny, a young married couple, Vincent, and Angelina Scallaci, and they named the child 'Pasquale.' The second-born was named William by Carl. William remained under the care of Carl's aunt, who had assisted in the deliveries. William was born with two different color eyes; his left eye was **blue** and the right one **brown**."

Vinny noted: "Strangely, young Pasquale experienced a similar mutation. His eye coloring however was strangely reversed, with his left eye **brown** and his right **blue**."

"When Helen left for Europe to continue her education, she took young William with her. Carl, his aunt, and uncle were the only other people to know of the birth of a second child.

"Carl kept in touch with Helen over the years, getting periodic updates on William's progress. I have not told anyone else about these journals. I have removed the incriminating journal pages and have them for you now."

"Jack, thank you for relinquishing the pages and for not telling anyone else about this!"

"My honor, Vinny."

"Jack, do you believe that Carl's injections into Helen played a role in creating the twins?"

"Yes, Vinny, I do."

"Me too!"

"Should we be concerned, Jack?"

"That's the million-dollar question isn't it, Vinny?"

"Jack, I'm going to have to discuss this latest news with Johnny. I'll wait until the investigation is all wrapped up."

"Sounds about right."

"Jack, it's been great to see you again, but I'm sorry it's under these circumstances."

With that, they both agreed. It had been a long day, and they should hit the rack.

The old man sat alone on the porch for a while to gather his thoughts. His mind wandered back in time to October 16, 1950, the birth of Patsy. Vinny arrived at the realization that although Patsy was raised as a "Scallaci" his own bloodline had been broken. His only child and future generations of grandchildren would not have Scallaci blood running though their veins, but his love for Patsy quickly erased those thoughts.

On the other hand, Laura and I had a wonderful dinner together. We shared a bottle of wine by the roaring fire. After we got finished, we took a cruise in my '55 Chevy. Laura took me to a secluded area on top of the mountain. When we got there, I found a magical spot. I left my car running so we could keep warm from the heater and popped my favorite romantic tune, "This Magic Moment" by Jay and the Americans into my eight-track. We started off with some passionate kissing that quickly escalated. I stepped outside, opened my car trunk, and pulled out one rolled up sleeping bag.

"Wow, you really do come prepared!"

"You know my old man taught me to be prepared for any type of situation."

I grabbed the sleeping bag, unrolled, and unzipped it. We now had a warm blanket. I laid it across the huge back seat, comfortably covering us. We were all alone, it was pitch black out except for the moon.

"Patsy, we don't need a blanket to keep us warm, you have me for that!"

We both laughed. You know what happened next. By then it was late, so we drove home and hit the rack in our own beds. While lying in bed, I thought to myself how happy I was that Laura told me she had a wonderful time tonight.

"You lifted my spirits at a time when I really needed it, Patsy."

We both slept in the following morning. When we finally did crawl out of bed, Johnny and my father were chatting in the great room.

"Good morning."

"You mean good afternoon. We have guests staying with us. The four detectives from the City and Yonkers will be staying with us until the investigation is all wrapped up."

"That explains the voluminous snoring and farting I heard last night. It must have been the fresh mountain air!"

Laura and I ate lunch, took hot showers, got dressed and were now ready to start our day. We joined Johnny and my old man as they relaxed by the fire.

20

The Bloodline Restored

Johnny began to speak:

"Sit down you two, I have the latest updates on the case. The police now know the names and dates of Carl's ten murders. They also have identified those buried in gravesites one through nine. The state police investigators, sheriff, and all four detectives are interrogating Otto at this very moment. With all this new evidence against him, he's probably singing like a bird."

Laura took the news of her Uncle Carl being a mass murderer pretty damn hard, as I am sure Johnny did, but he would never show it. He was one tough dude and Laura was one tough chick. Laura loved and trusted her Uncle Carl, who had always been there for her. I know this all came as a tremendous shock to Laura, Johnny, and to anyone else who knew Carl.

Carl, a successful and prominent physician, was the last person on earth you would ever suspect would be a murderous, cold-blooded psychopath. He was a wolf in sheep's clothing, no doubt about that! A real-life devil in disguise.

The phone rang, I answered. It was Jack asking to speak to my father.

"Hang on a minute, I'll get him."

"Follow me, Patsy."

"Jack, please hang on for a minute."

The old man looked at me, then gave me his car keys.

"I want you to take Laura out of the house for the rest of the afternoon."

"Sure."

I grabbed my leather jacket.

"Laura let's take a ride to the resort; I want to check on the progress of the barn construction. You can judge how the Halloween and fall decorations are coming along."

"Far out, let's split."

Again, the old man filled me in later on regarding what Jack had to say:

"State police investigators, our team, and the sheriff interrogated Otto, they presented the new evidence Carl had written in his journal. Otto who had been tight-lipped and had not cooperated with the in-vestigation at all, decided it was now in his best interest to come clean. We are all going to head over to Johnny's house where we will fill you in on the rest of what Otto had to say."

They arrived thirty minutes later. Jack continued to tell Johnny and my father what Otto had shared:

"I was born and raised in Germany. My father was caretaker of the Von Mueller Estate where I, my brothers, and childhood friend, Heinrich Von Mueller, AKA Carl grew up. As we became teenagers, many of us joined the Nazi Party.

"During World War II, I served as a sergeant in the Waffen SS. Heinrich, a captain, served in the Schutzstaffel SS. He was assigned as a medical officer billeted to Auschwitz Concentration and Death Camp. He worked alongside his friend and mentor, Dr. Josef Mengele. They were both members of a team of doctors responsible for the selec-tion of victims judged to be fit to work or destined to be killed in the gas chambers. In addition, they carried out inhumane experiments on camp prisoners, especially twins.

"After World War Two had ended, I became a prisoner of war, forced into labor by occupying Allied Forces for war reparations.

In1949, I became a free man, moved to New York City, and reunited with my old friend Heinrich (aka Carl). When the Muller family purchased the old mental hospital property in upstate New York, I relocated to the Adirondacks, becoming full-time caretaker. Carl became a fugitive, wanted for crimes against humanity. He was able to escape Poland toward the end of the war. Heinrich, while living in Argentina after the war, faked a horrific car wreck. He spent four months in a hospital, receiving plastic surgeries that altered his appearance.

"Carl and Johnny's father became a general in the medical corps and was able to escape Berlin before it fell into Allied hands. He was not involved in the extermination or experimentation of prisoners in concentration camps. He was a well-respected medical doctor and his patients were all high-ranking German officers. Carl, along with Josef Mengele, (AKA) the 'Angel of Death', one of the Holocaust's biggest villains with the many horrifying medical experiments he conducted were somehow able to dodge Nuremberg prosecution for 'crimes against humanity' committed during WWII.

"Carl, a prominent physician at a Bronx hospital, still harbored an unholy fascination with twins, believing they held the answers to the mysteries of how to cultivate and pass on superior Aryan genes. Carl wanted to continue his experiments and asked me for help in assisting him. I agreed to it. I got busy updating the old mental asylum's basement operating room and the morgue and piped in electricity, heat, and hot and cold running water.

"I ran strings of lights for the three main tunnels. When Carl was done with his human experiments, I would simply bury what was left of the corpses in their own separate graves. Carl knew Johnny's work schedule and picked those weekends he was working to carry out his plans. I told Johnny the abandoned hospital was not structurally sound. He instructed me to board-up all the basement and first-floor doors and windows. We reasoned this would suffice to keep anyone else out. I also told Johnny that I caught some local curiosity seekers trespassing on the property. That is why Johnny always wanted the entrance gates chained and locked at all times.

"Carl's preferred method of murder was cyanide poisoning. Johnny's father was not involved in any way, nor did he have any knowledge about what we were doing. I thought Johnny would like to know that. When I brought the pheasants that Jake and I had just butchered and cleaned, over to him, Carl told me, "Patsy and Laura were snooping around and found out that the old hospital was still in use after its closing in 1948. It will not be long before Vinny and Johnny put the whole thing together.

"Carl told me that Johnny, Vinny, Laura, and Patsy have to be taken out tonight by lethal doses of cyanide! Have your pistol ready at dinner, do not eat any pheasant roast, he told me. If anybody asks you why you are not eating, tell them your stomach is giving you problems. Everyone already knows I don't like pheasant."

Otto further quipped:

"Johnny's dog, Dempsey, spoiled our plan by eating a piece of the poisoned pheasant first, saving their lives in the process. The only reason Carl discontinued his horrific experiments was that his younger brother, Johnny, retired and moved up here full time. I was a good soldier and I always followed orders."

Jack added:

"With Carl's journal and Otto's confession, this case was quickly wrapped up. Tell Laura and Patsy that we now have assembled all the pieces to this bizarre puzzle!"

Vinny asked Tommy the state police investigator:

"Where is Bobby?"

"He's with the governor, mayor of New York City, and numerous New York police brass from different jurisdictions, addressing the media and public via a special news bulletin, exposing the details of this investigation. They shall discuss the particulars about the murderous Dr. Carl, responsible for killing ten people, eight of which were orphaned children."

Jack added:

"We have some big-time trouble brewing, Johnny. The Press is going to have a field day with this story! Not one of us on the investigation team mentioned that Carl had a half-brother, a highly decorated retired NYPD Sergeant. We will do everything in our power to keep your name out of this nightmare!

Vinny remarked:

"I also told Johnny that Uncle Pasquale will utilize his many connections with the New York City newspaper unions to assist in that secrecy, by leaving out some minor details on this huge news story."

Jack chimed in:

"Johnny just be prepared in any case. Now that all the facts of this case are in, it is up to the district attorney's office to prosecute. Because the case was closed, all four of us will be returning to the city tomorrow afternoon, right after filling out some final paperwork."

Johnny replied, "I want to take everyone out for dinner tonight at Swede's Lake and Mountain Resort. I won't take no for an answer!"

Everyone met at the restaurant including: Bobby and his team of investigators, Johnny, his girlfriend, Kathy, her sister, Linda along with her husband Robby, my old man, Laura and I, and the town's sheriff Richie and his deputies. When everyone arrived, we all sat down to a delicious dinner and drinks. I thought that this final get-together was Johnny's way of thanking the team for all of their help and to show them his respect. It was an exceptionally good night!

Before we left the restaurant, we exchanged our goodbyes with Bobby and his team, the sheriff, and his deputies. The two city detectives along with the two Yonkers detectives would be staying with us for one more night. When we got home, Laura and I said our good nights and goodbyes to the detectives, who would be gone by the time we woke up. They stayed up bullshitting and drinking a few brews. Laura and I were exhausted, so we hit the rack.

When we arose Sunday morning, Johnny and Vinny were already up, engaged in conversation out on the porch.

"Johnny, I have some additional news regarding the investigation. It comes directly from Jack."

"What is it, Vinny?"

"It's imbedded within the pages in one of Carl's journals. Johnny, it is shocking. The pages describe the birth of Patsy and an identical twin brother, William Muller."

Johnny read the pages and exclaimed:

"Yes, I can see that these pages are indeed shocking, Vinny. Helen took baby William with her to Europe those many years ago. I never knew!"

With everything we now know about Carl's background and eugenics-focused twins experimentation, it is quite possible that both Patsy and William are products of Carl's diabolic actions!"

"OMG, Vinny."

"I know. The journals indicate that during World War Two, Carl served at Auschwitz Concentration Camp under the command of the infamous physician, Josef Mengele."

"Vinny, wasn't Mengele's goal to create a master race of blonde haired and blue-eyed Aryans?"

"Yes, Johnny. Eugenics was based upon a devilish mission to perfect the human race. In its extreme racist form under Mengele, the goal was to wipe out all human beings deemed 'unfit,' preserving only those conforming to a Nordic lineage and bearing."

"How many people were affected, Vinny?"

"Hitler and his henchmen victimized an entire continent, exterminating millions in their quest to achieve a so-called Master Race."

"Vinny, I am beyond saddened, I am dumb-struck by this news. What should we do?"

"I think we take this one to the grave with us, Johnny. We have a special opportunity for good here. I think we should take that opportunity and make the Scallaci-Muller bond even stronger with our eternal silence!

"I agree, Vinny. We shall never speak of this again and these pages from Carl's journal shall be tossed into the fireplace, never to be seen again."

"Johnny, what about William and the **Muller Broken Bloodline**?

"Good point, Vinny, let us keep only the pages relating to William. We can track him down at a later date!"

"The journal pages burn beautifully, Vinny!"

"Yes, Big Man, they do!"

Both men paused a moment to gather their thoughts. When they did, they simply nodded and advanced into the kitchen. No further words were needed between the two, nor would there ever be!

"Let's eat, I'm cooking."

"A big country breakfast, Dad?"

"You bet, sweetheart. Everyone, this is the first day for putting this horrific nightmare behind and moving forward with our lives!"

We all agreed to that. After breakfast, Johnny and Laura strutted over to the kennel and picked out a cute as hell female German Shepherd puppy from Blitzkrieg and Schatzi's latest litter; they named her Duchess.

My old man and I had a talk.

"What are your plans for the future?"

"I'm not sure yet, I'll know better by tomorrow."

"Fair enough. I want to tell you that Giulia Castanza and I are now in a relationship."

"It's about time, Pop!"

I was happy for both of them. Giulia was my mother's best friend and was like a second mother to me.

"Oh shit, I forgot to call Joey."

"Joey, I'm sorry for not calling sooner."

"No problem, Patsy."

"When I get home, I'll explain."

"OK, sounds good."

"It's great to hear your voice again."

"I'm spending most of my time with my girl, Gabriella. That's where I'm headed now."

"Say hello to her and her brother, Ralphie, for me. I'll be home soon."

We said our goodbyes to each other and hung up.

We all spent the entire day just relaxing around the house, playing cards, and cuddling with the new puppy. My dog, Bruiser, and his new little sister, Duchess, got along great together. Johnny's girlfriend, Kathy, came over and cooked us a delicious dinner. That night, Laura and I had a long talk. Both of us knew this day was coming. Even though we both loved one another, I would not ever think of asking her to leave her slice of paradise up here in the Adirondacks. Even though I genuinely loved it up here, I was not yet ready to leave my family and the Bronx.

We were both incredibly young and had our whole lives ahead of us. We thought if it were meant to be, then sometime in the near future we would be reunited, but for now we would cherish the wonderful memories we shared.

"Laura, I will always be there for you in times of trouble."

"And I for you, Patsy."

We agreed that we would keep our romance our little secret, just between us. Come Monday morning, we all toured the resort to view the completed barn. It looked amazing!

Laura and her crew were busy finishing up with all the scary Halloween decorations. Johnny spent some time in his office talking with the new head of the overall construction of the resort, so it was just the old man and me.

"Have you figured out what you are going to do now that the investigation is over?"

"This coming Thursday will be October 16th, the day of my 19th birthday."

Yeah, I know that Patsy."

"I want to stay here, celebrate my birthday, and head home the following afternoon. Then take a week off, spend it with Joey and some of my other friends, and visit with all the Scallaci. After that, I want to return to work as a security guard as soon as possible."

"Wise decision, Patsy."

The next day, Johnny had my father, Laura, and me show him the secret passageway in his father's study.

Johnny told us:

"Carl wanted the study locked up after our father had passed to preserve the space just the way he left it. I had no problem with that. I never spent much time in the study when my father was alive. Both Carl and I had keys."

We opened the bookcase and ambled down the stairs. We navigated through the basement, opened the heavy-duty set of metal doors, and proceeded down the ramp to the tunnel. We proceeded to the updated operating room and morgue, located in the abandoned mental hospital's basement. From there, we headed to the brick-lined tunnel that connected the morgue to the cemetery.

When we got to the graveyard, Laura asked:

"Dad, can you help me in clearing the overgrown vegetation and spruce up the landscaping--planting shrubs and flowers?"

"Laura, that's a thoughtful and wonderful idea. I'm on it."

"Thanks, Dad. This is going to be a beautiful resting place for these poor souls that are buried here. Once transformed from eerie to beautiful, it will remain so all year round."

Thursday arrived, my 19th birthday! Johnny had just gotten a phone call from his girlfriend, Kathy, manager at the resort telling him about an electrical problem they were experiencing. My father and Johnny took a ride to Swede's to see what the trouble was. Laura had been busy doing laundry all morning. I thought to myself, "This is going to be some exciting birthday."

It was now afternoon and Laura had finally finished washing clothes. She jumped in the shower while I played with Bruiser and Duchess.

I sat on the porch celebrating my birthday with a few cold ones! Laura sauntered down in her bathrobe. She sashayed over, sat next to me, and whispered:

"Are you ready to open one of your presents?"

"Absolutely."

She took me by the hand and led me upstairs to her room. When we entered, I did not see any presents. Laura dropped her robe.

"Surprise."

Boy was I!

"What about Johnny and my old man?"

"Don't worry, I just spoke to my father - the electrical problem was a lot bigger than expected. They will be there all night working on it."

We stayed in her room until around 7:00 PM.

"Patsy, let's take a shower together."

"You bet!"

We did. This was without a doubt the best birthday present ever!! After we were done fooling around, we got dressed.

"Patsy, let's head down to the resort and see if my father needs a hand."

"Good idea."

We did just that. Having not driven it for a while, Laura wanted to drive her '58 Corvette.

We pulled into the parking lot and entered the restaurant's pitch-black corridor. I pulled out my trusty Zippo Lighter, using its small torch to navigate into the dining room.

"The blackened lights must have something to do with Johnny's electrical problem."

I started calling out to Johnny.

Suddenly, all the lights illuminated.

"Surprise, Surprise!"

The place was packed with people. I immediately noticed Jake, Jimmy, Jocko, Johnny, Kathy, the old man, the sheriff, his two deputies, the town's doctor, Johnny's lumberjack friends, my construction crew, and the resort's entire staff!

An excellent band called "Eddie and the Poets" performed. We all had a blast and a great night of drinking and dancing. The party lingered into the wee hours of the morning.

The sheriff told me:

"This is just what this town needed after all the painful drama; its spirit has been lifted!"

Needless to say, my father ended up driving Laura's Vette home and Johnny drove Laura and me." Yes, we both got blitzed and slept late the following morning because we were seriously hung over.

It was now Friday afternoon; we loaded the old man's Charger and my '55 with all of our gear. Laura and I gave each other a huge hug and kiss. To our surprise, Johnny gave my father and me a huge hug and a kiss on the cheek. Johnny was not a huggy-kissy type of guy. Johnny once told me, "That, that is an Italian thing."

"Vinny, thanks for being there once again, brother."

"No problem, Johnny, our friendship has always survived through thick and thin. I have something for you."

Vinny handed Johnny his Police Academy Notebook, Class of 1946.

"Far out, Dad."

"I thought I had lost this spare notebook a long time ago."

Johnny then shook our hands.

"Stay out of trouble, Patsy."

With that, Bruiser and I got into my '55, which I had been warming up for the last ten minutes. We were both sad to leave, but it was time for us to move on to new chapters in our lives. As we pulled away, I followed my old man and put in a Hollies tape that Laura gave me for my birthday. The first song that played was, He Aint Heavy, He's My Brother. This song reminded me of my father's and Johnny's friendship, which had always been a two-way street, with neither one ever keeping score. Their bond of brotherhood has rarely been experienced in life. They would truly die for one another, just like the Scallaci brothers. I have to say I have also been blessed with such a friend and brother, Joey Castanza.

Now back to my beloved Bronx, the Scallaci family, and all my neighborhood friends! Oh yeah, I forgot to mention, on my birthday October 16th, 1969, the amazing New York Mets, National League champions defeated the Baltimore Orioles, champions of the American League to win their first ever World Series! That same year in January, the New York Jets football team completed a major upset against the Baltimore Colts to win the Superbowl. Even though I was a diehard Yankees and Giants fan, I did root for all the New York teams.

The End

Acknowledgements

To my life-long friend James Gordon for his invaluable insight and tireless assistance with the production of this book.

With a BIG Thank you to Lisa Jones and her staff at outskirtspress. com.

Vast input is always required when writing a historical novel. This time Gaetano Bruno, Sammy DiBenedetto, Phil Gerardi, Josephine Biscardi, Maria Galuppo, Greg Boucher, Bill Wallace, Steve (Duke) Thomas, Steven Ruggiero, and Steven Tendler provided accurate historical content.

Printed in the USA
CPSIA information can be obtained
at www.ICGtesting.com
LVHW022327031023
759899LV00045B/1166